A FISTFUL

OF

FEATHERS

Book 1 of the Fraser chronicles

Linda Jones

This cover designed by Brett Burbridge
Original cover designed by Philip Jones and James Bank

This book is a work of fiction. Names, characters, places, and incidents
either are products of the author's imagination or are used fictitiously. Any
resemblance to actual persons, living or dead, events, or locales is entirely
coincidental.

Linda Jones Bavoom Publishing

www.facebook.com/LindaJonesukAuthor/

ISBN 978-1-9993248-1-0

For

My sister Pamela
Because I miss you…

Contents

1. The Clinic 1

2 Changes 7

3 Eavesdropping 15

4 Disguise 21

5 A Close Call 29

6 Caves 35

7 Red Hair and Blood 43

8 Bugs 49

9 Wings 59

10 Plans 67

11 Road Trip 75

12 Professor 85

13 Bird Talk.........................97

14 A Beginning.................109

15 Dundee 115

16 Learning Curve 125

17 Security 137

18 Break In 147

19 Glasgow 163

20 Hill Run 179

21 Watertight 196

22 Families 209

23 Competition' 219

24 Distraction 229

25 Show Time 241

26 Telling All 259

27 An Ending 269

About the Author 279

About Deadwood Hall ...280

Acknowledgments

My never-ending gratitude goes to Ray Hearne: a true oasis in my writing desert.

Thanks to all my friends and supporters in the writing groups I attend and who keep me sane. There are so many who have taken the time to read my work and encourage me.

To my niece, Summer Grace, and Anne and Dave who without even knowing it inspired me.

And most of all to my family, Phil, both old and young. Harriet and Joshua - and someone who is soon to arrive… Thank you x

.

1.The Clinic

Jo hated going to the clinic. The journey there was bad enough, mile after mile of mind-numbing boredom. When they finally arrived, the driver, as usual, strode beside him down the long corridor, his heels clipping sharply on the cold tiles. Then came the same menacing warning as he pushed open the waiting room door.

'You stay put, Ranson, or else...'

This visit was no different. Jo counted the driver's steps as he walked away; he waited for the swish of the heavy doors and that final click. It meant freedom, of sorts. Cautiously, Jo edged his way out of the small room and did his best to glance back up the now-silent corridor. It wasn't easy, the huge swelling on the back of his neck made everything - other than looking at the floor - almost impossible.

The place really gave him the creeps. Each time he came, he was marched past brightly decorated rooms where other patients were allowed to wait. He had to step through those double doors, where everything turned drab and gloomy.

Whether awake or in his nightmares, the corridor never altered. The walls were the same grubby beige colour, with cracks and flaking paint as the only decoration. On the floor were eight-hundred-and-twenty-three dingy grey tiles, each with a green crescent moon at its centre. Seven of them were broken, he knew because he'd counted them loads of times. Even the smell was always the same - a bit like the school toilets on a Monday morning; it reeked of disinfectant.

It was stupid having to wait in such a poxy hole, and even worse, he was starving. All he'd managed to grab that morning were slabs of bread and cheese. He studied the doors again, picturing what was on the other side. The vending machine wasn't far. He passed it every time he came, so he knew it was packed full: drinks, crisps, sandwiches, chocolates bars.

It was tempting, and he had money hidden in the waistband of his trousers. The driver checked his pockets every time he picked him up, but so far, he'd not found this emergency fund.

Jo's pulse quickened. The thought of filling his aching stomach spurred him on. Eleven strides, that's all it would take to reach those doors. His feet were already moving. He could be there and back in two minutes. Just three more steps. This time, he wouldn't get caught. He'd stuff his pockets full and...

Jo stopped dead, his heart pounding. Through the small frosted pane of glass in the door, the outline of the driver's hat was just visible. He must be talking to someone right outside.

It was like he was nine years-old all over again. That time, he'd made it all the way to the vending machine. He remembered putting in his money. The carton of juice, suspended, ready to fall. He stretched out a hand ready to pick it up and then...

'Gotcha...' Terrified, he was rooted to the spot. The driver's shadow had loomed over him, like a scary monster from a horror film. 'You'll be lucky to sit down this side of Christmas,' he'd hissed. 'Start walking.' The driver marched him straight back. Jo bore slap marks on his legs for days.

His heart still thudding, Jo turned back; it just wasn't worth the risk. Pushing his thick, sandy-coloured hair from his eyes, he kept his gaze fixed on the tiles, away from the other end of the corridor and the 'torture chamber'. He'd see that place soon enough. A few minutes later, a nurse in a blue uniform pushed through the doors. For a moment, Jo's spirits lifted. If it was Maggie, his favourite nurse, she wouldn't mind fetching him something from the machine. But it wasn't. He'd never seen this nurse before, and if she mentioned his request to the driver, Jo could say goodbye to his money.

Fed up, he waited for her to disappear before checking the clock in the room opposite. It was only quarter-past eleven. Doctor Bowden never got to the clinic before midday. He rummaged through the pile of magazines on the small table but they were all old copies. More cheesed off than ever, he slouched back in his seat.

'I hate this stinking place!' He kicked out at an unoffending chair so hard that it crashed into the wall. Chips of plaster puffed into the air like confetti. Seconds later, footsteps clicked rapidly down the corridor. He didn't care anymore if he got into trouble.

'Are you alright?' Concerned, the nurse stood at the door.

'Fine. I...tripped,' he lied, rattling the plastic chair back into place.

'Well, if you do want me, press the buzzer. I'm just having a quick bite before I start in the other clinic.' She walked off.

'Lucky you,' muttered Jo. His stomach growled noisily at the thought of food.

He waited until he couldn't hear the nurse's footsteps then pushed the small table under the window. Every visit he did the same thing. Scrambling on top, he pulled one of the plastic chairs up after him. It was dangerous, standing on the wobbly chair on top of the table, but it was the only way to see outside. The window was locked, of course. In the distance, he could just make out the edges of another building. It seemed to be empty. Even when they passed it in the car, he never saw anyone near it, not that he could see much. The tinted windows and the driver's shoulders usually obscured most of the car's windscreen.

'What are you doing, Jo?'

'*Whoa*!' The chair began to rock violently. He grabbed the windowsill, his heart thumping like a drum. 'Amy!' A curious face peered up at him. 'Why creep up on me like that?' He didn't mean to sound so cross. Her smile disappeared in a flash.

'I wasn't. Sorry,' she mumbled.

'It's okay, you just startled me. I thought you were the driver.'

'Oh, *him!*' She shuddered. 'What were you doing?'

'Just looking. I was hoping the window was open so I could do a runner.' He said it with a smile, but he meant every word. 'Are you okay?' he asked her, as he climbed down. The swelling on her neck wasn't as big as his, but he could see it had grown from the last time they'd met. Even with her shoulder length hair it was obvious.

She bowed her head letting her hair cover her face. 'Suppose,' she shrugged. 'I'm hungry. I've been here for hours already. I've been doing those exercises like you showed me though and they've helped loosen me up lots.' She checked over her shoulder. 'It's been hard, keeping it secret when I do them, especially as they moved me to another place last week. It's not fair, Jo. I'd just got sorted and everything.'

He could tell by her sad eyes that it had not been a good move. He had only met Amy a year ago. Until then, he'd been convinced that he was the only one in the whole world with such a swelling on his neck. Even more shocking, Amy swore that she'd seen at least two other teenagers with the same 'thing'.

'Are you still on that farm, with those Bigwells?' she asked.

'I am.' Jo smiled. 'It's almost a year now and I'm still going to that school. Doc Bowden hasn't found out.'

'Does Bert Bigwell still make you do all the farm work?'

'Yeah, but I don't mind.' He grinned. 'Every time I come to the clinic, he panics. He thinks I'll tell the doc about all the stuff I have to do around the farm. But I'm not going to say a word, as long as I can carry on going to school.'

'Well, I think you were really brave standing up to Bigwell,' she said. 'And I can't believe you got one over on the doc.'

'I just hope it stays that way.'

'Me too. Do you know it's my birthday next week? I'll be eleven.' There was no excitement in her voice. Jo noticed how pale her cheeks were and wondered how bad things had become.

'Well, happy birthday from me,' he said, as cheerfully as he could. 'Mine isn't until April, then I'll be fourteen. I'll probably spend it with the pigs. They're always good for a laugh.' Amy only managed a feeble smile.

'Tell you what, how about we play some stupid games?' he suggested 'Anything you like, your choice.'

It didn't take much to bring Amy's sparkle back. 'You're so silly,' she said, twenty minutes later. 'That sounds nothing like a cockerel.'

'It's got a sore throat! Anyway, I think that makes you today's grand winner.'

'Have you got any friends at that school?' she asked him as they fell silent.

'Just the one, Dan Fraser. But he's not going to be there for much longer. He's moving away.' Just saying it made Jo's emptiness feel ten times worse.

'Oh, I'm...' Amy stopped abruptly. Her eyes grew wide. 'It's Doctor Bowden!' she mouthed.

'He'll go straight to his room, don't worry,' Jo whispered. They waited in silence until they heard his door click. 'Go, while it's clear. Jo said. 'Remember, not a word about school or the farm.'

'Promise.' She flashed him a quick smile then she was gone.

Jo sank onto one of the hard chairs, the familiar knot of anger beginning to tighten. Why was this happening to them? Why couldn't they just cut the stupid lumps off? It wasn't fair - none of it was fair. He'd get away from the Bigwells, go to another doctor, or the police. The same thoughts ran through his head a dozen times a day. What was the point of anything? He was just useless.

By the time Doctor Bowden buzzed for him, Jo hardly had the energy to stand. Stepping out into the corridor, he glanced longingly towards the doors that lead out to freedom. He turned back toward his nightmare. It would take just nine short steps to reach Bowden's office. Nine, eight, seven...

The examination was the usual torture, except this time, Bowden didn't take any blood. Jo gritted his teeth, determined not to yelp as cold fingers prodded. He knew better than to complain. At last, Bowden barked, 'Put your shirt back on.'

Jo dared to ask a question. 'Doctor Bowden, when will it stop growing? Only, it seems to be getting worse.'

'Nothing to worry about,' Bowden said curtly, still looking down at his notes.

Jo threw caution to the wind. 'Can't you just cut it off, or do something? You have to, it isn't fair!'

Cold, dark eyes glared at Jo under thick eyebrows. He had a small, pointy beard, splattered with grey. It wagged like an angry finger when he spoke. 'It will all be over soon. That, I promise.' Bowden's words held no comfort.

'What do you mean?'

Bowden's pale lips curled into a smile that was about as warm as an ice cube. 'Just what I said. Another few months, Ranson, and it will all be over. Now, get dressed!

2 Changes

Bert Bigwell leant on the gate of the small farm as Jo wound his way up the narrow track. His beady eyes gave nothing away. Dirty brown hair stuck out from under the felt hat he always wore; scruffy whiskers covered most of his face. He was not a particularly big man, but he did have a hard hand and didn't mind using it. His wife Jane wasn't much better.

'You're late,' he announced, as Jo came into earshot.

'There was lots of traffic,' said Jo. 'What do you want me to do first?' There was no point arguing unless he wanted a backhander.

'You' sort them chickens. Feed pig and the goats. Weekend, both sheds need cleaning proper. I want...' The list went on and on.

By Sunday evening every muscle in Jo's body hurt. He lay on the rickety bed in the smallest bedroom of the cottage, desperate for sleep. He'd managed to sneak some of Jane Bigwell's painkillers from the drawer in the kitchen. Hopefully, the pain would die away soon. Bowden's prodding and poking at his neck hadn't helped, and clearing out the pigsties had made things worse. It didn't help that there was only a week left at school. Some summer holiday he was likely to have. All he had to look forward to were the dirtiest, foulest jobs Bert could find for him.

Feet stomped up the stairs to the bedroom at the other end of the hall. That would be Jane, off to bed. Bert would be up shortly. He was probably having a few extra swigs of the gin he kept hidden. Jo groaned as he tried to turn over. Every spare blanket he could find was piled against his side, in an attempt to support his back.

His head was still full of the clinic and Bowden's words. What had the Doctor meant. Was he going to operate? That smile - Jo shivered at the memory. There was no way he'd trust Bowden to do anything.

He must have eventually dozed off. When he woke, he was smiling for a change. Though the dream quickly faded as the bleak room came into focus. He could remember a woman's laughter. Not his mother's; she'd died when he was born. The woman in his dream must have been at the first place he'd stayed in when he was small. The memory of warm arms and feeling safe was rare. At least the Bigwell's farm was better than the last place where the doctor had dumped him: The Suttons, where the smell of stale milk and soggy cabbage stunk the place out. He was only there for five weeks but it felt like a lifetime.

The cracked clock on his table showed 5.10 a.m. He'd miss the school bus if he didn't get a move on. Rolling out of bed, he tried to ignore the sharp pain. I should be used to this by now, he thought miserably.

Finally dressed in his oldest clothes, he limped downstairs. Ozzie, the chocolate Labrador gazed up at him. 'We'll let the chickens out then I'll feed the pigs and goats,' he told the waiting dog. 'Everything else can wait till this evening.'

It was impossible to move fast. Everything hurt ten times worse than usual. 'I hate him, Ozzie,' he muttered. 'He could've helped me with the pigsties at least.' The dog raised an ear, then cocked his leg against the wall.

'Yeah, my feelings exactly, Oz.'

In the distance, the church clock chimed seven. He was running late. Pouring a last bucket of feed for the chickens, he limped back towards the cottage. At least the Bigwells wouldn't be up yet.

The effort to climb the stairs left him hot and breathless. He sat on the toilet seat, trying to find the energy to strip off. He stank of pig and goat. Washed at last, he stood up to reach for his shirt. It had a couple of small holes and the colour had faded, but at least it was clean.

'Ow!' he groaned, as an agonising pain shot across his back and sides. It felt like someone had grabbed his neck and shoulders and was now tearing them apart. Nausea twisted his stomach. He clutched the taps as the room began to spin. His knees were like jelly; all he could do was slide onto the toilet and rest his head on the cold sink. He closed his eyes. He mustn't faint, he couldn't let the Bigwells know.

It seemed to take forever before the pain eased. When he opened his eyes, he caught a glimpse of his ashen cheeks in the tiny shaving mirror. A bell ringing in the distance registered in his fuzzy brain. It was already half-past seven. The Bigwells would be up soon. Wincing, he tentatively prodded his neck. It all hurt so much.

'This can't be right.' He prodded again, not believing what he felt. The lump from his neck had shifted, and not just a bit- more like half way down his back! What if he couldn't stand up?

The thought goaded him into action. He moved his arms, wriggled his feet; they still worked. Using the sink as a crutch, he stood up, blood pounding in his ears as he fought for balance. It was minutes before he found the courage to move. Taking it slowly, he pulled on most of his clothes, apart from his socks. Stuffing them into a pocket, he thrust bare feet into his shoes. Dan could help when he got to school. That was if he could get his trousers to stay up. As he tried to fasten them, he realised the whole of his back must be swollen. Hoping the old belt he wore wouldn't snap, he cinched it another notch.

Bert's echoing snores followed him as he limped down the stairs. He didn't bother with the larder, the thought of eating just made him feel sick. With the faintest click he closed the back door. Now all he had to do was get down the shale path before Bert did his usual trick, and stuck his head out of the window to call him back.

By the time Jo reached the bus stop, he was shaking so much he could hardly stand.

'Are you alright? You don't look too good,' said the bus driver as Jo limped off the vehicle.

'I'm okay,' he promised. 'Late night, that's all.'

He made it to the heavy school doors only to wonder if he had enough strength to pull them open. Then he heard a familiar Scottish voice call his name.

'Hey, Jo, wait for me. You'll never guess what I've got. There's a...' As his dark-haired friend, Dan, drew level, cheerful banter faded into stunned silence. 'Hell fire!' Dan turned, checking to make sure no one was close. 'What happened?' He didn't wait for an answer. 'Inside, now!' He pulled Jo's bag onto his own shoulder.

'I'm okay, honest,' Jo protested

Dan was having none of it. 'Shut up and walk,' he ordered, steering Jo to the disabled toilet. 'Inside,' he insisted. With the door locked, he paced impatiently until Jo's shirt was finally off. His finger trembling, he pointed at the long mirror. 'So, did Bigwell beat you?'

Jo rarely looked in mirrors. Most of them were set too high over fireplaces or sinks anyway. It was only when he was forced to stand in front of the body-length ones at the clinic that he had the opportunity to look at himself, but even then, he tried not to. He knew what to expect, or so he thought.

'No, he didn't.' Jo's jaw gaped as he saw the damage. He was speechless. Twisting one way then the other, he tried to work out what had changed. 'Wow, no wonder the bus driver gave me some funny looks. He must've thought I'd been in a punch-up or something.' He fingered his neck and face. A deep red tinge to his skin had spread up the side of his head, neck and across his back. On a positive note, with the large swelling gone from his neck, his shape looked almost normal.

'Look at this, I've got a neck, and it even moves!' He tried to turn his head and immediately winced. 'Ouch, maybe not too much yet.'

'Your back's really swollen,' said Dan. Jo shivered as Dan slid his cool fingers over Jo's hot, tight skin. 'It's like the swelling's split into two separate halves, one each side of your spine. Weird.'

'Hey, who're you calling weird?'

'Keep quiet, I'm still looking,' Dan scolded. 'The swelling has moved down over your shoulder blades. Can you still move them?'

Jo tried rolling his shoulders. He yelped as pain shot from his sides and stomach. 'Wow, won't try that again for a while.' He was grateful that the pain seemed to disappear quickly.

'This is not good,' said Dan, for once deadly serious. He walked around his friend, peering closely at the damage. 'Do you realise you could be bleeding to death? Your whole back and sides are bright red.'

'Don't be stupid.' Jo shifted uneasily. 'You don't die from a bit of redness. Do you?' He was beginning to feel light-headed. 'Anyway, what do you know about it?'

'I know because of Dad. He's always doing first-aid at that outward-bound place.' He again ran his hand over the surface of Jo's back. 'It looks to me like fluid is seeping into the soft tissue. If it carries on, it can cause really serious problems. I'm not winding you up.'

Jo turned so he could look Dan in the eye. 'I am not, repeat: not, going to let them drag me off to that stinking, awful clinic! That place gives me nightmares. And if they send me to an ordinary hospital, Bowden will only find out and drag me back there anyway. He really scares me, Dan.'

'I know, mate. I'll think of something. Just don't blame me if you drop dead, okay? Now give me a sec and let me think.'

Minutes later, they were in a shower room in the gymnasium's changing rooms. Dan persuaded Jo to strip off and sit on the floor, so that the cool water could flow over his swollen chest and back. 'We'll just give it a few minutes. I don't want to give you hypothermia. Hopefully, it'll help close the small capillaries and give you chance to clot. That's as long as you haven't a major bleed.'

'Cheers for that happy thought, Danny boy! But I bet you can't spell half of that, can you? Still, at least one of us listens in anatomy classes, I suppose.' Jo's jaw cracked as he yawned loudly.

'Just because I'm dyslexic and can't read the damn textbook, doesn't mean I can't understand what's in there. Anyway, Dad's got these cool audio books that go with his first aid and stuff.' Dan sprayed the cool water over Jo's neck and face, laughing as he spluttered. 'There you go, that should keep you awake.'

'So, did you see your dad at the weekend?' Jo finally asked.

Dan immediately brightened. 'Yeah - and it's all sorted, at last. I can't believe I'm really going to move to dad's place.'

He sounded so happy. Jo tried to stay cheerful, but he was about to lose his one and only friend. 'Sound, just a few more days and you'll be living in Devon.'

Dan shuffled uncomfortably. 'I don't mean to go on about it.'

'You don't. Honestly, you deserve a medal after putting up with your mum for all this time.'

'Yeah, she's been a bit extreme. But you could try and visit?'

'And there's as much chance of that happening as winning a marathon.' said Jo. 'Anyway, chances are they'll move me on pretty soon.' That was another thing Jo really didn't want to think about.

'How long have you been at the Bigwells now?'

'Just a year, and that's a record. Last place was for all of five weeks.' He could feel Dan studying him but his neck hurt too much to look upwards.

Dan left Jo alone for a few minutes. Jo wasn't sure whether it was the cold shower that had done the trick but he was feeling a lot less light-headed when his friend returned. Dan handed Jo a couple of towels.

'How did you manage to get hold of these?' Jo asked.

'I told the receptionist you'd fallen in a pile of horse muck on the way to school.'

'You did not?'

'Yep, and she believed me. I said you'd got a change of clothes, so we're good to go.'

Glancing in the mirror Jo could see he looked a great deal better. Much of the swelling had gone from the side of his face and neck, although the redness was harder to disguise.

Dan's answer was to cover it up with a healthy dollop of talcum powder. 'Just tell them you've got an allergy,' he said. 'That way, no one thinks you're contagious, and the teachers won't send you home.'

Linda Jones

3 Eavesdropping

With only the occasional odd glance from his classmates, Jo managed to survive until the end of the day, although his neck and shoulders hurt quite a bit.

Dan was unusually quiet when he walked Jo the bus stop after school. 'What's up with you?' asked Jo

'I'm worried how you're going to manage tonight. Only, it's a bad idea to start lifting sacks of feed. It could start the bleeding off again.'

The problem had been on Jo's mind for most of the afternoon. 'I'll think of something,' he promised, hoping he was right.

As Jo reached the farm gate he hunched inside his oversized coat, pulling it around him more tightly. With a bit of luck, he could get to his room unseen. He'd pretend he'd been throwing up, that might work.

'You're home early.' Bert's gruff voice greeted him from across the yard. He was kneeling on top of the chicken shed roof, a hammer in one hand. Jo just nodded and moved a little faster along the path. 'Have you finished for the summer? It'll be about time.' Bert's beady eyes were still watching him.

'The last day's Thursday,' Jo shouted. He lengthened his stride hoping to reach the kitchen door.

'Come here!' Bert ordered, and slid down off the shed.

'I'm feeling sick, and I need to take my...'

'Come here,' he demanded again.

It was no use. Dragging his feet, Jo edged over.

'So, what's happened to you?' Before he could even think of a reply, Bert yanked Jo's coat and shirt to one side. 'Well, it looks like you've had a spot of bother,' he cackled. 'Shame, just when you were getting useful too.' He spat to the side. 'Get to your room and stay there.' He pointed with a dirty finger towards the cottage. 'I don't want to hear nor see you.'

'But why...'

Bert growled and took a menacing step forward. 'I said get, or I'll be dragging you up those stairs.'

Limping as fast as he could, Jo made a quick detour to the larder for food and more painkillers. He wasn't going to starve this time.

He tried to stay calm. He had a feeling he knew exactly what was about to happen. The day he threatened to tell Doctor Bowden about all the work he was expected to do on the farm, Bert had locked him in his room and left him there for almost three days. With only a bucket for a toilet and a single bottle of water, the experience had left him shaken and more than a little scared. He stuck it out, though, and got his own way about going to school. A few days after things calmed down, Jo waited for Bert and his wife to go to the pub. He found the key to his room and snuck out to get a copy made. It used up quite a bit of his precious stash of money. Still, it looked like it was about to pay dividends.

Five minutes later Bert's voice echoed up the stairwell. 'Are you in your room yet?'

'I'm in the toilet,' Jo yelled back. He was busy wetting a couple of scraggy old bath towels to wrap around his back and middle. No sooner had he pulled the bedroom door closed the floorboards in the hallway creaked and a key grated in the lock. Pushing down a shiver of fear, he gave it a few minutes before pulling up the floorboard near his window. There was the key, safe and sound.

With one of the cool towels wrapped snugly around his middle, he crept to the other side of the room. The tatty rug was soon pulled aside and another floorboard slid away. Months ago, he'd made several small holes so that he could glimpse the kitchen below. They were right next to the large, oak beam and almost invisible. Perfect for listening to the

Bigwells and avoiding any nasty surprises coming his way. Putting a glass beaker over the top, he leant over. The kitchen was usually the place where they sat and talked but they could be ages yet. He'd almost convinced himself that nothing was going to happen, when he heard the familiar squeak of the kitchen door.

'No Jane, we can't put it off. Not if we know what's good for us.'

'Well, it's not fair. And it's right before his holidays and all.' She almost sounded concerned about Jo until she continued, 'I mean, what will we do about all the jobs? If you think I'm getting out there and mucking out those pigs, you'd better think again. And anyway, the doctor won't know if we don't tell him? He never did find out about the boy going to that school, did he?'

'Get away, woman, and do something useful. It was made very clear what would happen if I didn't report it, so hold your bleating tongue.'

Silence. It took a moment for Jo to understand what was happening. Bert must be searching for his glasses. The sound of pots and pans thudding heavily onto the Aga made him jump. Below, Bert swore loudly. 'Will you shut up, you fat lump of... Oh, sorry, not you! I, umm...right.' Bert cleared his throat and began to explain. Screwing up his eyes, Jo concentrated hard.

'Yes, it's definitely changed. No, he's still walking round. Course he hasn't been doing anything he shouldn't.'

'Liar!' Jo mouthed at the ceiling. Silence again. Bert was listening to whoever was on the other end of the phone.

'Nine? What, tonight? No, that'll be fine. That's not a problem. I've already got him locked up. Yes, and I won't say a word, not to worry.'

Jo hardly registered the ding of the receiver as Bert hung up. He was too stunned. They were going to drag him off before he even had a chance to get away. It was already five o'clock. No way was he going to be able to sneak out in daylight.

'That's that,' Bert's voice echoed through the tumbler. 'Tomorrow morning, at nine someone will come for him. The doctor said, to make sure he's got all his stuff with him. Mind you, that won't take long, will it?'

Jo didn't hear the coarse laughter; he was too busy thumping the air with relief.

When Jane Bigwell pushed open his door an hour later, he was staring out of the tiny window, trying to look fed up and defeated.

'What do you want?' he asked, hardly bothering to look at her.

'You're to pack your things in your bag. And mind, don't take anything that don't belong to you.'

He almost laughed. 'Can I have some food then, and use the toilet?' Not that he expected her to agree.

'There's a bit outside on a tray, and you can use the toilet if you're quick.' She waited outside the toilet, as if she expected him to make a sudden dash for freedom.

The 'bit' on the tray wasn't much. Still, along with the biscuits and slice of cake he'd nabbed earlier, the dried- up slice of ham and bread would do. He pulled open the drawers of the old chest in his room and banged the tiny wardrobe door a few times for show. Everything he needed was already packed in his school bag. There wasn't much, just a couple of changes of underwear and socks, along with an old pair of shorts and the three T-shirts he owned.

His remaining clothes amounted to just his school trousers and shoes - the only jeans and trainers he possessed were covered in pig muck. Most importantly, he retrieved his eighty-nine pounds and fifty pence from one of the hollow legs making up the metal bed frame. All he had to do was wait for the Bigwells to go to bed and head for the only person he could trust.

Being summer, it took ages to get dark. Finally, in the distance, the church clock chimed ten. Jane had already gone to bed; Bert would come up soon. Ear pressed against the door, Jo listened for tell-tale signs. It wasn't long before he heard the creaking stairs and Bert huffing and blowing. Gradually, the noise in the cottage began to settle. After half-an-hour he could make out grunts and snoring. It was time to go.

Easing the door open, he looked back into his room. With the light off, the rolled-up blankets and pillow made a good-enough dummy. It should fool the Bigwells, if they even bothered to check on him in the night. His shoes tucked under his arm, Jo stepped into the hall and locked the door.

'Let's do this,' he murmured, and stepped out into the darkness.

Linda Jones

4 Disguise

Exhausted, Jo leant on the high gate that blocked the path to Dan's bungalow. It had taken him almost an hour-and-a-quarter to limp a mile and a half. Now, it looked as if the gate was going to stop him dead. Fumbling in the dark, it seemed to take forever to find the latch. 'Why won't the stupid thing move?' He bit back a yelp as his knuckles grated against the hard metal. Finally, it slid across and he limped on. At least finding the right room was easier. The Dr Who stickers plastered all over the window were the giveaway. He tugged at the handle of the French doors, expecting them to be locked, but they flew open and he almost fell.

'Dan, wake up,' Jo shook him a couple of times. 'Quiet!' he urged, as Dan suddenly bolted upright.

'What the… Why are you here?' Dan switched on a small lamp and blinked sleep from his eyes. 'Although, that's probably a stupid question,' he added. He pointed to the end of the bed. 'You'd better tell me the worst, Jo boy.'

Curled on his side, Jo began to breathe more easily. 'Can I have some of your water first? I've got to take some of these tablets. My back's killing.'

It didn't take long to explain everything. By the time Jo had finished, Dan was wide awake. 'That doesn't sound good. What'd you reckon they'd do to you at that clinic? Operate, or what?'

'I don't know for sure, but I really don't want to find out. That place gives me the creeps, big time.'

'So, what are you going to do?'

Jo was unsure why, but Dan's question made him feel angry. 'Right now, I want to get as far away from that torturer Bowden, the stupid clinic, and the Bigwells, as I can. After that, well, maybe I can find out who I am, or at least where I'm from. Who knows, I might even find someone who knows what the hell's wrong with me! Sorry.' Jo sank back, feeling hopeless. 'It's not your problem. I shouldn't get you involved.'

'That's a load of bull.' Dan's eyes were alight. 'First up, I am involved. Second, this is what we need to do. I've sort of got it planned.'

'What'd you mean, you've sort of...'

Dan's teeth flashed white. 'It's Dad's favourite motto. Be prepared; planning and preparation.'

'You're a complete loony, Danny boy.'

'You can use the flat over Mum's clothes shop,' Dan said, ignoring him. 'No one's renting it at the moment. Stay until Wednesday morning then get a train to Devon. I've got the perfect solution. Remember me telling you about that pop-up tent, the one I got with my birthday money? You can camp till I get there. Honest, it'll be sound. I've got everything you'll need.'

'If you say so.' Jo was too tired to argue.

Sneaking back out was easy. The small Northamptonshire town didn't run to CCTV, and they didn't meet a soul.

'Just out of interest, when exactly did you plan all this?' Jo asked as they walked, keeping to the shadows.

'In geography. The Bigwells would have to be blind not to have noticed the changes to your neck.'

'Suppose. It's pretty radical, though, thinking all this out.'

'You think?' Dan shrugged it off. 'We can take a short cut up by the bakery. Come on.'

The flat was great. The double bed took less than a minute to make up. Throwing his clothes in a heap on the floor, Jo crawled in, exhausted.

'Stay away from the windows, and don't, whatever you do, answer the front door. I've got a key to let myself in.' Dan dodged around the small flat, pulling curtains and checking the bathroom. 'No one's in the shop tomorrow; Mum's off to a fashion show. I'll come in before school and drop off some food and stuff. Use the shower and TV. Just make sure you stay out of sight. Are you sure you'll be alright?'

'Brilliant. Positive.' Jo yawned so wide he thought his face would crack.

'I'll see you tomorrow then,' Dan called.

Jo was asleep before the flat door had closed. Nothing disturbed him. Not the hum of the early morning traffic, the postman, or even Dan, calling in as promised before school.

When he finally opened his eyes, the clock above the electric fire showed 11.15. He laid on his side, trying to adjust to his new surroundings. Reluctantly, he rolled to the edge of the bed, his stomach growling with hunger. 'Not too bad,' he murmured, as he cautiously stretched, although it hurt quite a bit when he moved his neck. Maybe a shower would help.

Limping into the bathroom, he pulled aside the shower curtain and almost fell over in fright. Dan really should have warned him about the wall of mirror tiles! His panic over, he let the water run over his sore neck and enjoyed the luxury of fragrant-smelling soap. The warm water certainly helped to loosen him up.

Once dried, Jo wiped down the mirrors with one of the damp towels. He took a good, long look at himself. The redness had definitely faded from his face and neck. Around his shoulders, the swelling and red glow was still there. The whole of his back, right down to the base of his spine, was swollen. It was still tender, but again, not quite as bad. He prodded his back with a finger; it felt a bit squashy, not hard like it was yesterday. Was that a good thing?

He didn't have a clue.

His neck was definitely easier to move after the shower, and he could almost stand up straight. Turning from side to side, he studied his profile. The swelling around his middle just made him look large rather than deformed. Still, he could take it easy for the rest of the day. With any luck, by tomorrow, things should be even better.

Stomach still growling, he pulled on a towelling dressing gown and went in search of food. Dan had been as good as his word. He found an envelope pinned to the fridge.

'J seepig mk in fige C U Lar D' He grinned as he interpreted his friend's note. Dan had also left cereal, some rolls, and stuff to put in them. With a tray beside him, television remote within reach, Jo settled onto the large, comfortable sofa.

By 7pm he had eaten just about everything Dan had left. He was trying to decide whether to watch another film or not, when he heard someone open the front door.

'Only me,' Dan called out.

'Did you bring any food?' Jo asked, as he stood up to meet him.

'Wow! You look better.' He circled Jo sounding surprised. 'You must be four inches taller at least.'

'You think? I'm just standing a bit straighter that's all What's happened? Is there any news?' He sniffed at the bag Dan carried. Something smelled really good.

'I'll tell you everything, but first, curry. I picked it up on the way. Mum thinks I'm at Chris's for the evening.'

They ate in silence for a few minutes, too busy with their rice and chicken to talk.

'Well, there's good news and not so good,' Dan announced, as he nibbled the corner of his Naan bread. 'The good news is no one has any idea where you are. The school secretary told me that the Bigwells rang school this morning and were in a right state. As far as I can tell, the police haven't been told. The secretary was really miffed about that. But guess who collared me on my way home this afternoon?' Jo shook his head. 'Bert. He wasn't happy. Especially when I told him I didn't know where you'd gone.'

'He didn't try and hurt you, did he?'

As if! I convinced him I didn't have a clue where you were.'

'So, the bad news is?' Jo asked, his heart sinking.

'You know that BMW with the tinted windows? The one you say takes you to that clinic.'

'What about it?' An icy stream of fear trickled down Jo's spine.

'Well, one like it has been outside the school and around the town. I've seen it at least three times.'

'Great!' Jo panicked. 'What if they spot me leaving tomorrow? I'm not exactly easy to miss, am I?'

'It's not a problem because I've got a cunning plan,' said Dan.

'Be serious, Dan. That driver, I'm sure he's really dangerous.'

'And?' Dan shrugged it off. 'Just trust me, okay? You want more of this food or shall I chuck it?' He refused point blank to say more; instead, he held up a DVD. 'Fancy watching the latest Superman?'

Despite his lack of exercise and the worrying news, Jo still slept like a log. It was Dan's cheerful call that woke him with a start.

'Who's that?' he began, trying to work out where he was. By the time he made it out of the bathroom, Dan had sorted breakfast.

'So, what's this genius plan?' Jo asked, eyeing the bags and suitcase Dan had brought with him with a growing sense of unease.

'Eat and I'll explain. It's raining, which makes the disguise much easier to pull off.'

'Disguise?' Jo spluttered, almost choking on a mouthful of cereal.

'No one will give you a second glance once I've finished. Trust me.'

Twenty minutes later, Jo sat on a stool whilst his friend calmly applied make-up to his lips and eyes. 'Please tell me you're not serious?' Jo pleaded.

'They'll be looking for a teenage boy with an odd shaped back and a limp. They won't be looking for a woman with grey hair, a scarf, wearing slacks and a baggy coat. Cool, huh? I got the whole lot in a charity shop after school last night.' Dan stood back and studied his friend with a serious expression. 'You look a bit like my great aunt Betty.'

'I can't believe I allowed you to talk me into this,' Jo moaned.

'Just put these reactor-light sunglasses on and go take a look in the mirror.'

Jo stared at his reflection in the bathroom. A grey-haired woman looked back. Her face partially hidden by the glasses and a scarf, she bore no resemblance to him whatsoever. He had peach coloured lips and rouge on his cheeks. As for the rest of him, he twisted round, trying to see what he looked like. The grey slacks were held up by an elasticated waist. The enormous pink blouse had a high neck that concealed the redness. Over everything was a large, grey, plastic mackintosh. Dan had even brought an old pair of trainers that belonged to a boyfriend of his mum's. They were a size nine and fitted like a glove. Jo started to shake as laughter bubbled up.

The taxi was due at 8.40am. They sheltered in a shop doorway a few doors down while they waited.

'Don't forget the envelope,' said Dan. 'I've put it inside the case, where the zip is. I prepaid the taxi, remember, so don't let him tell you any different.'

'You already told me.' Jo wasn't sure who was more nervous.

'There's my mobile number and Dad's address: 6 Florentine Lane. And his house telephone number, and there's a couple of other useful things in the envelope. I know you haven't got a mobile yet, but you can use a phone box to ring me. Umm, what else? Did I tell you about the train ticket?'

Jo smiled at his anxious friend. 'I need to pick it up from the ticket office, and it's under the name of Mrs. James. I buy one to Leemouth when I get on the train at Bristol, right?'

'Yep, then they can't connect the name to you. I wish I was coming.'

'I'll be sound, Dan.'

'Sure you will. Did I say money for the ticket is in the envelope?'

'Dan! I've got money. You shouldn't have.'

'You've got some money but I think you'll need it all, for food and maybe to pay for a camp-site. Anyway, when you're on the train, check the envelope. I've put some ideas as to where you could stay. What else? Everything is double-wrapped to keep things dry, in case of bad weather. Did I say that?'

The taxi came around the corner. Jo's stomach did a backflip, and for a moment he wanted to run in the opposite direction.

Dan gripped the handle of his school bag so tight, his knuckles turned white. 'We'll be down Friday afternoon or Saturday at the latest, and then you can come and stay. You'll ring me, promise?'

'I promise, and thanks, Danny boy. I don't know how I'll ever make this up to you.' Jo's throat was tight.

'Oh, don't worry about that, Jo boy. I'll think of something.'

Linda Jones

5 A Close Call

'**Excuse me, madam, can I help?**' Blood rushed to Jo's cheeks as an elderly man held out a hand for his case.

'Thanks, sorry. I've a bit of a cold,' he squeaked, as the man slid the case onto the train.

'I'm off to find my seat. Have a good journey.' The man smiled then disappeared to the right. Jo checked his ticket. Carriage B; left. Excellent, he would be well away from the good Samaritan.

He gave it ten minutes before he disappeared into a toilet and changed. The teenager that slipped out looked nothing like the grey-haired woman. It was another twenty minutes before he felt brave enough to hunt down a drink. As he got near the counter, the man who'd helped him onto the train was standing just in front of him. Jo almost turned and ran. Gritting his teeth, he kept his cool and waited. The man staggered past with his drink without even a glance in Jo's direction.

Dan was a genius, he decided, as he sipped his juice. The taxi ride had been a cinch. No one on the station even looked his way. The worst part had been the wig; it made his scalp itch like crazy. Catching sight of his reflection in the window, Jo grinned. Dressed in various cast-offs, from an old boyfriend of Dan's mum, he almost looked cool. He just needed a mobile or earpiece plugged into his ear, and he'd looked like any other teenager.

The novelty of travelling by train quickly wore off. The seats were uncomfortable, the carriages, hot, and as for the food, no way could he afford to eat much. He arrived at Bristol and had an hour-and-a-half to wait until his next train. Back on board, the journey, again, felt endless and boring; with nothing to do, apart from watch the alien scenery slide by.

When he finally arrived at Leemouth station it was almost four o'clock. He was hot, sticky, and desperate to eat. Pulling the rattling case into the street, Jo turned the corner, away from the noise and clatter. He sniffed the air. It smelled fishy, and there was something else he couldn't identify. A sign to his right read, To The Sea Front. There's bound to be a cafe there, he thought, the excitement rising.

As he rounded the corner and caught sight of the sea, he couldn't help but gasp. The noise was incredible. Screaming gulls dived and soared. Waves pummelled the shoreline, sending spray high into the air. He'd seen photographs of the sea, of course, but this. He stood, unable to drag his eyes away.

'Son, you're in the way. Could you shift?'

Jo shook like a dog and looked up. The man's eyes were lost under a wide-brimmed hat. 'Sorry, I, umm, I was just thinking,' he mumbled, embarrassed.

'Not a problem, only I've got my bike to put away.' The stranger pointed to a black tricycle and the garage door behind Jo.

'Oh, sorry,' he said again. Jo dragged the case across the road and leant over the sea wall.

A few minutes later the same voice interrupted. 'It won't be going anywhere, you know.'

Jo tore his eyes away to gaze up at the smiling man. 'The truth is, it's the first time I've seen the sea, and, well...'

'Just don't be like most of the daft grockles. Tourists,' the man added, seeing Jo's blank expression. 'They stay in the sun all day and end up looking as pink as the shrimp I sell.' The man shrugged, turning to go. 'See you around, maybe, if you fancy some shrimp or fish.'

'Talking of food,' Jo's stomach rumbled noisily. 'Can you tell me where there's a cafe?'

'See that blue sign over there, by the candy-floss stall? Go up the street to the right of it, and there's a nice little place.

Tina's, it's called. That should suit.' With a final wave he was gone, leaving Jo to find the cafe.

With his stomach full of the best fish and chips he'd ever tasted, Jo turned his attention to deciphering Dan's note. It mentioned a campsite not far from the seafront. His back was too sore to think of walking, so he pulled the rattling case over to the taxi rank and grudgingly paid three pounds for a lift.

The campsite looked huge, but empty. He signed in, scrawling 'Craig Wilson'. It was better to be safe than sorry and it wasn't a name he would forget - Craig was the worst bully in their school.

'There's loads of room because the schools haven't broken up yet,' the receptionist said. 'It's not until next week that things get mad.' She handed Jo a green wristband. 'Make sure you wear it on site, please. If you follow the red route, you'll end up with a sea view.' She gave him a small map.

Five minutes later, Jo arrived on plot 223C. It was hard to ignore his pain but he still had the tent to put up.

He unzipped the bag containing the rolled-up tent. 'Yeah, right, Dan, fool-proof you said.' Without much hope, he gave the unpromising looking contents a shake. Instantly, a small tent sprang into shape, floor and all. 'Wow! That is so sweet.' He could hardly believe it was that simple. All that was left was the slotting together of a couple of rods. He found the pegs, and the small hammer, and spent a few minutes knocking them into the grass. The bed inflated easily enough; it had a brushed cotton lining and a pillow at one end. He quickly undressed and climbed into his sleeping bag. With the tent flap open, he just lay gazing out at the huge sky, watching as the stars winked into life one by one.

By seven the next morning he'd already been awake for quite a while. The night had not been the best. He'd rolled off the bed several times, and woke, shivering with cold and pain, on a few occasions. Not that he was bothered. At least there were no pigs or goats to muck out.

His stomach started to complain loudly. With a sigh, he tore his eyes away from the view and found his wallet. He'd have sixty-two pounds left once he paid for last night's camping; he'd have another thirty to pay if he stayed until Saturday. But he also needed to eat. For all he knew, Dan's father might refuse point blank to let him stay. If that happened... He bit his lip, refusing to even think about that.

Pulling on his clothes and the sunglasses, he took a walk along the path towards the toilet block and shop. It promised to be another glorious day.

'It must be from lying so flat,' he muttered, as he tried to shake off his stiffness. Everything felt weird. Being several inches taller than usual made him feel like a giant, and his balance was all over the place. The prickling sensation around his spine was definitely not helping.

In the shop, Jo smiled at the assistant then wandered down the cluttered aisles. The shelves were full of different types of gadgets, such as torches, and strange looking knives, each with a dozen blades. At the far end, he picked up a tiny blue gas canister mounted on a stand. He was so absorbed with the portable stove and how it worked that when the bell on the shop door jingled, he didn't even bother to look up.

'Do you recognise him?'

Jo froze to the spot. That voice. It was like he'd been doused in a shower of ice. Desperately, he glanced around. There was no other way out. He was trapped! All he could do was crouch behind a tower of boxes, and hope the driver from the clinic didn't come looking.

'Take another look, will you?' that was definitely the driver talking. How had he found out where he was? Jo didn't daren't risk a look. Sweat ran into his eyes, and he could feel it trickling down his back.

'I'm sorry. I don't recognise the boy at all,' the assistant said. 'If you'd like to leave it with me, maybe he'll turn up. Do you think he's come here especially, or are you trying the whole area?'

'He could be anywhere.' The driver's voice was gruff and unfriendly. 'A friend of his lives nearby, so it's worth checking. More likely he's gone up country.'

Jo heard the door jingle and held his breath. Was that the driver leaving or someone else coming in? Should he look?

'I'll come back later and do a proper search. I've left a photo at reception with a contact number. If he turns up, he should be easy enough to spot. There is a reward, by the way.' The door jingled again.

Jo waited, every second agonising. He hardly dared believe he'd gone. Clambering to his feet, he glanced through the window, and immediately ducked. The driver turned and scanned the path, as if he knew he was being watched.

'Are you alright?' the assistant called.

'I just dropped my money,' Jo lied, pretending to search the floor.

He didn't dare go out of the shop on his own. He waited for some other campers to finish their shopping then sidled out behind them. Limping as fast as he could, he made it back to the tent in record time, and almost fell inside. Zipping it up, he wrestled to control his breathing.

'Hell, that was so close!' He buried his head in his shaking hands. There was no way he could stay there now. Even if he disappeared for the day, they could be waiting for him when he got back.

Concentrating on packing up the tent helped him calm down. By the time everything was neatly stowed away he felt a lot better. He debated whether to just leave and not pay but figured that would be noticed. Gathering his courage, he pulled on Dan's beanie hat and sunglasses and began the trek back to reception.

By the time he arrived his nerves were, again, a jangling mess, but he pulled the hat down over his ears and pushed open the door. Hopefully, the receptionist wouldn't recognise him from the photograph the driver had left.

She was busy talking to a couple at the desk when he walked in.

'I'll be with you in one moment,' she called.

Pretending to look at some pamphlets pinned to the noticeboard, he tried to spot the photograph. It wasn't there. He edged over to the counter and leant over a little; his heart skipped a beat. It was right below him, poking out from under a letter. It was so close. He quickly scanned the room. There was a security camera but it was trained on the safe at the back of the office. If he dangled his fingers over the counter...

The couple and the receptionist were still talking. No one noticed the small photograph disappear. Finally, the receptionist moved towards him. He was ready. 'Here's my wristband and the money. Thanks, but I've got to go or I'll miss my dad.'

He didn't give her a chance to reply; he just walked away without looking back.

6 Caves

He sat right at the back of the bus, constantly checking to see whether the black BMW was following. He was halfway to Stetton, the next town along the coast, before he finally allowed himself to relax. As soon as he arrived, he ditched the rattling case in one of the luggage lockers. He would pick it up later when he'd found somewhere to stay. First, he needed to eat.

Stetton was more upmarket than Leemouth. There were no fish or candy-floss stalls. Instead, neat little shops filled the alleyways, alongside expensive-looking restaurants. He finally found a café that served an enormous all-day breakfast. Full again, and feeling a whole lot better, he treated himself to a chocolate and orange ice-cream.

On the sea front, the beach stretched away to the right into a small harbour Away to the left, the sands seemed to go on forever, heading away towards some towering cliffs. Running along the coast road was a small electric train. Its carriages were painted in a series of jaunty colours. Jo cast a nervous glance over his shoulder. There were fewer people about and most of those seemed to be elderly. If the driver from the clinic decided to check along the coast road, he would be very easy to spot. Maybe he ought to take a trip on the train? It would keep him out of the way for a while.

The carriage he was in pitched and rolled, which shook his back. He was almost tempted to get off halfway it hurt so much. A neat row of bungalows and chalets, were the last buildings they passed before the train finally rattled to a standstill near the towering cliffs.

'How often do you run?' he called out to the driver. They were well over a mile from the town and there wasn't a building in sight.

'Every half hour, give or take. The last run is about seven.'

At least that would give him plenty of time to recover, Jo thought, as he limped away.

Dense woodland spread up and over the top of the cliffs. It looked difficult to walk through, let alone camp in. Ahead, he could see a sandy beach, but a jagged spur of rocks ran from the cliffs almost to the sea, cutting the beach in two. The widest bit of sand was on the furthest side. It looked as if there was a gap in the rocks, but it was a long way down the beach, almost at the water's edge.

Jo limped his way along a well-used track to the sand. In several places there was evidence of old bonfires and fire pits, but nothing recent. The cliffs were steep, which made it impossible to see to the top. Bushes and small, straggling plants clung to the rockface. Taking off his socks and trainers, Jo followed the jagged line of rocks, enjoying the new sensation of sand between his toes. Halfway down the beach, he turned and looked back at the cliff.

'Yes!' At his shout a gull flew into the air, sending up a spray of sand. Against the grey rock a dark hole stood out. A cave? It could be just what he needed.

Deciding to try and clamber across the top of the rocks, he pulled his trainers on, but even though the rocks were dry, his feet kept slipping. Hot, sticky and with several new bruises, he finally made it across. Jo limped as fast as he could back up the beach - only to find what he had hoped was the entrance to a cave, was hardly more than a dent in the wall of stone.

He kicked at the sand in disgust. 'Well, that was a waste of space, and I'm parched!'

The cliff curved gently away, making it impossible to see what was around the next bend. Not sure why he was bothering, Jo started to walk again. He'd only gone a few yards when his foot became caught in a piece of driftwood half buried in the sand. He fell, landing on his knees with a thump.

'Ow! Stupid...' he began, only to gasp in astonishment. 'Yes!' The cave was almost invisible. seaweed and debris were piled up at one side, almost obscuring the entrance.

Jo scrambled inside. The cave wasn't huge, but he could stand up with a bit of room to spare, and it was plenty deep enough for the tent. There were no signs that anyone else had visited recently. Not surprising, he thought, thinking of the effort it had taken to get there.

Exhausted by the time he got back to the town, he spent the afternoon asleep, tucked up against the sea wall. He woke with a start, hearing five o'clock ring out from the town hall clock. For a moment, he couldn't work out what was wrong. A large gull was pecking at something, right by his toes. He flicked a foot to send it hopping away then winced as pain jabbed at him.

He needed to move before he seized up completely.

There were even fewer people on the streets now. Feeling more conspicuous than ever, He hurried to the station to retrieve his case. Leaving the old-lady disguise in the locker, meant he had loads of room to stash the food and drink he bought from the small shop. Boarding the train, he gritted his teeth. He could put up with the discomfort; he just wanted to get out of sight.

Jo got off near the bungalows. Hiding behind a stone wall, he waited for the train to trundle back toward the town. The last thing he wanted was for the train driver to know he was heading to the beach.

The case was easy enough to pull along the tarmac road. Trying to lift and pull it through drifts of sand and across large pebbles was definitely not. Soon, the pain was so bad he felt dizzy and sick. He wasn't even at the gap in the rocks yet, and he still had to get all the way back up the other side.

'Why didn't I think of this?' he moaned. He leant against a larger rock to catch his breath. Something wet dripped onto his cheek.

'Thanks,' he yelled at the sky, 'Just what I needed!'

Glancing back toward the towering cliffs, the sky was a solid blue. He looked to the horizon. Heavy black clouds were scudding towards the shore.

Jo gaped in horror. The storm was the least of his worries. Huge breakers were only yards away from the gap. If he didn't reach it in the next few minutes, there was no way he'd be able to get through!

Pulling and pushing as best he could, he finally made it and gave one last huge tug. The case bumped and skittered over the jumble of pebbles, as water lapped at his feet. He'd only tugged it a few yards up the beach when a wave crashed into the rocks, shooting a towering spray of water high into the air. The salt stung his eyes.

Dark clouds moved in with the oncoming tide and with them, driving rain. Miserable and soaked through, he kept going as best he could, but the wheels of the case kept digging in. Thunder rolled, like doom-laden drums, the forks of lightning a terrifying accompaniment. He began to think he'd gone the wrong way, when finally, the cliff loomed over him. Shivering, he searched for the torch and turned it on. It was hard to see anything in the pouring rain. He staggered to take shelter under the rocky overhang. Where was that opening? Even with the torch, he could hardly see more than a few inches in front of his nose. Another huge fork of lightning lit the beach like a beacon. Mere feet away was the pile of driftwood. He'd made it!

Limping inside the cave, Jo collapsed in a soggy heap. He had no idea how long he laid there, propped up against the case on the sandy floor. Pain was the only thing he was aware of. It burnt like hot knives until he thought he'd pass out. Slowly, it eased off, enough for him to realise just how cold and wet he was. His fingers numb, he wedged the torch in a crack in the rock and fumbled to open the case. It took precious seconds to rip the wrapper from some chocolate.

'Energy, eat something,' he muttered through chattering teeth. It helped to hear the sound of his voice, and the taste of the chocolate was incredible. Outside, the rain still drove down. Fingers aching from the cold, he began to pull off his wet clothes, throwing them into a corner. 'Good old Danny,' he said to himself as, naked and shivering, he pulled out dry clothes from the plastic bags and rubbed a towel roughly over his skin. He couldn't put the jeans and the big, brown hoody on fast enough. Wrapping his sleeping bag around him, he waited for some warmth to return to his fingers and toes.

'How did I mess up so badly?' Outside, the storm picked up, the wind howling across the mouth of the cave. But there were no Bigwells, no driver, and no crappy clinic, he reminded himself; that thought cheered him enough to sort out some food.

He ate in the dark to save the torch's batteries. The bread rolls filled with ham and cheese tasted like heaven. Now he was dry and beginning to warm up, he found the storm kind of exhilarating. Putting the tent up was even easier second time round, and soon he was wedged inside, staring out at the raging storm.

'Who'd have thought I'd get this far?' he said into the darkness. The fear and danger of the last few hours were all but forgotten. For tonight, at least, he was safe. Yawning, he tried to get comfortable. Hopefully, he'd sleep.

After hours of tossing and turning, Jo finally hit on a solution. Propping the case up at a forty-five-degree angle, he covered it with the slightly deflated bed. He lay, face down, stretching over it, so his chest and stomach were supported. With his head resting on spare clothing at the very end of the case, he let his arms hang down and gently rest on the floor. With the sleeping bag unzipped and pulled over the top of him, he closed his eyes. Within minutes, he was asleep, hardly stirring until the morning.

He woke to a glorious day. Apart from stiff knees and hips from sleeping in such a funny position, the rest of him felt amazing. Being raised up off his back and sides like that had worked a treat. When he stepped outside, he saw the sun edging its way across the curving headland. Standing as tall as he could, he raised his arms, yawning and stretching.

'What was that?' Jo danced around, almost falling over with fright. Something was on his back! Jumping on the spot, he tried to dislodge whatever it was. Wafting a hand up and down, he shook his T-shirt, hard. He stared at the ground, his skin crawling. He fully expected to see a spider or beetle he'd dislodged. Nothing moved.

Turning slowly, he looked all around. The sensation had gone. Whatever it was must have flown away, he decided and shrugged.

'Mega hell!' There it was again. Something big was fluttering on his back. He could feel it, even stronger, if anything. Trying desperately to look over his shoulder, Jo twisted an arm, feeling as far up his swollen back as he could. For an instant, he could have sworn he felt something quiver under his fingertips.

With a yelp of fright, he wrenched off his T- shirt and swung it round in a circle. Nothing fell out or flew away that he could see. Turning the shirt inside out, he looked carefully. There wasn't even a stray grain of sand. He was being silly, he told himself; it was just one of those 'sand hoppy' things. Reassured by his logic, he eased the T-shirt back on. Breakfast would probably help.

Tucking into cereal and warm milk, he considered what to do with his day. Dan would be arriving in Leemouth, hopefully. With luck, he wouldn't be on his own for much longer. Should he try phoning, or leave it until tomorrow? It would be risky going into town. What if the driver was still around? Then again, would it be any different tomorrow? Questions rumbled around in his head as he ate. Knowing

Dan, he'd probably wait until they were back in Leemouth before he told his dad anything. Jo couldn't even begin to think how his friend was going to explain. He couldn't see why Mr. Fraser would want to help him out anyway.

A dark gloomy sensation rose from the pit of his stomach. Mr. Fraser would insist on sending him back to Bowden and that stinking clinic. He'd have to live with yet another faceless couple, who wouldn't give a damn. He couldn't bear the thought, but what else was there? What was the point of even trying? Who would ever take a bumbling idiot like him seriously, especially looking like he did?

From nowhere, two gulls almost fell from the sky, landing in a squawking heap only feet away. Immediately, they began squabbling, flapping and running around each other like two angry, old men. They looked so funny, Jo couldn't help smiling. With a sigh, he threw off the black mood.

'You won't get me, Bowden, no way. Even if I have to live in a stinking cave for the rest of my life, I won't be coming back!'

Linda Jones

7 Red Hair and Blood

Deciding that it wouldn't be any safer waiting until the following day, Jo had a quick wash in a rock-pool and changed his T-shirt. With Dan's small backpack slung over his shoulder, he opted for the shorter route across the rocks.

The bus-stop sign by the bungalows had just come into view when he was brought to a shuddering halt. A huge dark shadow loomed near an overgrown bush. Was it the driver? Instantly, Jo's mouth went dry. His first reaction was to turn and run– but run where?

'Oh, sorry, I didn't mean to startle you.'

Astonished, Jo could only gape at the slim girl who stepped out. 'It's, umm, I just didn't see you,' he managed to stutter. He couldn't help staring. Set in the palest skin he had ever seen were a pair of deep green eyes, framed by black mascara. Bright red hair spiked up at all angles. Teamed with cut-off jeans and a T-shirt covered in multi-coloured swirls, it was hard to know where to look first. Dragging his eyes back to the road, he pretended to look for the train. Those eyes were so intense. Trying not to make it obvious, he stole another quick look, only to find the girl was staring at him. His heart sank. What if she'd seen a photograph and recognised him?

'You've been camping down on the beach, haven't you?' she said. 'Did you manage alright last night? Only that storm was bad.'

'Storm? Yeah, it was. How'd you know about the beach?'

'I saw you get off the train yesterday with that case.' She grinned. 'It must've taken you ages to drag it all the way along the road.'

'You watched me?' Jo's face turned red. 'How did you know I wasn't staying in one of the other bungalows?'

'Yeah, right. So, why didn't you go all the way on the train? That's what I couldn't work out.'

'It's no big deal. I, er, thought I could get down to the beach just along there.' Jo pointed vaguely towards the road. 'I was wrong, though. Have you lived around here long?' he asked, hoping to get her off the subject.

'My gran lives in one of the bungalows. I'm living with her.' Her green eyes narrowed to a hard stare. 'Just so you know, I don't tell tales. If the cops are looking for you...'

'No, nothing like that,' he interrupted. 'It's not the police, honest.' It suddenly seemed very important that she believed him. 'I'm waiting for a friend of mine. He's moving down here this weekend and I - I ran out of money.' It wasn't a complete lie.

'Well, I'm Lucy Abbot,' she said with a wide smile.

'I'm Jo R...'

'Don't tell me, then if anyone asks, I won't have to lie. I'll just call you Jo, and you do sort of look like a Jo.'

'What's a Jo look like?' he asked, bemused.

'A boxer or rugby player, I'd think. Do you play?'

Flabbergasted, he shook his head. Was she blind?

'It's the big build,' she continued. 'Your back and shoulders. How old are you?'

'Thirteen. I'll be fourteen in April.'

'Wow, I thought you were loads older. I'm fourteen in October, so we're only a few months apart. You must be in the same year at school as me.'

He nodded. This was weird. He was having a normal conversation with a girl. Lucy chatted easily as they travelled. He joined in where he could, trying hard not to sound too dim. What did you say to girls, anyway? He was curious though. He wanted to ask her why she lived with her grandmother but somehow couldn't find the right words.

'Can I ask you something?' Lucy said. 'You don't have to answer if you don't want to.'

'Sure, if you want.'

'Will you be safe? I mean, someone is looking for you, aren't they?' Those green eyes wouldn't look away.

Jo hesitated; there wasn't much point in denying it. 'I was telling the truth about the friend. I just need to stay out of sight until tomorrow. Don't worry about me, I'll be fine.'

'Who is it? Family? Police?'

'I don't have any family. Seriously. My mum died when I was born, apparently. I've no idea who my dad is, or was. Like I said, it isn't the police.' Jo noticed the terminus approaching. 'Looks like it's time to get off,' he said sadly. Despite the pain in his back, the journey could have gone on for hours for all he cared.

Lucy turned as he limped off the carriage. She reached out and touched his hand. He felt a pulse of heat shoot up his arm and into his head.

'Nice meeting you, Jo. If you happen to be around the area anytime, it's number 4 Track End bungalow.' With a final wave she was off.

'Yeah. Bye,' he managed. His skin still tingling, he watched her spiky red hair disappear into the crowd. Realising he'd been staring at the same spot for over a minute, he gave himself a shake. That driver from the clinic could be lurking anywhere. He needed to keep moving or get out of sight.

Jo found a cafe and filled up on hot food. The shop was packed with tourists; no one gave him a second glance. At three o'clock, he nervously made his way towards the phone box near the bus station. Surely Dan would be at his dad's by now?

Once inside, he pulled Dan's list of instructions from his pocket, but as he did so something small and square fell out. The photograph from the campsite! He'd forgotten all about that. Intrigued, he flattened the edges. His face, partially covered by his long, floppy hair, stared back, pale and gaunt. Then, his shoulders had been distorted, his neck all but swallowed up by the swelling. It was his first ever school photograph, taken not long after he'd arrived at the Bigwells' farm. He looked so different now. Jo smiled, suddenly feeling a lot safer. Stuffing it into his pocket, he picked up the receiver and dialled.

'That number is not available. Please try again later.' Frustrated, Jo pushed the door with more force than he intended. It slammed into the wall, making a passer-by jump. 'Sorry,' he mouthed. He'd give it another ten or fifteen minutes and try phoning again.

Over an hour later, Jo anxiously pushed in the now-familiar numbers. What if Dan had written the number down wrong? If it didn't work this time he would head back to the cave and just go straight to the house tomorrow.

'Jo, is that you?' Dan sounded worried. 'Don't say anything, just listen. There's been a complication.'

'What do you mean?'

'Just listen,' Dan insisted. In the background Jo could hear someone calling an order. 'I've only got a minute until Dad gets back. Don't worry, you'll still be able to come to us, but...'

'But what?'

'It's the Bigwells, last night. There was a fire and their whole house went up. It was on the news and everything. They pulled out two bodies this morning.'

'What? It was an accident, right? Jo suddenly felt cold. This was unreal.

'That's not what the police said. Apparently, they were stabbed before the fire. I'm really sorry, Jo.'

He couldn't take it in. He'd hated the Bigwells, but murder? 'Are you sure?'

'Very. I had to tell the police about you leaving Wednesday morning. They were starting to think, - well, you can imagine.'

'You've got to be joking. Me?!'

'Don't panic, you're in the clear.'

'Did you have to go to the station? What did your dad say?'

'I did my usual fast talking. Look, I'll explain more when I see you. I've got to go, he's on his way back. Come to the house at lunchtime tomorrow and I'll have everything sorted.'

'Dan, wait! That car, the black BMW, it's down here, looking for me.' Jo thought he heard a faint 'ok' before the phone clicked off. Somehow, he managed to stagger onto the street. Dead? How could they be dead? and, if Dan was right…murdered? Clutching his bags of food like a life-belt, he hurried onto the train, his head buzzing with the news. Why kill them? Maybe it was a robbery, but the only things of value on the farm were the animals. Jo shivered, even though the sun was warm on his back. What if he'd still been there? Would they have stabbed him too?

The truth hit him like a stone. It was his fault they were dead. They'd been killed because he'd done a runner. What other reason could there be? He couldn't shake the terrible feeling of guilt.

By the time he reached the cool darkness of the cave, he felt more confused than ever. Why was he being chased? Why did Bowden want him so badly? Bowden's final words at the clinic echoed inside his head: It would all be over soon. What had that meant?

Food helped a little, and he desperately tried to think of other things; Lucy, mostly. She had to be the most extraordinary girl he'd ever spoken to. Not that he'd had many proper conversations with girls with which to compare, he thought. Counting her and Amy, that made a grand total of two.

Despite his worry, he couldn't keep his eyes open. It was still light outside, but he propped up the case, like he had the night before. He was soon comfortable, though he had to admit, it was a weird position. Still, if it worked, what did he care? Without the added distraction of a storm raging outside, he soon dropped off to sleep.

At some point during the darkest hours, Jo woke with a groan. Two sharp, hot tracks of pain raced down his back.

'What now?' he mumbled, fumbling for the torch in the dark, but as quickly as it had come, the pain disappeared. 'Must've twisted or something,' he muttered, still half asleep. Jo lay over the case again. His back burnt and stung a little but he could ignore that, he'd had a lot worse.

8 Bugs

Opening his eyes, Jo sighed with pleasure. In the distance, he could see the long line of breakers making their way up the beach. Everything looked perfect in the morning sun. He decided to have breakfast then go for a paddle.

'Ow!' he yelped. He'd tried to pull off his T-shirt, but it was stuck fast to his skin. Jo twisted, trying to see what had happened. The bile rose in his throat as he saw the edge of the shirt was covered in blood. He hated the sight of blood, especially his own. He already felt a bit sick. Perhaps it was just a cut; he must have caught his skin on the zip. But even as he thought this, he knew it couldn't be true.

Limping outside, Jo cautiously sat on a rock, trying to find the courage to pull off his shirt. Gritting his teeth, he gave it a quick, hard yank. 'Hell, hell, HELL!' Sweat ran down his face, into his eyes. Trembling, he waited for the worst of the stinging to stop before easing the T-shirt off.

His jaw dropped in horror; there were two thick lines of congealed blood running down the back of the shirt. Something wet and warm dripped onto his hip. Swallowing hard, Jo glanced down. A small pool of red had formed on the rock beside him. It was too much and his stomach heaved.

Despite the heat he shivered with shock. For several minutes he just sat there, waiting for his stomach to settle. When he finally dared to glance down again, he was relieved to see the drips had stopped, and now he looked properly, there wasn't that much blood anyway. Wiping his trembling fingers on his shirt, he decided he should probably check the damage.

He started at the bottom left of his back, though it wasn't easy feeling his way. Halfway between his side and his spine there seemed to be a ridge, just a few centimeters wide, which ran right up his back, almost to the top of his shoulder blades. Tender to the touch, it also felt wet and sticky. His skin had obviously torn on the top of the ridge, as the two edges sat slightly apart. The other side of his spine felt exactly the same.

What's that all about, he wondered? He prodded around some more but was afraid he'd start bleeding again. At least it didn't hurt that much. Maybe the swelling on his back had got so big it had just burst? Perhaps that's what Bowden meant - that it would just pop and go away? Whatever, he doubted gaping wounds were good news. At least in a few hours he'd be able to show Mr Fraser. He would know exactly what to do.

Nibbling on a bread roll helped to settle his queasy stomach. He sipped tepid water, watching the white foam of the waves curl up over the gap in the rocks. The tide was still high and there was no way he was climbing over the top again. Still, it gave him time to consider his other problem: what to do with the case. Given the state of his back, there was no way he could drag it with him.

Rinsing the bloody T-shirt in a rock-pool, he left it to dry in the sun, while he scooped out a shallow pit at the back of the cave. He took his time; his back stung but it didn't ooze too badly. Putting the tent and other bits inside the case, he placed it in the pit, covered it over with sand and, piled up some driftwood at the entrance. Unless you knew it was there, the cave was almost invisible.

It felt like hours later when he finally limped onto the road. A train was just pulling in, so he slipped a cleaner shirt over the top of the one he was wearing and sidled on board. No one seemed to notice the extra passenger. As they chugged passed the bungalows, he looked wistfully at the bus stop, but Lucy was nowhere in sight.

He spent an uneasy time on the bus to Leemouth, constantly checking the traffic for any sign of the driver. When the bus arrived at the seafront, the streets were packed.

There were so many holidaymakers, it was practically impossible to see the sand for all the umbrellas and windbreakers. At least that made it harder for anyone to spot him.

The queues for the taxis seemed to stretch for miles. Jo decided it wasn't safe to just stand there, waiting. With a sigh, he dug out Dan's directions from his pocket and tried to work out which way he needed to go. It was a good thing he could remember the name of the road, he thought. Dan's writing was almost impossible to read.

In the end he headed into a newsagent to ask for help. 'Have you any idea where Florentine Lane is? he asked the assistant.

She pointed vaguely to the left, 'It's roughly a quarter of a mile away, up Summerton Hill.'

'Thanks,' Jo turned, heading to the door.

'Did you know there's blood on your T-shirt?' she called after him.

Hastily, he nodded. 'I fell on some rocks. It's just a graze.'

Once out of view, he checked his reflection in a shop window. Just a few red spots, nothing too bad, he reassured himself.

Jo found Summerton Hill without a problem. From what he could work out from Dan's writing, Florentine Lane was the first turning on the left near the top. Dan could be a genius, but giving directions wasn't one of those skills. Hot and sticky, Jo got to the end of the long lane to the left without spotting a single building. His back and legs were already throbbing.

'Why didn't I just wait for a stupid taxi?' he muttered. The turning he needed had to be further up the hill, on the right, not the left. Back at the start of the empty lane at last, Jo sat on an old tree stump to catch his breath. Wearily, he glanced up, trying to judge how far he had to go, and had to stifle the gasp of horror.

He couldn't believe it. The driver stood at what Jo guessed was the turning into Florentine Lane. If he hadn't been sitting exactly where he was, he would never have spotted the glint of binoculars. Shaking, Jo moved into the shadow of the hedge. This was all he needed!

Two very long hours later and the driver still hadn't moved. There was no way he could risk going back down the hill, Jo decided. He would have to go back along the empty lane again and climb through the wooded area at the other end. If he made it through the trees to the top, he should be able to cross the road when the driver wasn't looking, - unless there was someone else on look-out as well. He'd have to risk it. He couldn't just sit there and do nothing.

The woods were not as dense as he first feared. Even so, his back ached badly, and he knew there was fresh blood clinging to his T-shirt. As the trees thinned out near the top, he caught glimpses of the road. His heart pounded in his chest. Every time he stepped on a twig it sounded like a crack of thunder. He crept on, hardly daring to breathe.

'Georgia, Georgia...'. Jo dropped to his knees, the music sounded so close. Hiding behind a tree trunk, he snatched a quick glance. The BMW was just yards away. Someone was in the driver's seat, changing channels on the radio. On his hands and knees, Jo crept on. His back hurt so much, but what else could he do?

Playing it safe, he made his way down the other side of the hill before making a dash for it. It was probably only ten feet of tarmac but the road felt a mile wide. Panting hard, he waited, expecting to hear the sound of feet running after him.

Nothing. All he could hear was the blood pounding in his ears. Just a bit further, then I'll stop, he thought. His head throbbed but he couldn't give up now. Step by painful step he crept on, until he found a more sheltered area. He sank to the floor, grateful for the shade. Downing the last of his drink, he rested his head against the tree. Immediately, his eyes began to close.

'Can't sleep, that's stupid.' With an effort he pulled off the extra T-shirt and turned onto his knees, ready to hoist himself up using the tree trunk.

'Aargh!' He couldn't stop moaning with pain, as ribbons of fire tore across his back. Fighting to stay conscious, he leant his head against the bark.

Suddenly, he felt something large and wet moving over his skin. 'No, no please!' he groaned. It was terrifying! With a dreadful comprehension, he knew that, whatever it was, had come from inside him. Petrified, he clung on to the tree. His T-shirt kept moving up and down, like something was pushing, trying to get out. I'm going to die, he thought, right here, in these woods. Whatever it was inside him would eat its way out and leave him to bleed to death.

Frightening, blood-soaked images raced through his head. Overcome with terror, Jo fell to the floor. The fear and shock were too much; he slipped into unconsciousness.

He came to with a start. Curled on his side, he had the strangest feeling someone was watching him. Blinking dust from his eyes, he caught a sudden movement in the tree above. A grey squirrel sat on a thick branch, its tail in one paw.

'Hi,' he rasped, then remembered the driver and clamped his lips shut. At least I'm not dead, he thought, as he wriggled his arms and feet. Taking a deep breath, he moved a hand around to his back, only to snatch it away. It hadn't been a dream after all. Whatever had come out of his back wasn't moving, but it was still there.

He swore under his breath. Somehow, he had to get to Dan's. Counting to three Jo rolled onto his knees. That part was easy. Getting to his feet took way more effort. Finally up, he clutched at the tree for support. He could feel a weight on either side of his back, dragging and pulling. Was this thing still alive? Dreading the answer, he concentrated on trying to ease the pain and pressure. Hunching his shoulders forward, he rolled them back, hoping it would stop the pulling at least.

The oddest thing happened. There was a strange, nudging sensation, like he was being poked firmly in the back, followed by two audible clicks. Jo stood still, waiting for the next wave of pain and weirdness. Plucking up the courage, he moved his neck from side to side. Still nothing happened. His T-shirt now lay flat against his back. The pulling and dragging had completely gone.

Nothing made sense at all. He didn't care how or what had happened, he just wanted to get to Dan. Managing to retrieve his bag he took a few cautious steps. He still felt woozy but he couldn't stay where he was. Keeping to the densest part of the wood, he walked for several minutes before he began to breathe a little more easily. It still hurt, but not so he couldn't move.

He had no idea what time it was when a row of semi-detached stone cottages came into view. He knew Dan's father lived at the far end. He just hoped they hadn't gone out, thinking he wouldn't turn up.

The wood thinned out quickly, the last trees lay some yards away from the fence. Jo was just about to step around the last trunk when he stopped short and sniffed. Cigarettes. Someone was smoking close by. The hairs on his neck stood on end as he spotted grey curls of smoke drifting through the air. They were coming from a large bush close to Dan's cottage. He didn't need the shiver of fear to warn him that wasn't Mr Fraser or a neighbour.

Moving back a few paces, Jo sank to the grass and buried his head in his arms. Why were they doing this to him? He just didn't have the energy, not any more. How was he supposed to get to Dan now?

It was his aching back that finally made him move. If he stayed put, they would catch him anyway, so he might as well try something, he reasoned. The logic helped – a bit.

The fence around Dan's cottage looked new and was easily six foot tall. The one next door, however, wasn't as high. Creeping back along the tree line, until he was sure he was out of sight, he made a dash to the long grass abutting the neighbour's fence. Jo breathed a sigh of relief - not only was the fence low enough to climb over, the two cottages shared a flat roof space. Even better, he could see a set of metal steps fixed to the wall.

Before he could twitch a muscle, a man's rough voice had him dropping to the ground. Jo held his breath, as two heavy black boots approached. He just prayed the grass was high enough to cover him.

'Nothing. You? Maybe he's gone back to the farm? Well, it was only a suggestion.' The man sounded indignant.

Jo tensed as the boots moved even closer. This was it. Any second now he'd be spotted; another foot and the man would fall over him! The footsteps stopped. The man was so close, Jo could see the stitching on his shoes. Grass tickled Jo's nose but he daren't move a muscle.

'I'll give it another couple of hours then I'm done. Not a chance, you aren't paying me enough for an all-nighter.' Jo heard paper rustling and a chewing-gum wrapper fluttered to the ground near his chin. The man turned and stomped back towards the bush.

Jo felt drained. The man must've been blind not to have seen him, he thought. Once he was sure the man was back in the bush, he gathered his courage and scrambled over the fence. Staying low, he limped as fast as he could to the metal steps. The first rung felt solid enough, but each step jarred his back. It was slow going. He crawled onto the roof and was forced to swallow a yell of fright as something large and furry wrapped itself around his leg and began to purr.

'Go away! Shoo!' he whispered. The purring sounded like a drill; the man would have to be deaf not to hear it. Trying to ignore the friendly tabby, Jo crawled over the small divide between the cottages. All that now stood between him and safety was a flimsy net curtain.

Suddenly nervous, Jo was rooted to the spot. Through the fine mesh of the curtain, he could see the outline of a man sitting at a desk, a phone in his hand. Seconds later, the figure spun in his chair.

'You'd best come in,' said a calm Scottish voice.

Still unable to move Jo just stared. The curtain was pulled aside. 'Jo?' Mr Fraser took one look at Jo's pale face and reached out. 'Just give me your hand, lad. That's it. Slide your way in.' Lowering him gently onto a chair, Mr Fraser shouted, 'Dan? Get your backside up here, now!' Dazed, Jo heard someone mumbling and muttering as feet thudded up the stairs. Mr Fraser turned his attention back to Jo. 'Don't worry. We'll soon have you sorted, lad.'

Jo's head swam. He shook his head, trying to stop the buzzing.

'What's wrong, Dad? Do the police want to speak to me? Oh, wow!'

Jo felt someone shake his arm. He managed to open one bleary eye. 'Hi, Dan. Sorry, but they're watching. The men...' Jo tried to point, desperate to warn them.

'First, I need to call a doctor...' Mr Fraser began.

Jo shook his head furiously. 'No, no, you can't. You mustn't. They're outside. Smoking in the bush. The man, - please, don't call anyone. I'll be okay.'

'He's delirious,' Mr Fraser muttered.

'No, I don't think so, Dad. It's like I was trying to tell you. They were looking for him back at the school and they must have guessed he'd come here.'

Jo came to enough to nod vigorously. 'Two of them are at the end of the lane, another in the bush outside. I had to come through the woods.'

'Jo, listen to me.' Mr Fraser shook him gently until he opened his eyes. 'Have you fallen over? Your T-shirt, it's covered in blood.'

'It wasn't a fall. The bleeding's stopped now, but you won't believe... I just need to sleep.' Jo could feel his thoughts slipping away.

'Pull that bed out, now,' said a distant voice. Jo found himself on his side, laid on something soft and warm. A firm hand smoothed the hair from his forehead, and with a grateful smile, he slipped into a deep sleep.

Linda Jones

9 Wings

A wood pigeon's call briefly roused Jo early on Sunday morning. His eyelids fluttered open. For a moment he expected to see the dusty, drab bedroom at Bigwells' farm. Confused, he blinked hard, before spotting the curled-up figure of his friend in a sleeping bag. He was safe, and grateful not to be alone. He pulled the cover up over his back and closed his eyes again.

He came to in fits and starts, aware of voices in the hallway. 'Just stick your head in. If he's still asleep, leave the poor lad.'

The door opened with a creak. Dan peered through the gloom. 'You awake, Ranson?' His 'whisper' was loud enough to wake the dead.

Jo grinned, 'I am now,'

'About time. Just a sec.' Dan strode to the window and threw open the curtains. Light flooded the room. 'You took your time getting here. I was so worried, and Dad was close to calling the cops.'

Jo remembered the moment he first saw Mr Fraser, phone in hand. He started to open his mouth to explain but shook his head instead. 'I'll tell you and your dad everything that happened later. It'll take forever.'

'I suppose so. Hang on then.' Dan yelled into the hallway. 'He's awake Dad.'

Jo prepared for a barrage of questions. Instead, he was greeted with a wide smile and a firm handshake. 'Nice to meet you at last, Jo. Let's try and get that T-shirt off. I've been checking through the night; it's stopped bleeding. If you're anything like Dan, it takes hours just to peel off a plaster.'

Cautiously, Jo stood up. Mr Fraser gave the shirt a tentative tweak. It was well and truly stuck.

Dan stared, wide eyed. 'You look like you've been stabbed. 'Did someone hit you and it burst open, or what?'

'Daniel, do you mind?' said his father. 'Go and sort some breakfast while Jo has a shower, that might help.'

Feeling very nervous, Jo followed Mr Fraser. He was told to stand under the shower-head, fully clothed. 'Let the water soak through,' said Mr Fraser, 'I'll wait outside. Shout if you need me.'

Jo tried to relax. He let the warm water run over his hair and into his clothes. Yesterday felt like a dream. He'd lost a bit of blood that morning, and then the panic at seeing the driver again. The climb through the woods and then that 'thing' crawling on his back. Did it actually happen? Reliving the sensation of that wet, bony shape on his skin, Jo knew it was real. At the thought, his back gave an almighty quiver. He was forced to shove a fist in his mouth to deaden the scream.

'Are you alright, Jo?' Mr Fraser peered around the edge of the shower door, his face a blur in the steamy haze. 'It looks like it's coming loose. Here, let me help.' Before Jo could stop him, Mr Fraser began to ease off the T-shirt.

The terrible dragging sensation was back, only worse 'No, honestly…' Frantically, Jo tried to pull it back down.

'Stop worrying. I've seen people in far worse shape. You're as bad as Dan. That's it, over your head. What is it with teenage boys? They think they've…'

As the shirt dropped to the floor, Mr Fraser's gentle teasing stopped, replaced by a stunned silence. Jo was too scared to say a word.

Dan's voice echoed up through the house. 'Dad, shall I put the sausages in yet?'

'Aye, go ahead. We'll be down in a bit,' Mr Fraser answered, his eyes still fixed on Jo's back.

Shaking with fear, Jo rolled his shoulders in a bid to ease the pressure. Again, he heard two faint clicks and immediately the dragging sensation disappeared.

Mr Fraser turned off the shower, wrapping Jo in a soft towel. 'Hey, come on, look at me. Jo, it's going to be okay.'

Mingling with large drips from his wet hair, Jo couldn't stop the tears. 'I don't know what's happening to me,' he stuttered. 'I'm so scared. This thing's in my back and it keeps trying to get out. I, - I think it's feeding on me!' The words just tumbled out. 'Am I turning into some sort of monster?'

'You're not alone now. Whatever it is, we'll sort it. I promise.' Mr Fraser continued to talk, to reassure. Slowly, Jo's desperate fear drained away with the water. 'No more questions for now. I'm going to stand right by that shower door while you finish up. Can you manage that? Here you go, have some shampoo, and when you've done, I'll find you a spare toothbrush.'

When he'd finished drying, Jo pulled on some borrowed jogging bottoms.

'Now you're calmer, I'm going to take a closer look,' said Mr Fraser.

Jo was just grateful the mirrors were still steamed up. Mr Fraser said nothing for a few moments.

'So? What do you think?'

'I can't even begin to imagine how you've coped - you must have been terrified. As for what 'it' is,' Mr Fraser ran his fingers over both sides of Jo's back. As he did so, Jo felt something quivering under his skin. 'Now, would you just look at that?!'

'Look at what?' Jo tried to twist round.

'It's alright, Jo. I think I can promise that 'it' won't be eating any part of you. However, 'it' isn't going to be leaving any time soon, I'm afraid.'

'What do you mean?' Jo asked,

Mr Fraser shook his head. 'I'll find you a T-shirt then we'll eat. You must be starving.'

'Mr Fraser?' Jo called, but he was already halfway down the stairs.

'So?' asked Dan, as soon as Jo wandered into the kitchen.

'So, what?' Jo sniffed the air, enjoying the aroma of sausages and bacon.

'Aren't you going to show me?'

'Not until after breakfast, Dan, I've already told you,' his father interrupted. 'Now, let's see how many sausages you've managed to cremate this morning.'

Breakfast, far from being burnt, tasted wonderful. Jo was starving again. Dan's appetite easily matched Jo's.

'I think I'll need a second mortgage, given the rate you two eat,' said Mr Fraser, as they polished off the last of the toast.

'It's alright, Dad,' Dan mumbled, with a mouthful of food. 'Once I've got used to the sea air and everything, it'll be fine.'

'I'll hold judgement on that.' He smiled at Jo, 'Now that you're fed and watered, Jo, I think it's time you paid your dues.'

'Oh. I've only got about thirty-five pounds left. I, er…'

'Dingbat, Ranson.' Dan looked at him pityingly. 'He doesn't mean money. Your story, - what happened? It had better be good, though, or he might change his mind, ay Dad?'

The first part was easy. Mr Fraser looked horrified as Jo described his struggles on the beach during the storm. For the most part, he just sat and listened. The most difficult bit was trying to explain what had happened to his back at the cave.

Dan interrupted. 'What do you mean 'something on your back'? Like a bat or insect?'

'I thought it was, at first.' He glanced over at Mr Fraser who just nodded. 'Carry on, Jo. Stop interrupting, Dan, and you might find out.'

When he got to the point where he was in the woods above the house, Dan's eyes were enormous. 'No way! You've got to be joking. Something came out of your back? Is this for real?'

'Yep.' Jo nervously watched his friend's expression, wondering how he would react.

'Well, if this 'thing' came out of your back, what did it look like?'

'I couldn't see it, could I? I only managed to feel it a bit with my fingers. It felt sort of long and bony.'

'Urgh, that's gross. So, what happened then?'

'Don't know. I heard these two clicks, and the next thing, it's not there anymore. At least, not out on my back.'

It took about ten seconds for Dan to catch up. His mouth fell open. 'You're seriously telling me that there's something living inside your back?' He looked disgusted. For some reason, Jo felt ashamed.

'No, of course he's not, Dan,' his father interrupted. 'Although, I can understand why you'd think that, Jo.'

'If it isn't living inside me then…is it dead?' Jo wasn't sure which was worse.

'Gross!' Dan looked absolutely horrified.

'Please, boys! No, Jo, it's not dead. You've got it wrong. You're thinking they're some kind of creature, aren't you?'

'They? There's more than one?' Jo paused, stunned. 'Well if it's…if they're not creatures or bugs, what are they?'

'I'll tell you what I think but I'm not sure I believe it myself. Very briefly, I saw what appear to be wing-like structures. They're really small at the moment, about half an arm span.' He pointed to the distance between his wrist and elbow. 'That long bony thing you say you felt would be the main part. Wings are quite similar to the arm. If you look at a bird's wing underneath all the feathers, you'll see joints...'

Dan and Jo stared, open mouthed.

'Wings? You're telling me I've got, - wings? But that's impossible.' Mr Fraser had to be mad. Was he saying he was some sort of a monster? It was a dream. In a moment he'd wake up. He had to.

'I'm pretty sure that's what I saw and felt. Mind, I'm no expert,' Mr Fraser continued.

Incredulous, Dan shifted his gaze from his stunned friend to his father. 'How the hell can Jo have wings growing out of his back? That's just, just, well...?' He was like a goldfish, his mouth opening and closing.

'It does go some way to explaining why those men were so keen to find you,' Mr Fraser said thoughtfully.

'Dad, you're not listening.'

'We definitely need an expert, and the sooner the better,' Mr Fraser continued, ignoring Dan.

'Can't you explain, Dad? This is too weird.'

'No, I can't. I don't have that sort of knowledge, and I'm not prepared to guess. Now, let me think about what we need to do, okay?'

'Wings?' Jo shook his head. Nothing was making any sense whatsoever. He felt completely numb. He couldn't look at Dan. There was no way his friend would want him to hang around, not now.

'Hey, it'll be okay,' Dan whispered. 'Don't look so scared. Honest, you'll see. Dad will sort it.'

Jo glanced up to see his friend looking almost as worried as he felt. With an effort, he tried to shake off the awful sense of dread.

He needed to think about something else before he went mad. 'So, did your dad believe me yesterday, about the men watching?'

'Oh yes. He ended up asking Mrs Pretherton, the old lady next door, to help. She's a bit odd,' he said touching his head. 'Sorry, Dad, but she is. Anyway, Dad nipped over the roof and asked her to call the police. He was worried in case someone had tapped our phones. He told her, he thought someone was hanging around outside. Next thing we know, there's this almighty row in the road. Mrs P had only gone out and threatened to land him one with her walking stick. She was alright, though, the police came hurtling up the road just as Dad got to the gate. You should have seen her have a go at the man! Anyway, to cut a long story short...'

'Is this the short version?' Mr Fraser interjected.

'Dan ignored him. 'Anyway, next thing, the bloke ran away. He was seen running out of the woods at the top of the hill. And the other good news is, she also got a couple of number plates. One off that BMW you're always on about, and another from this blue Peugeot parked next to it. Mrs P went for a walk with her dog. She said she didn't trust the police to do a 'proper job!'

'Sound.' Jo managed a smile. 'Didn't the police come here as well?'

'They only asked us if we recognised the man's description, and that was it. Best thing is, a police car's been around at least three times.'

'So, I'm safe for now?'

'Aye, but you stay inside, at the back of the cottage and away from the windows.' Mr Fraser smiled, softening the warning. 'Now, I need to do some bits and pieces, so I'll see you later, lads.'

It was weird, everything being so normal. Jo sat with his friend in the small back room of the cottage, watching DVDs, but images of vultures and huge eagles with terrifying talons kept popping into his head. He couldn't concentrate. Dan pulled out a video game but playing that wasn't any better. He was rubbish at them anyway, but losing four times in a row was the pits. 'How come you're so good at these?' Jo asked, frustrated, as his on-screen soldier died yet again.

'You know Dad carted me off to see that dyslexia expert? He was well miffed when they said it's really good for me to play them. They help with hand-eye co-ordination, apparently.' Even as Dan explained, aliens fell in droves. He swore as an attacker crept up and started blasting him.

The words were hardly out of his mouth before Mr Fraser called from the kitchen, 'Fifty in the box, Daniel, or wash up. Which is it?'

'Huh?' Jo asked.

'Sorry, Dad, I'll wash up,' he called. 'Swear box, Jo. I've already had to put a couple of quid in.' He pointed to a large wooden box on the mantelpiece. 'He's a bit mental...'

'I heard that.'

'Sorry!' Dan called back. 'Well, he is,' he whispered. 'It's still better than being at Mums', by miles. Right, it's your go. Line them up.'

'If you want to go to the beach, or something, you don't have to stay in just because of me,' Jo said, uncomfortably aware of the bright, blue sky.

'Just because I'm beating you, loser. No, I want to be around when those bat-wing 'things' pop out. That, I've got to see.'

'Do you think this is funny?' Jo snapped, and threw down his controller. Just the mention of them made him feel ill.

'Don't get all shirty on me. I wasn't there on the beach, was I? And Dad said...' Red-faced, Dan tried again. 'He told me when we were making lunch that you could've died. Not just because of your back. In the storm, with hypothermia. My brilliant idea of camping almost got you killed. Seriously! So, like it or lump it, Ranson, I'm not going anywhere.'

'Well, if you put it like that.' Jo tried to look glum. 'Suppose I'll have to put up with you for a bit longer, Danny boy. Let you carry on winning.' He grinned and picked up the handset. 'Okay, go for it. I'm prepared to be annihilated.

10 Plans

Apart from lunch and tea-time, Jo hardly saw Mr Fraser. He assumed he was reading or on the computer in the attic room.

'Was that Dad calling?' Dan turned down the volume of the film they were watching.

'Boys? Kitchen.'

'Maybe he's made supper?' Dan said hopefully. They hurried through, to find the old pine table covered, but not with food.

'Wow, isn't it a bit early for Christmas, Dad?' There were two mobile phones, alongside a laptop and two iPods. A large, blue sports bag lay to one side, with several pieces of clothing draped over the top.

'Right, Dan, the mobile your mother gave you…'

'It's upstairs.'

'No, it isn't, for now it's in my safe.' He held up his hand to ward off the argument. 'There's a small chance it could be tagged. Someone could be listening in or trace us through the signal. For now, we're all going 'pay as you go'. No frills, I'm afraid, but at least we can all stay in contact. Here you go. Make sure you don't use your old one if you still have it, okay?'

Jo looked down at the first mobile he'd ever owned. 'Thanks, Mr Fraser.'.

'Wouldn't get too excited,' Dan murmured, 'They don't do a lot.'

'A further warning,' Mr Fraser added in a serious tone. 'Don't activate your phones in this house. I'm being ultra-cautious, but if someone's scanning, they'll pick up the signal and all this effort will be lost. And the laptop, for the same reason; we'll leave yours behind for now, Dan. Don't worry; I've made sure I've some games to keep you going.' He leant over to hoist a carrier-bag off the sanded wooden floor.

'Sweet, Dad, and thanks.'

'For you, Jo,' he passed over the sports bag. 'You'll find clothes, the usual teenage stuff. A pair of slippers. No wearing shoes in the house, please. And these.' He handed over a pair of walking boots and trainers.

'Wow!' Jo was gobsmacked. No one had ever bought him new things before. 'Thanks, Mr Fraser. I don't know when I'll ever be able to pay you back.'

'When did you sneak out and get all this lot, Dad?'

'Mrs P went shopping. I nipped over the roof earlier to pick it up. You wouldn't have heard anything over that row you were making. The iPods are yours as well, and you can use those straightaway. You can change what's on there once we're on the move.'

'We're leaving? When?' Dan looked up at the clock.

'Sooner, if I could, but there's one more thing I need to sort. We'll go at midday tomorrow.'

'Where are we going, or is that a secret too?'

'To Uncle Ian's. Do you think you can cope?'

'Wicked. He's really cool, Jo. So, how're we getting to Scotland? By train?'

'Yet to be arranged. I'll tell you when I know.'

It was as Jo was packing up the sports bag to take upstairs that he remembered what he'd left behind in the cave. He swore and was instantly embarrassed.

'Sorry, Mr Fraser only I remembered something I should've told you earlier. It's the case and Dan's tent. I had to leave them in the cave, and the disguise. That's still in the locker at the station.'

'Not to worry, give me directions. I'll have someone pick them up for us.'

'I should've remembered sooner, sorry.'

'They'll be safe enough, Jo. Tomorrow, though, the same rules apply. Fifty pence a time for swearing or a job around the house. Fair enough?'

'Sure.' Jo grinned. 'I'd better go find that locker key for you.'

Dan insisted on Jo using his bed, whilst he slept on the floor of his bedroom, which Jo appreciated, given how difficult his back made trying to sleep. 'What does your dad do for a job?' Jo asked once they were settled.

'He moves packages around the country, makes sure they arrive and stuff. Logistics, or something like that. All I know is, he gets to play around with computers a lot. He used to work abroad but not anymore. I think he did some sort of sneaky stuff for a bit, like MI6. And don't bother asking, because he never told me much.'

'Sneaky stuff? What sort of a job description's that? Hey, I wonder what the careers advice teacher would say, if we put that down as a career option?' There was muffled laughter from the floor. 'Dan, do you think Doctor Bowden knew about these wing things? Only, - why would he let them keep growing?'

There was silence. For a moment Jo wondered if his friend was too embarrassed to say anything.

'Oh, he had to have known,' Dan finally said.

'You think? But why didn't he cut them out? What's the point? It's not like they're big or anything. They're just stupid, runty things.' Even as Jo spoke about them his back twitched.

'Because he's an evil, sadistic, monster and I really hope Dad and Uncle Ian meet up with him one day in a very dark alley!'

Jo shivered in the darkness. He'd never heard his friend sound so angry. 'Sorry, I...'

'Don't you dare apologise to me, Ranson. Like any of this is your fault. Anyway,' Jo could sense Dan's smile even through the shadows, 'You're safe now, so that's all that matters.' He yawned. Jo automatically joined in.

The following morning, they woke with a start as the room flooded with light. 'Sorry, boys, I know it's a bit early. Dan, I've left cereal on the table. Please stay away from the phone and the front sitting-room window. If anyone calls, make sure Jo stays out of sight.'

There was a grunt from Dan's sleeping bag. Bleary-eyed, Jo looked up and nodded. 'I'll only be a couple of hours. See you later.' The door clicked shut.

'Seven. Is he for real?' Mutinously, Dan pulled the curtains closed again and jumped back into his sleeping bag.

He must have fallen asleep, because the next thing Jo knew Dan was shaking his arm. 'Wake up, it's only a dream. Jo!

'What? What's up?'

'You were. You kept moaning and muttering. What were you dreaming about?' Jo shook his head. Whatever it was had gone. 'It's almost nine,' said Dan. 'I suppose we'd better move.'

'If I was still at the farm, I'd have done almost four hours' work by now,' Jo said, carefully rolling to the edge of the bed.

'Slavers, that what they were, they had to be.'

'Nah, they got paid lots of money for looking after me. I used to hear them discussing it, though they were supposed to keep it secret.' He looked up to see Dan watching him intently. 'Do you want to use the bathroom first?' he asked. Talking about it always made him feel bad. It was like no one had ever really cared about him, only the money they'd received.

While Dan sorted out tea and toast, Jo carefully stretched and rolled his neck and hips. His back felt huge. It was like his muscles had doubled in size.

'What are you doing?' Dan asked, turning to watch.

'Just loosening up a bit.' He had only been stretching for a minute or so when he felt the familiar quivering, 'Oh, oh!'

Dan's jaw dropped. The teaspoon he held hung in mid-air, forgotten. 'Hell fire, your T-shirt…' He pointed wordlessly with the spoon, his eyes like saucers.

Hands still out in front of him, Jo could feel pressure as the shirt rose and fell. Sweat ran into his eyes. He tried to wipe it away, but the shirt moved more frantically than ever.

'What do I do?' Dan begged.

'How should I know?' Trying to hold back the panic, Jo shut his eyes, not daring to move.

'Think! You told us those wing things went back in alright the first time. So how did you do it?'

'I don't know. They just sort of did it on their own.'

'Jo!' Dan stood in front of him. 'Open your eyes and look at me.'

Slowly, Jo opened one eye and looked at his friend. Even through the dread, he realised they were now the same height. When had that happened?

'Does it hurt?'

'Not as much as the first time,' Jo admitted. 'Still pulls, though. Feels like it's, - they're falling off my back.'

'Concentrate, they have to go back in.'

'You think?!' Jo tried rolling his shoulders and realised there was a problem. 'Umm, Dan,' he looked at his friend's white face. 'I think one of the 'things' is caught up in the T-shirt. You're going to have to take a look.'

'You're winding me up?' said Dan. Jo shook his head. 'Right.' Dan blinked, hard. 'So, I'll just take a quick look?' He lifted the back of Jo's T-shirt. 'Okay,' he squeaked, and quickly cleared his throat. 'It's caught alright. You're going to have to take it right off.'

'Are you sure?' Jo tried his best to hold on to his panic but it wasn't easy.

'No, but there's no way those wing things are going back stuck like that.'

'Just do it then,' Jo said, gritting his teeth.

'Count of three. Ready?'

There was a slight moment of pain as Dan jerked the T-shirt away, then the dragging sensation he'd had before. Dan gave a gasp as the T-shirt fell to the floor. 'You should see this. I'll get a mirror.'

'I don't want to!'

But it's...wow! There aren't any feathers yet. You can sort of see where they'd grow. Or maybe they're more like bats'? And Dad was right, they look just like arms with joints. Like an elbow. That must be...'

'Dan,' Jo hissed, 'I don't want to know.'

'They're amazing, honest.'

Jo's temper started to fray. 'Dan!'

'Sorry. Just try and get them back in then.' He ran a finger over Jo's right side. 'Can you feel the difference? This one on the left is...'

'That's my right side,' Jo corrected.

'Whatever, can you feel the difference? The other one's all folded up. This one is half open.'

Jo was about to say no, when he realised that wasn't true. 'Yeah, it feels like its stuck halfway.' He shrugged his right shoulder.

Dan squealed excitedly. 'Do that again.'

'Do what?'

'Shrug, you wally. When you did that, the wing moved.' Jo did as he was told. 'Can you feel that?'

'Sort of.' The pulling wasn't so intense and the weight seemed to have moved further up his back.

'That has to be the answer,' Dan declared. 'Think about it. You've got those two openings running down your back. I bet, if you move your shoulders the right way, the wings will slip inside.'

Jo knew he was right. He leant forward just a little and lowered his head. Pulling his shoulders forward he then rolled them back. Two loud 'clicks' followed.

'Yes! Dan punched the air. 'You did it, Jo. Nice one!'

Jo felt his way to a kitchen chair and sank down. His knees felt like jelly. 'Thanks. Sorry to put you through that,' he managed.

'Get real! That's better than Terminator 5 any day.' Dan flopped onto a chair. Despite his bravado he looked a little shaken. 'Tell you something, though.'

'What's that?'

'Glad there wasn't any blood. Not sure what I'd have done. Still, pretty cool having a friend with wings.' He grinned, back to his unflappable self.

'Yeah, well, I can't believe I've got a friend who dresses like that. Did you have your eyes closed this morning or what?'

'Nothing wrong with what I'm wearing.' Dan rubbed the fabric of his lurid purple shorts.

'Not if you're blind,' Jo began to laugh. 'I mean, orange and purple; seriously?'

Not long after they'd cleared the breakfast things away, Mr Fraser reappeared. 'Good to see you boys are finally up. Any chance of a coffee, Dan? Then I can fill you in.'

They sat around the kitchen table as he sipped his drink. 'It's almost ten and we need to leave in forty minutes. Have you both finished packing?' Jo nodded. Dan looked at his feet. 'I'll take that as a no. You've got twenty minutes, okay?'

With dire warnings ringing in his ears to pack his toothbrush, Dan headed upstairs. The kitchen fell silent. Jo wondered if he could find an excuse to leave as well.

'You'll be pleased to know, Jo, I've arranged to have the case and tent picked up. They should be safe and sound by tonight.'

'Great. That pop-up tent of Dan's was amazing.'

'Aye, it's a clever piece of engineering.'

Jo shuffled nervously as Mr Fraser studied him for a moment. 'Jo, I'm going to have to ask you to trust me. It's really important we get you away, so we can sort out what the hell's going on. Now, I know the local police have managed to chase off those men who were doing surveillance; however, I'm not convinced we're in the clear.'

'Have you told the police about me?' Jo asked, surprised.

'No, it didn't seem wise. I've a friend who's checking the area for me. As soon as I get the all clear, you're going to pay a brief visit to Mrs P.'

Jo's heart sank. 'Aren't I staying with you and Dan?'

'You'll be there about ten minutes, half an hour at the most. Mrs P. happens to have a garage, with a door that leads straight into the house. A friend of mine will pick you up. I promise, Jo, in two hours or so we'll all be back together.'

'Okay, Mr Fraser.'

'Good. There's one other thing. I'll shout Dan and explain to you both.' He waited for him to appear. 'Dan, meet your cousin, Jo Fraser. I'll be Uncle Simon. We'll forget Ranson, even with Uncle Ian.'

'Why not change his first name as well?' asked Dan.

'No point. It's Ranson that'll stick in people's minds. Anyway,' he smiled, 'I happen to like the name Jo. It suits him, don't you think?'

A memory of spiky red hair and green eyes flashed into Jo's head. He turned away, his cheeks burning.

11 Road Trip

Two hours later, and Dan and his father sat in their car, waiting for Jo to show. Dan checked his watch for the hundredth time. 'How long now?'

'Four minutes and counting. Jo is fine.' His father didn't bother to hide his smile. 'There's more traffic on the roads they've taken, so be patient.'

'Suppose.' Dan glanced at the large brown signpost on the other side of the hedge. It had a castle and a picture of a duck, but as soon as he tried to read the words, the letters turned into a jumble, like a bowl of alphabet soup. He sighed and dropped his gaze.

'Are you alright with all of this, Dan?' Mr Fraser twisted in his seat to look at him properly. 'Only, I haven't asked you, have I? If you wanted, I could find someone else to look after Jo and sort this out.'

'Not a chance! You don't want to, do you?' He was suddenly unsure of what his father was really getting to.

'No, I don't, and not just because Jo's your friend, though that would be reason enough. I'm in this all the way, whatever it takes. Deal?' His father held out a hand to shake.

'Deal. I'm sorry about me, though,' he added quietly.

'Sorry about what?' his father sounded baffled.

'Not being able to read and stuff. It's stupid.'

'Daniel Fraser, you're not stupid, or silly, or thick, or any other daft thing you want to call yourself. So, stop beating yourself up. How many lads your age could have done what you did for Jo, huh?' He held his eye until Dan grudgingly nodded.

'Suppose you're right.'

'I'm your father, of course I'm right.' He ignored the snigger and pointed to a dark, sleek camper van that had just pulled in. 'So, what do you think, is it good enough?'

Dan was out and inspecting the exterior of the van before his father could open the boot of their car. He whistled as he inspected the wheel arches.

'Cool huh?' A voice came from just above his head.

'Ra…Jo,' Dan corrected himself. 'Am I glad to see you.'

The van, built to suit British roads, was quite narrow but a good length. Every centimetre was decked out with the newest and best in technology. Easily big enough for six, it even had a satellite dish. Dan sighed happily, as he finished checking the cupboards. 'All we need now is a couple of surfboards and we'd be away. Are we driving all the way there in one hit, Dad?'

'I thought we'd camp for the night. We may as well make the most of it. Buckle up, we need to get going.'

They parked up for the night just inside the Scottish border at the back of a small café. It was definitely a step up from the tent. Comfortable though the van was, Jo had to admit there'd been a thrill to sleeping outside. There was something really special about going to sleep to the sounds of the sea.

They were woken early, as several large lorries rattled out of the car park. 'What's the time?' Dan yawned, groaning as he caught sight of the clock on the radio. It's only six.'

'Up, Dan,' his father insisted. 'I want an early start.'

Dan grudgingly got out of his sleeping bag and sat scratching. Jo yawned, surprised that he'd managed to sleep so well. He stayed where he was however, suddenly unsure.

'Come on, lazy. One up, all up,' Dan sounded exactly like his father.

'You go first, then there'll be more room.' The truth was, Jo felt very uneasy, but he waited until Dan had finished dressing before he said anything. 'Mr Fr…Uncle Simon? My back, you know, the wings - well, most of the stuff happens in the morning, when I first get up. It's just, I'm a bit worried. What if something happens when I go to the toilet or café?'

Mr Fraser turned to look at him. 'Now, that's a sensible question.' He sat on the edge of Jo's bed. 'Tell me again about yesterday. Dan gave me a brief version, but I'd like to hear it from you.'

He nodded occasionally as Jo explained. 'So, certain movements seem to be the trigger? Once the wings have had some exercise, they slip back in and don't cause you a problem, is that right?'

'I hadn't thought of it like that,' Jo admitted.

'Dan, make sure all the blinds are down. I suggest, Jo you get up, do your exercises and we'll see what happens.'

Dan perched on the small table, swinging his legs, while Mr Fraser stood to one side. Embarrassed, Jo removed his top and began by raising his arms to shoulder height. Having people watch felt awkward. Within moments, he felt the familiar quivering.

'Here we go,' he warned. Jo tried to tune out Dan's whoops of excitement and concentrate. He was much more aware of every sensation and grateful to find there was hardly any pain, just a slight stinging. As the wings slipped out of their sacs, he could sense them expanding outwards. It was so strange. It made him feel queasy. Dan may have been excited but all Jo felt was dread.

'I know I only saw them briefly but they've grown in just two days,' said Mr Fraser, moving closer. Jo didn't think that was good news but he kept his mouth shut. He felt a tickling sensation as Mr Fraser touched a wing. 'There's an oily coating, which we wouldn't have seen before because of the blood. It must act as a lubricant, I suppose. Now, let's see if you can get them to fold away, Jo?'

Concentrating hard, Jo shrugged his shoulders firmly. Immediately, he felt the wings close up.

'Yep, that's it,' said Dan.

Lowering his head, Jo rolled his shoulders back then pulled them forward. Nothing happened.

'Nope,' Dan said, a little unhelpfully. 'I think it was the other way around. You sort of pulled your shoulders forward and then...' He demonstrated.

'And rolled them back?' Jo finished the manoeuvre and heard the welcome 'double click'. There was a sudden explosion of laughter.

They turned to see Mr Fraser doubled up, his face buried in a towel. 'Sorry. I'm so sorry,' he gasped, trying to get control. 'You've no idea how surreal this whole thing is. And Dan there, so cool.' He bowed low. 'I take my hat off to you both. You're amazing.'

With the wings back in, Jo's mood began to lift. 'Everything feels okay now, Uncle Simon. There's not even a tremor.'

'Good lad, just be careful not to over-extend and you should be fine. Finish dressing and we'll go find some breakfast.'

'What time is Uncle Ian expecting us?' Dan asked, as they walked towards the smell of cooking bacon.

'I'm hoping to get there for about four.'

'Is he still working at the university, or has he retired?'

'He's part time. He's only fifteen years older than me, Dan, not a hundred and fifty. Anyway, it's a good thing for us he still has contacts, given our little problem.'

'What does he mean, Dan, about the contacts?' Jo whispered.

'Not a clue, it must have something to do with him being a professor, I suppose.'

It was almost five o'clock when Mr Fraser finally announced that they were only ten minutes away from his brother's house. Turning right, the camper van sped along an increasingly narrow lane with high hedges on either side. Jo strained his neck trying to see ahead. He couldn't spot a house anywhere. He was just about to ask Dan where the village or town was when the van turned again. This time, they drove up a rough track, which wound this way and that for a quarter of a mile.

'And we're finally here,' Dan said wearily.

Astonished, Jo saw they'd driven right up to the doorway of the strangest shaped building he'd ever seen. The bungalow was so low, the roof seemed to touch the floor. It would be impossible to see it over the hedges of the lane.

My brother has an unusual taste in architecture,' Mr Fraser said, as he pulled open the van door. '

'And there you are,' a deep Scottish voice called. Jo caught a glimpse of dark, greying hair before Dan jumped out.

'Uncle Ian!'

Jo suddenly felt nervous.

'Come out, Jo. I want you to meet my older brother.' Mr Fraser smiled encouragingly as he hung back.

'This is my best friend, Ra – Jo,' said Dan, ignoring the glare from his father.

'Jo, is it? Well, good to meet you, laddie.' Uncle Ian was tall, with dark eyes and a mass of hair that stuck out everywhere. 'I'll not be shaking your hand yet, but come on inside and we'll find you all a drink.' Jo noticed mud plastered over his wellington boots. The thick woollen shirt he wore was darned in several places.

Dan grabbed Jo's arm, pulling him towards a large wooden door under an archway. 'Just wait until you see inside. Leave your shoes here, under the porch.' He pointed to the low shelf that held shoes and slippers. 'It's like a Hobbit's burrow, only not round. You'll see.'

Intrigued, Jo slipped off his new trainers and stepped inside. The wooden floors were covered with thick rugs; light flowed down from tall lamps sat against the hall walls. Wood and white plaster, interlaced with pictures and sculptures, filled the space with rich colour. Despite the low roof, windows were set along the wall. He only had a moment to absorb it all before Dan pulled him through another door.

'And the kitchen,' he announced, letting Jo walk first into the large, welcoming space. Copper and steel pans hung over a large Aga. They gleamed against the oak beams. In the centre sat a large, old pine table, with big comfortable chairs tucked underneath. A rocking chair, covered with a multi-coloured throw, nestled in the corner.

Somewhere outside a dog barked. 'That's Rory,' said Dan. 'He can be a bit of a pain until he gets to know you. So, what do you think?'

Jo tried to take it all in. 'It's brilliant. I can see what you mean about hobbits. I sort of expect a dwarf to come banging on the door any moment.'

'The rest of the place is just as cool but I'll save that till tomorrow.'

'Is your uncle married?' Jo asked.

'Divorced, I think. Must run in the family, I guess.' Dan grinned. 'There's a cousin too, but I never get to see her. She lives in America, or Canada.'

Before he could expand, the kitchen door swung open and the brothers walked in.

'Put the kettle on then, Dan. Now, Jo, most folk call me Prof, or Professor. It's up to you, of course.' Jo just nodded, a little intimidated by the large man. 'Right, Daniel, let's sort food out. I'm sure you'll be hungry.'

Mr Fraser pulled out the chair next to Jo, watching as his brother bustled about his kitchen. 'You'll be as safe with Ian as you are with me, so you're not to worry about anything,' he promised. 'I haven't said anything yet about your little problem and I don't intend to until the morning.' Jo watched the slow flicker of a smile and couldn't help grinning back. 'It isn't often I have the chance to rattle my big brother,' he whispered. 'It should prove interesting.'

After supper, they walked to the end of the long drive with Dan's father. Jo spent most of the time gazing upwards. 'I can't believe how many stars you can see here. It's even better than at Stetton.'

'Aye, and wait until we go up into the hills. It gets better,' Mr Fraser promised. 'Dan, just under the top of the hedge near the gate is another barrier. Can you pull it across for me?'

'I didn't know that was there,' he said, sounding surprised. He swung across two metal bars, which Mr Fraser then slotted into a metal clasp on the other side.

'We don't need to use it often. We're not likely to get many burglars this far north.'

'So, what's it for?' said Dan. 'It's not likely to stop anyone getting in. They'll just slip underneath.'

'It completes a circuit. If you look to your right, you'll see two green lights.' Both boys stared into the dark corner. Sure enough, two twinkling lights blinked back. 'That means the connection is complete. When we get back, I'll switch the matrix grid on.' He laughed, as they stared blankly. 'And you haven't a clue what I'm talking about. Essentially, there are lasers set into the ground, and at various heights around the gardens, which detect motion and weight. When I'm more awake tomorrow, I'll explain it better. I promise you both, though, if anyone tries to get close, we'll know about it.'

They walked back in near-silence.

'Dad, are you still worried about someone following us?'

'I'd be stupid not to. Never assume, that's the first rule. Always check, double check, then put in extra safety. That way, hopefully, there won't be any little surprises waiting around the corner.'

Jo peered up at the tall, slim man. Even in the dark, he could sense how alert Mr Fraser was, his watchful eyes were everywhere. Jo trusted him and liked him a lot, but he was beginning to wonder what exactly he did do for a living.

He and Dan shared a large room. It had two single beds and oak beams, with cobwebs caught at their edges. The little window beside Jo's bed opened onto the garden. Jo lay on his stomach over some pillows, enjoying the breeze and the sweet smells wafting on the night air.

Dan fell asleep almost as soon as his head hit the pillow. Maybe it was the lack of exercise but Jo didn't feel sleepy at all. His head was too full of thoughts, mostly about the following morning, and the professor. Every time he thought about it, his stomach cramped up with nerves. What on earth was he going to say? What if the professor thought he should go back to Doctor Bowden? With so much to worry about, it took a while to register the voices. He deliberated whether he should pull the window shut, but curiosity got the better of him.

'If you told me more, I'd be able to say,' the professor said gruffly. 'Why be so devious? You could just tell me.'

'Devious? Now that's the pot calling the kettle black. I learned from the best, Ian. So, don't go accusing me of being devious.'

'Aye, well, some of us had the sense to try and leave that behind.' There was a clink of glasses before the professor spoke again. 'I cannot understand why you stay in exile all the way down there, Simon. It makes no sense.'

'It's part of the deal. I am not letting Caroline keep Dan on her terms. She'll pack him off again first chance she has. As for letting me bring him back up here, she won't even consider it, and right now, I'm not prepared to ruffle the waters. Not until certain things are in place, at least.'

Jo glanced at his sleeping friend. He had no idea what they were talking about.

'Aye, well you'll do what you must.' There was silence for a while. He thought they'd moved away when the professor spoke again. 'So, young Joseph, you've known him long?'

'Dan has, about a year, I think.'

'There's an edge to him. Wary, I'd say. I thought he was going to bolt when you first introduced me.'

'Would you blame him? Have you seen the state of your hair? I cannot believe they let you near any student looking like that. As for the edge, when you know his story you'll understand. And don't ask, I'll not be going into it tonight.'
Someone scraped a chair back. Jo ducked quickly.

'Well, the morning will do, though I'm intrigued, Simon I must admit. I'm glad you had the sense to come to me, whatever your worries. You know I'll do my best for you.'

The murmur of voices drifted away, until all Jo could hear was the occasional branch stirring in the breeze.

Linda Jones

12 Professor

Rain pattering on the roof woke them both. Dan raised his head and yawned. 'Good old Scotland. If it isn't raining, it snows. Don't worry, it'll probably clear up later, usually does. I'll go and give Dad a shout, see what he wants to do.' He yawned again and lazily rolled out of bed. 'Did you sleep alright?'

'Pretty much,' said Jo, although he felt guilty about his eavesdropping.

A short while later Dan reappeared. 'Dad said come into the kitchen, and try not to let anything happen yet. Don't bother getting dressed,' he added with a grin.

A few minutes later, Jo nervously pushed open the kitchen door, not quite sure what to expect. The smell of sausages cooking made his mouth water.

'Jo! There you are.' Mr Fraser waved him over with a smile.

'Come and explain to my brother about the clinic and the Bigwells. That's as good a place to start as any, I think.'

When Jo finally stuttered to a halt the professor said, 'So, you've been moved from pillar to post since you were a wee lad? And this clinic where they sent you, they never told you where it was?' Jo nodded, unable to work out the professor's train of thought. 'I see. Now, you say there was a swelling on the back of your neck but it's moved. Have I got that right?'

'Yes, Professor.'

'And what did the Doctor say was the problem? I suppose you'd be too young to understand X-rays and scans...'

'I never had any,' Jo interrupted.

The professor frowned, 'They must have. It makes no sense.'

'Not once. I was examined each time, though. They took measurements, lots of blood and things, but I've never been X-rayed, or scanned for anything.'

'Well, I'll be...'

'It gets stranger, Ian, trust me,' said Mr Fraser. 'Jo, tell him what happened when you were camping in the cave.'

By the time Jo finished, the professor was on the edge of his seat. 'I think you'd best just show me, laddie.'

With a sigh, Jo slipped off his top.

'Do you mind if I touch your back?' the professor asked politely, but Jo could tell the man was struggling to contain his excitement.

'Okay,' Jo said, hoping the wings wouldn't suddenly spring into life. Dan was sitting almost in front of him, a wide grin hidden behind a hand.

'Do you feel me pressing?' The professor ran his fingers up and down Jo's sides. 'Lift your arms up for me, straight in-front of you. I just want to check muscle strength.'

Immediately, his back began to quiver. 'Umm, Professor,' Jo murmured. 'I really wouldn't stand too close if I was you.' He couldn't stop it. As soon as his arms were shoulder height, it happened. He felt the two wings flip out, unfolding against his back.

'What the...!' the gasp was followed by an almighty clatter. The professor gaped up at him from the granite floor.

As Jo spun around to help. one of the wings jabbed Mr Fraser in the arm. Dan was bent double laughing, helplessly.

'I'm so sorry,' said Jo, terrified the professor was having a heart attack or something.

'He's fine, Jo. Don't you worry.' Mr Fraser lent down to hoist his much larger brother to his feet. The professor said absolutely nothing. Reaching out with a shaking hand, he gently turned Jo around to stare, wide-eyed, at the wings. There were a few minutes of silence, broken occasionally by Dan's muffled giggles.

Mr Fraser leant over to whisper, 'Stop looking so worried, Jo, everything's fine. And I owe you one!'

It took a small scotch and a plateful of breakfast for the professor to lose his glassy stare. Swallowing the last of the amber liquid, he eyed his brother who was calmly sipping tea. 'You could have warned me, Simon. Heavens, I could have had a coronary.'

'Rubbish, you've the constitution of an ox. Anyway, Dan's well up on first-aid. We'd have resuscitated you, wouldn't we, boys?' He ignored his brother's grimace.

Still feeling guilty, Jo stole a glance across the table and saw the professor staring back at him. He felt his cheeks turn scarlet.

'Don't you go worrying. It's that prat of a brother I should scold.' A smile lit the professor's lined face. 'Mind you, if he'd told me I wouldn't have believed him. So, there's no winning really.'

He poured himself a mug of tea. 'Let's finish up here and, if it's alright with you, Jo, I'll do a quick examination. The sooner we make a start, the quicker we can sort this out.'

'My thoughts exactly,' Mr Fraser added brightly.

'I'm still not speaking to you,' the professor said, winking at Jo.

The office was a light, airy room at the front of the bungalow. Like the rest of the place, it had dark wooden beams. The walls were lined with numerous bookcases, stacks of magazines piled beside them. On the large desk was a statue of a sitting Buddha. Next to it was a photograph of a much younger-looking professor. He was with a young girl; she had long black hair and sparkling eyes, and looked about ten years old.

Next to the photograph was a small gold-coloured statue, though it was hard to make out what it was. Jo was still trying to work out if it was a leprechaun or the figure of a running boy, when the professor spoke.

'Sit here, Jo.' The older man pulled up a stool with a low back and turned his own large, leather chair to face him.

'We'll start at the beginning. I'm going to ask you lots of tedious questions, which I'll record here.' He held up a notepad. 'I'll not be putting anything on disk until I've worked out a secure code,' he added, more to himself than Jo. 'Any questions, ask away, though I'll not necessarily have the answers yet.'

Despite not being able to answer many questions, Jo noticed the notebook filling up rapidly. The professor listened carefully and took notes, making no judgements. He carefully recorded Jo's measurements: height, weight, chest size, then suggested he flipped out his wings.

'But I've never done it like that before, Professor. It's only ever sort of…happened.'

'If it doesn't, tomorrow will do. However, I think you might be surprised. I'll close these, just in case.' Leaning over, he dragged deep red curtains across the metal rail.

'Okay, if you think so.' Jo tried shrugging his shoulders. Apart from jerking his chest muscles up and down, nothing happened. He tried the arm exercises. Still nothing.

'Think about how you put them away and reverse the process,' the professor suggested.

It worked like a dream. No sooner had he started to hunch his shoulders and roll them forward than the quivering began. Seconds later, out popped the wings.

'Well done! Doesn't hurt, does it?'

'Not any more. It did the first few times. I thought I was going to die.'

'Aye, I can believe that.' The professor sounded angry.

'Is everything alright?' Jo turned, worried he'd done something wrong.

'Laddie, take no notice. Let's make a start.'

After about fifteen minutes Jo's back began to ache. Before he could even mention it, the professor tapped him on the shoulder. 'You're tired, and I've got just about all I need.'

The double click reassured him everything was safely tucked away. Jo turned with a shy smile. 'I am sorry about this morning, you falling over like that.'

'You think nothing of it. I'll bide my time and catch my brother. Revenge, Joseph, is always a dish best served cold.'

'Will you be able to help me?' Jo asked as he pulled on his top.

The professor drummed his fingers on the table. Jo was beginning to feel very uneasy, when he finally spoke. 'That depends on what you mean by help, Jo. If, for instance, you're asking if I can get rid of those things for you, well, the answer is, I've no idea. Whether I should, of course, even if I could, would be your choice anyway.'

'I see.' Jo didn't see. If anything, he felt even more confused.

'No laddie, I doubt you do. Let's wait until I can do some tests then we'll talk about it.' The professor stood up and pulled back the curtains. Light flooded in. 'The sun's decided to come out and play. I see. You get along and enjoy it whilst it's here. I'll be out soon.'

'Everything okay?' Mr Fraser called from the kitchen.

'Yep, brilliant. The professor's finished with me for now so I'm off for a wash.'

'Dan's feeding the chickens and picking up the eggs. Hopefully, he won't break too many. I'll just take Ian in a coffee, see if I can't sweeten him up at bit.'

'It was funny,' Jo said, matching Mr Fraser's grin. 'Though I didn't expect him to fall over like that.'

'His expression will live with me for a very long time, Jo believe me!'

Jo spent the rest of the morning with Dan, walking around the property. There was a large poly-tunnel for growing vegetables, as well as another plot with beans and potatoes to the west. To the north side of the garden was the large chicken coop and run, as well as the familiar snort and snuffling of a pig.

'Do you really like pigs?' Dan asked, as his friend made a fuss of the sow and eight tiny piglets.

'I do. Apart from you this last year, they were the only friendly contact I had.'

'Not much to choose between us then?'

'Not really, just the smell. But when you shower, you're not so bad.' Jo managed to duck; as a handful of straw sailed past his head.

'Let's see if there're any plums left,' Dan suggested. 'Uncle Ian had masses last year.'

As they walked back towards the bungalow, Jo pointed at a glass structure that was almost the length of the property. 'That's a weird lean-to, or is it a conservatory?'

'More like a conservatory, I suppose. Uncle Ian uses it to do his martial arts. He'd like a Dōjō but they cost masses.'

'Aren't they extinct?'

'Duh! That's a dodo, ding bat. Dōjō is the Japanese name for a training hall. Dad will probably use it as well, but I can't take you in to show you without permission.'

'What martial art does your dad do? Judo?'

'That, Aikido, and some other stuff. He'll explain. I did a bit of judo, until Mum put a stop to it,' Dan said sounding glum.

'Yeah, but now you'll be able to do it again, won't you?'

They hadn't walked more than a few paces when a dark bundle of fur ran out and started barking at Dan's feet. 'Rory, it's me!' He bent to let the dog smell his hand. Still unsure, the dog sniffed more closely. Deciding Dan wasn't the threat, he moved on to Jo.

'Just stand still and let him sniff,' Dan advised.

Jo let the little dog circle him until, gradually, the barking quietened. Slowly offering a hand, the dog's nose twitched furiously, then he felt his fingers being licked. 'Hello, Rory, nice to meet you.' The little dog looked up, gave a strange yap then sat down, its tail wagging furiously.

'Wow, you must smell good. It normally takes him a week to decide not to eat you,' said Dan. With the dog at their heels they carried on walking. Dan fell silent and, for some reason, kept snatching furtive glances at Jo.

'What's up? Jo asked. 'Have I got a bogey on my face or something?'

'It's difficult to say, it would blend in so well.'

'Dan!'

'Dad wants me to ask you about the clinic,' he blurted. 'He wants to see if you can remember anything.'

Jo stopped dead. Rory sat at his heel expectantly. 'What for? He won't send me back there, will he?' Just the idea made him feel sick.

'No! What are you like? He wants to track down someone who worked there. He hopes they might be able to tell him something more about that Bowden.'

'Suppose that's okay then,' Jo said, feeling a bit silly.

'So…?' Dan urged as they walked on.

'What do you want me to say? I have no idea where the clinic was and I was never told anyone's surname.' Jo hesitated, realising that wasn't exactly true. 'Though now I come to think about it one of the nurses, Julian, told me his. I think he got into trouble because of me.'

'What happened?' asked Dan.

'It was about eighteen months ago, I think. I'd always wanted to see my birth certificate, so I asked Julian about it. Up till then nobody would tell me anything. Anyway, he said he'd have a go at getting hold of a copy. A couple of weeks later, one arrived in the post. All it really told me was the name of my mum. 'No fixed abode' it said, but it did show which hospital I was born in. When I next went back to the clinic, He said he'd found it among some notes in Bowden's desk. Julian was furious…not with me. I'd never seen him so cross.'

'Cross about what? Didn't he say?'

'Just something about it 'not being legal'. I don't know, it was ages ago.'

'So, you said you knew his last name?'

'It was something like…Trainum? No, maybe more like Transom. I'm not sure.' Jo screwed up his eyes as he tried to remember.

Mr Fraser walked around the corner at that moment carrying a small basket. 'I wondered where you two had gone.'

'Dad, Jo was trying to remember a name of one of the nurses from that strange clinic. Weren't you?' he urged.

'He was Julian. His last name sounded a bit like, - Trainum or Transom?'

'Let's see.' Mr Fraser thought for a moment, 'Maybe Julian Trantham?'

'Yes,' Jo said, amazed. 'That's it exactly. How'd you work that out?'

'I just thought what the names might sound like if you whispered them to someone that's all.'

'That's so cool.'

'Experience and luck,' Mr Fraser admitted. 'Did you know him well?'

'More than the others. I remember being really upset once. I'd missed a school party because of that stupid clinic. He and another nurse, Maggie, took me into a corner and we played games. I'd forgotten all about that.'

'Excellent. And I'd guess Mr Trantham told you his real name. Can you remember when you last saw him, or this other nurse, Maggie?'

'Not for over a year now. I was telling Dan, he got me a copy of my birth certificate but he ended up leaving, or something happened. I saw Maggie a couple more times. She told me Julian had decided not to work there anymore. I was really upset.'

Mr Fraser took a ripe plum from the basket, handing it to Jo. 'How about I try and find him?' he suggested, handing another plum to Dan.

'Can you do that? Won't there be loads of Julian Tranthams?' Jo asked, not daring to hope.

'Possibly. But I doubt many of them are nurses, or at least we can hope not. How about we see what else you can remember? It might come in useful.'

They sat in the kitchen while Mr Fraser took notes and asked simple questions. An hour later he sat back and read through what Jo had remembered. 'Julian Trantham. Nurse, aged 40-50. Maggie, 45-55. Clinic on the outskirts of Oxford, because you remember seeing motorway signs over the driver's shoulder. The clinic driveway goes through large grounds with lots of trees. The driveway divides into two, going towards two separate buildings. The clinic is two storeys high and brick built. You only saw the second building from the outside, which was larger, and several storeys high. It had no name and looked derelict. There are at least three other children with similar neck problems. Amy is one but you don't know the names of the others.'

'It doesn't sound much,' Jo said.

'Rubbish! You've done really well. You've named all those families you stayed with. If anything else pops into your head, jot it down or come and tell me.'

The kitchen door opened and the professor walked in. 'Have you done, Simon?'

'For now. I'll make lunch if you like,' he offered.

'Aye, I need a word with young Joseph.' The professor sounded serious.

'Has something happened, Professor?' Jo said, instantly worried.

'Ian! Stop scaring the lad.' Simon glared at his brother.

'Sorry, Jo, there's nothing to worry about,' the professor assured. him. 'I just want to talk to you about doing a couple of tests. Some X-rays and an MRI scan. That stands for 'magnetic resonance imaging'. Have you heard of that?'

'Yeah, a bit,' Jo admitted.

'We can't just use any hospital, for obvious reasons. Fortunately, because of the university, I'm able to use the medical facilities of a nearby private clinic. Simon has agreed to help me with the MRI scanner. We'll do the tests tonight, if you're up for it, brother. I've already cleared it with the chief technician. I've told him I've a skeleton embedded in clay. He seems to have swallowed it.'

'Won't you get into trouble, Professor?' said Jo.

'We think it's worth the risk, don't we, Simon?'

'Oh, aye, if you can get me in the place, I'll do my part.'

'But is it safe, Uncle Simon?' Jo demanded.

'Safe? The scan, you mean? You'll have to ask Ian about the effects of the MRI, but I'd think so.'

'Not that. I mean, what you two are planning to do. What if you get caught?'

'I'll not pretend there aren't a few risks - of course there are. We'll be as careful as we can,' said Mr Fraser.

'It's just…I couldn't bear it if something happened to either of you. I'm not worth that.'

Mr Fraser put his mug back on the table. 'We won't take silly risks, Jo. But you're more than worth the effort. We'll do this, and whatever else it takes. Isn't that so, Ian?'

'Aye, that's nicely put. So, about eight o'clock tonight, boys, Simon and I will go and sort the machines. The clinic isn't far; you two can wait here until we're ready for you.'

It sounded easy enough, but Jo paced and fretted for most of the afternoon and evening, positive something would go wrong. It was a relief when Mr Fraser finally came for them.

The MRI machine was strange and noisy. As he clambered into the car after it was all over, Jo's head was still ringing.

'What was it like?' asked Dan, as Jo eased his back against the seat.

'Loud, like a drill. I had to wear headphones, and it had this narrow bed that slid inside the machine. Really weird.'

'Uncle Ian said he got everything he needed. So that's good.'

'Yeah, though I'm glad it's over.' Jo closed his eyes, wishing he could stop the drilling noise still in his head. Moments later, Dan elbowed him.

'Wake up. Uncle Ian's calling you.'

'Just a quick X-ray,' the professor explained as Jo hurried over. 'I promise, no more than twenty minutes.'

'How come you get to use these machines? Are you a doctor?' probed Jo, as they walked to the next cabin along.

'Aye, but not the sort you're thinking of. I use the machines to look at bits of bone and fossils. Anything caked in mud that I'd damage if I washed it.'

'So, what are you a professor of?'

'My brother would say the meaningless.' He smiled. 'But that's no answer, is it? I'm a Paleo-Osteo-archaeologist. I study ancient bones, among other things.'

'Like dinosaurs?'

'That's it, though not just dinosaurs. I look at human remains, as well as sea and land creatures.'

'Wow, sweet,' said Jo, impressed.

'Aye, it can be. Most of the time it's just boring paperwork, but it has its moments.'

As they walked up the steps and into the much quieter cabin, Jo asked, 'Am I one of those moments, Professor?'

The professor stopped to face him. 'Jo, you're worth a hundred times any of those moments. But do you know what? If I could, I'd give them all up to put you back as you should be. Now, let's get this over with. I need my bed.'

13 Bird Talk

Something cold and wet brushed across the back of his neck. Jo woke with a start, his heart thudding. Several times he'd woken during the night, nightmares still hovering. This, however, was definitely real. 'Rory, do you mind?' He pushed the furry bundle off the bed. 'Go wake Dan up. Go on.'

'Oy, get off!' Dan cried, as the cold nose found its way under his bedding. 'What's the time anyway?' he asked as he tried to find his watch.

'It's just gone eight,' said Jo, 'and I'm starving.'

The wings co-operated for a change, waiting until Jo had eaten before they started to quiver. 'Professor, I can feel them moving,' he warned.

'Take yourself off to my office and I'll be along shortly.' He paused for a moment. 'Would you mind if I took a couple of photos?'

'No, not at all,' said Jo.

'Can I come in with you?' asked Dan.

'If Jo doesn't mind, though you sit quiet, because I've a few bits I need to check out.' By the time the professor stepped through the office door, Dan had pulled the curtains closed. Jo was trying hard to wait but the wings were growing restless.

'Good control,' the professor remarked. 'Now, let me just find that camera.'

'Hurry, it feels like I'm about to burst open,' Jo begged. When he was finally able to let them out, Jo could clearly feel them fluttering from side to side. The professor took what felt like a million photographs.

'We're all done for now, lad.'

'So, what did the X-rays show?' Jo asked, as the clicks told him all was safely stowed away.

'No idea yet, I haven't even got them downloaded. It's going to take a while to sort everything.'

'Oh, okay.' Jo tried not to sound too disappointed.

'I'm going to spend an hour now. You two go find Simon. I'm sure he's got something planned.'

'You didn't really expect to hear anything yet, did you?' asked Dan, as soon as the door closed behind them.

'Suppose not. I don't know. It's just...' He cut the conversation short as Mr Fraser walked out of his room.

'Are you all done?' he asked, ushering them into the kitchen.

'Yes, thanks.' At first, Jo thought Mr Fraser was wearing his pyjamas, until he took a closer look. His black trousers were loose fitting, and completely plain. The jacket was tied with a black belt, though it had several flashes of colour sewn onto one of the ends.

'What are you doing now, Dad?' asked Dan.

'I've just finished the download for Ian and thought I'd do some Tai Chi, loosen up a bit. Why?'

'Jo was interested, that's all.'

'And you're not?'

'Well, yeah...but what if Mum finds out?'

'You're with me now, Dan. We'll just make a point of not rubbing it in.' He smiled. 'Go check your case. Your "Gi" is in the bottom; there's also a spare set of mine Jo can borrow.' Dan was already out of the door. 'Go after him, Jo, he probably didn't hear me. I'll meet you in the conservatory.'

Dressed in loose-fitting, white cotton trousers, and a thick, white cotton jacket, Jo did his best to tie the white belt.

'Here, let me do it. I'll show you properly later.' Dan pushed Jo's fingers away and deftly tied it. 'There you go. Now you at least look the part. Just do what I do, okay?' Nervously, Jo copied Dan as he stepped out of his slippers and bowed low before entering the glass-fronted room.

The walls were plain, the wooden floor springy underfoot. Multi-coloured mats lay in a neat pile. On one wall was a wire-fronted cabinet, holding several wooden sticks. The room was big anyway, but Jo noticed that the glass doors opened onto a large grassed area, which easily tripled the space.

'I don't know if Dan's explained, but when I'm teaching, you call me 'Sensei'. It means master and teacher. Judo and tai chi are some of the skills I teach.' Mr Fraser smiled. 'Ian thinks practising tai chi would help build up your muscle strength, and I agree. Now, before we start, there's a greeting every student makes to the master. Copy Dan, he'll show you.'

Immediately, Dan knelt; first, onto his left knee, then he lowered his right. He sat back, eyes straight ahead, with his hands flat on his thighs. In a smooth, effortless action, he bowed forward from his hips. Placing his two hands in-front of him on the floor, his head level with his shoulders, he waited. Jo tried to do the same. He was sure he'd got bits wrong but he managed to end up in a similar position.

'Very good,' said Mr Fraser. 'Now, we'll start with meditation.'

That sounded easy. Trying to empty his mind and concentrate on his breathing wasn't. 'Why is it important, Sensei? Everyone breathes,' he asked, once they'd finished meditating.

'Ah, but learning to control your breathing is key. Not much point creeping up on someone only to give yourself away gasping for breath. Now, have you ever seen tai chi practised?'

'Only on TV. Don't old people in China do it?'

'Not just the elderly, Jo. Tai chi involves most of the movements used in all other martial arts. The only difference is the movements are done slowly. It concentrates on precision and balance, which all help to make you supple.

We'll start with simple moves that we can adapt for you. If it hurts, say so; none of this should give you pain. Though you will ache until you've built up your muscle strength.'

The movements demonstrated did look effortless, Jo had to admit, until he tried them for himself. 'Wow, is it supposed to be this hard?' Jo rubbed his aching arms.

'It'll get easier. It'll certainly help build up the muscle along your shoulders,' Mr Fraser promised.

Half an hour was more than enough. Jo watched from the side as Dan and his father practised basic throws on the thick mats. They also did something called 'kata', which they did kneeling and standing. It involved some very complicated hand movements.

'That is so cool,' Jo said, impressed. 'I'd no idea you could do all that, you never said.'

'No. Well, you had other things on your mind,' Dan panted.

'That was fantastic, Uncle Simon. When can I do it again?' Jo asked, as they cleared away the mats.

Mr Fraser laughed. 'Let's see if you're still as keen in the morning!'

The days fell into a routine. Each morning, he and Dan would crawl out of bed and stagger into the kitchen. After breakfast, the professor spent half-an-hour checking Jo's measurements and taking photographs. Jo would wait expectantly, sure the professor would tell him what he'd found out. When a whole five days had gone by and there was still no news, his mood plummeted. It didn't help that his nightmares were getting worse. The latest woke him in the early hours, as a scream caught in his throat. He'd seen razor-like talons instead of hands, and feathers sprouting everywhere. He shivered in the dark. Running a shaking hand over his face, he swore he could feel the beginnings of a beak. It took ages to go back to sleep. Even tai chi the following morning didn't shift the gloom.

'Are you almost ready?' Dan pulled on his socks. They were supposed to be changing to go out for the day but Jo was too busy staring at his reflection.

'Sort of, I suppose.'

'Have you got a spot or something?' Dan said as he watched his friend examine his chin.

'It's nothing. Do you think we need a jumper?'

'It's Scotland, you always need one. What's up? Did Uncle Ian say something?'

'Nope. Do we need to take any money?' he asked, wondering what Mr Fraser would say if he said he didn't want to go.

'I doubt it. We're going hill walking again. Anyway, if we don't have any, Dad will have to cough up for drinks.' Dan narrowed his eyes and studied his seemingly disgruntled friend. 'I bet I can guess what's rattling your chain.'

'Yeah...?' Jo picked up his water bottle from the shelf and threw it with some force onto the bed.

Undaunted, Dan continued. 'Has to be. Caught you at least five times checking out your neck and nose. Then there's all that hand clenching. Would those long showers be to determine if you're growing a tail?'

'SOD OFF!' Furious, Jo stormed to the door.

'I'm right, aren't I?' Dan called. 'You're all wound up because you are convinced you're turning into some kind of bird.'

Jo whirled round and strode back to the bed. 'This is so funny, isn't it, Dan? Go bury your stupid head!'

'You are not a bird,' Dan said flatly. 'You are not growing a beak. And last night, when you were getting changed, I saw no sign of a stupid tail. Nothing, Jo, you're winding yourself up over nothing. Before you go off on one, five quid says I'm right. And it's my last fiver because Dad's got the rest in the swear box!'

The absurdity of the bet broke the tension. Jo slumped down beside his friend, sighing mournfully. 'The professor hasn't said a word, Dan. What if it's because it's bad news?'

'That's rubbish. I've asked as well. Dad reckons it takes days to sort out a normal scan. Yours is way more complicated.'

'But what if I am...changing. I keep having these dreams,'

'When I was still living with Mum, I used to dream all the time about stupid things. They didn't come true though.'

'Yeah? Like what?' scoffed Jo. Like there was anything that could faze his friend.

'She tried to get me to do modelling,' he admitted, his cheeks scarlet.

'No way!' The idea was so ridiculous Jo began to laugh. 'You?'

'I got out of it with my usual flair. Pretending to throw-up over her favourite producer worked pretty well. Most of my dreams involved being dressed up in ball-gowns and stuff. Not quite the same, but enough to give me some pretty scary moments.'

'She didn't really make you, did she?!' Jo asked, mortified for his friend.

'Nah. But it didn't stop me having the dreams.'

'Sorry I had a go,' Jo said, already feeling better.

'It's okay. And I promise, if you do start growing a beak, I'll be the first to tell you.'

Admitting it to Dan definitely eased some of Jo's worry. The dreams disappeared or, at least, he didn't remember them. He felt safe, like he was inside a bubble, where only the four of them existed. It was the best feeling ever - until he thought about his wings.

It also helped that most days they were out on the hills, walking. The weather made little difference. If it rained, they wore wet weather gear; if it didn't, they carried it, just in case. Jo knew he was getting fitter. Every day he could do just a little more tai chi, walk an extra mile or so. He ignored the changes to his back. If he didn't think about it, it was easy to pretend he was normal.

On their twelfth morning in Scotland, they took a breather after finishing tai chi. The professor eyed his younger brother with a challenging glint. 'How about showing young Jo some Filipino skills, Simon? Escrima, if you think you're up for it?'

'Is that a challenge, old man?' Mr Fraser teased.

The professor didn't answer. He walked over to the wall where the wooden sticks hung in the case. Taking two of the shorter ones, he threw one to his brother.

'They're 60cm long and 2.5cm thick,' Dan whispered, as he and Jo hurried to the edge of the room. The conservatory windows were already wide open, so there was plenty of space for manoeuvre.

'They look lethal,' muttered Jo.

'I haven't seen Dad do escrima since he won in London a couple of years ago.'

'What did he win?' Jo whispered back.

'European championship...'

As though responding to an unseen bell, the two men strode forward, stopping a few yards apart. They bowed, not taking their eyes off each other for a second. A moment later, they touched sticks and they were off. Jo watched breathlessly. Twirling and swinging, the sticks whipped through the air. Sometimes blocked by the opponent's arm or hand, the two fought in what looked like an endless dance, their feet and hands a blur.

'Don't they hurt each other?' whispered Jo, as a sweeping attack landed on the professor's thigh.

'Only if you're not very good,' said Dan. 'You learn to control the power so you hardly touch.'

'Can you do this?' Jo was transfixed by the swirling figures.

'You've got to be joking. Can you imagine the damage I'd do? No, I haven't enough control - yet.'

'Wow, cool or what?!' Jo gasped. Mr Fraser vaulted effortlessly over the top of his brother's head, landing with the stick aimed directly at his neck.

'Enough!' The professor stepped back and bowed in submission. Immediately, Mr Fraser dropped the stick to his side and bowed too. 'Well fought. I'd forgotten how skilled you are, Simon.'

'I had a good master,' Mr Fraser replied with a grin.

Once the rituals were complete, they headed back to their rooms to change. 'Your uncle taught your dad then?' Jo asked.

'When they were in China, I think. Uncle Ian married a

Chinese lady and lived there for ages, before I was born though. He and Dad are half-brothers; same father, different mothers.'

'Did your dad live in China for long?'

'I'm not sure, I know he went all over the East. He even spent some time as a monk in Tibet.'

'No way!'

'Freaky stuff, he had the shaved head and everything. He still meditates every day, though he eats meat now. Weird, huh?'

'And some,' Jo agreed. Over a bowl of steaming vegetable broth, Jo couldn't shake the images of Dan's father in monk's robes. Lost in thought, he stirred his soup aimlessly.

'Got a lot on your mind, lad? The professor waved a plate of bread under his nose.

'Oh, um, sorry. I was just thinking about the escrima you were doing.' He smiled to cover the lie.

'That tai chi's starting to pay off,' the professor said. 'Your muscles are looking much healthier.'

'Does it happen that quickly?'

'Aye, it can. I was a bit concerned when I first saw the state of your shoulders and upper back. Not your fault, but you need to keep those muscles healthy.'

'So, I should keep doing the tai chi?'

'It can only help. Not just with muscle tone but your posture and balance. After all, you've got a bit more to contend with than most.' He smiled reassuringly. 'In a day or so I'll have your results and then I'll be able to give you more meaningful advice. For now, though, you're doing fine, so stop worrying,' he ordered.

'I'll try.' Jo looked sheepish.

Later that afternoon, he'd just got to a good bit in his book when the door to the sitting room burst open. Dan hurried in. 'Guess what?' he demanded.

'How am I supposed to know?' Jo closed his book with a sigh and sat up.

'Dad said we're going on holiday, staying at a hostel near Dundee. And, he's been asked to be a judge at a senior judo competition up there. How good is that?'

'Great, staying in a hostel sounds way cool. But why are you so excited? Don't you do that sort of thing with him all the time?'

'This is different. Didn't you hear? He gets to be a judge.'

'Is this special or...?' Dan wasn't making a lot of sense.

'He hasn't been a judge for years. Mum managed to get in the way of that.'

'What's she got to do with anything? I thought she ran a clothes shop?' Jo said, even more confused.

Dan flopped onto the footstool with a sigh. 'She does, but she hates Dad having anything do with sport, and especially martial arts. She thought he should run around after her all the time.'

'If she hates sport so much, why did they get together?' Jo asked.

'She fancied him, I suppose. I think she thought he'd just drop everything and do what she wanted.' Dan shrugged. 'They met at one of those big arenas in London. Mum was modelling and Dad was in a display team. Anyway, one thing led to another and, hey presto, here I am.' He cleared his throat, looking at some distant spot on the wall. 'Dad being Dad, they got married, but I can never remember them being happy. They were always arguing.

He wanted to set up an outward-bound centre with Uncle Ian but Mum, well, she refused to have anything to do with it, or Scotland. She told him that unless she could stay in England, she'd take me away and never let him see me. In the end, he bought her the shop and he moved to Devon.'

'Selfish or what?' Jo said, before he realised how it must have sounded. She was still his mum.

'She's always trying to stop him doing martial arts, especially competitions,' Dan said sounding grim. 'Well, she couldn't stop him, but she's been trying everything to stop him teaching me. She even went to a solicitor and tried to get a court order.'

'What?! That's unbelievable.'

'Like I'd ever say Dad made me do it. That's what she expected me to say. But in the end, just to stop her nagging, I gave up the classes I was taking. Dad was furious, but at least he didn't have to listen to her rant on all the time.'

'That's really crappy, Dan. You should have said something.'

'Yeah, well, it's over now. And anyway,' he said slyly, 'I've finally got my own way.'

'What made her change her mind about you living with him?'

Dan edged closer and lowered his voice. 'You remember I told you she kept dumping me at the shop, leaving me on my own to run it? I hated it, and it wasn't even legal. If anyone asked, I was supposed to say I was sixteen and the other assistant was on their break. Well, during the Easter holidays I was in there for three full days, while she and her mates went off to a fashion show somewhere. She'd timed it so Dad and Uncle Ian were away as well, so I couldn't even tell them. I was so fed up. Then I found this number for a hotline where you can report things.'

His voice changed to mimic a worried woman: 'There's a young boy left to run this shop alone and he can't be more than thirteen! Two days he's been here, I checked!' He grinned as Jo started to laugh. 'And sure enough, these inspectors turned up at the shop and caught me there on my own. She got fined and threatened with court action. It took her a while to work out who'd made the phone call.'

'How come she didn't throttle you?'

'She threatened to smash all my computer games and console. I just told her I'd tell everyone I knew about the fines and stuff, unless I could come to Dad. Strangely enough, she had a sudden change of heart, and here I am.'

'Nice one, Danny boy.' Jo had to admire his friend's nerve. 'So, will we get to watch some of the judo competition?'

'Definitely.' Dan beamed. 'We're there for two whole weeks. The competition isn't until the end of the second week, he'll still be able to join in all the other stuff.'

'Is it just us three then?'

'No. Dad and a couple of others run a youth club in Leemouth. He's arranged for a group of them to come up. We were supposed to be going with them to Dartmoor, camping, but this'll be way better.'

At teatime Mr Fraser explained more about the holiday. 'Dundee is perfect for hill-walking, with loads of places to canoe and climb. Ian pulled some strings, so it's all sorted. You two will have one of the en-suite rooms at the hostel, Jo, so no worries. Two of the group are taking part in the senior judo competition, so we'll all spend a bit of time each day helping them practise. Does that sound alright?'

'Bang on, Uncle Simon. I can't wait.'

14 A Beginning

The following day packing started in earnest. Mid-afternoon, the professor stuck his head round the bedroom door, as Jo hunted down a missing T-shirt and trainer. 'Has Rory been in here?'

'Yes, but I could have sworn I left my trainers on the porch.'

'I'm sure you did, laddie. Try under the rocking chair in the kitchen, or failing that, in his basket by the back door.'

Jo did as he suggested. He swept his hand under the chair and out came his trainer, followed by the T-shirt and a pair of boxers. He could have sworn he'd already put them in the wash. Mr Fraser wandered through as Jo stood up, clothes in hand.

'You're now an official member of the Fraser clan.' He laughed, taking the dusty clothes. 'He only does it to family. I'll pop these in with the last wash and they'll be ready for tonight. Now, Ian wants a word with you in his office. It seems he's finally managed to make some headway with the scan.'

'Right now?' Jo's stomach seemed to drop like a stone.

'it's better just to face up to it, Jo.

'I suppose.'

The professor was sat in his usual chair, with a row of photographs placed across the desk. Each one had a grid drawn over the top. With numbers and letters down the sides, they looked a bit like a graph. At first, Jo thought they were of different fossils. Then he looked closer.

'Is that what they look like?' He turned away, disgusted. In truth, he felt a bit sick.

'Come and sit down and tell me what you see,' said the professor.

'They look like skeleton or dinosaur wings-something out of a horror film.' Jo stole another glance. 'I mean, look at them! He stabbed a finger at the nearest photograph 'Dan called them amazing. How can those be amazing?'

The professor said nothing. He picked up another pile and laid them, one at a time, directly below the others. 'Take another look and tell me what you see now.'

Stomach churning, Jo leant forward a little and shook his head.

'I don't know what I'm supposed to be looking for,' he mumbled.

The professor pulled the nearest two photographs closer to Jo and pointed. 'What would you say if I told you that this one on the top line is from the first set of photographs, and this one here, from another set four days later?'

Jo gazed down, wishing he was anywhere else but in that room. 'They're bigger, I suppose. And that bit there,' he pointed to the lines of membrane snaking across the width of the wing, 'there seems to be more of it.'

'Good.' The professor laid out another line of photographs.

This time Jo didn't wait. 'Bigger again, especially that bone, or whatever it is, across the top.' Jo followed the sweeping contour with his finger, seeing for the first time the fine detail of joint and ligament attachments. 'What are all these? Is there something wrong with the photograph?' He bent closer. Tiny flecks were noticeable on the last few pictures.

'There's nothing wrong with the photograph. Take a closer look.' The professor handed Jo a large magnifying glass.

'Feathers. Tiny ones.' Jo looked up for confirmation.

'Aye, you can just see their tips. If it's the same as with other wings: there'll be a set of downy feathers first, you know, like chicks have. These will then be shed, followed by the growth of your first set of flight feathers.'

'Flight!' Jo felt his heart skip a beat.

'Let's not jump the gun.' The professor sighed and rubbed his forehead. 'I've the initial results from the X-ray and scan, Jo, and there are things you need to understand.'

'Is it really bad?' Jo was suddenly afraid.

'I don't mean to scare you, lad! It's a good thing I wasn't a medical doctor. Most of my patients would have died of shock. Shall we ask Dan to step in? It might be easier to have someone else listen with you.'

'Please,' Jo said, immediately relieved.

It wasn't long before Dan hurried in. 'What've I done now?' he asked.

'Nothing I know of,' said the professor. 'Why, is there something you want to own up to?'

'No, just checking. So, what's up?' The professor quickly explained about the photographs. Dan picked them up and began to study them intently. 'They've really grown. Are these feathers?' He pointed to the spots.

'Aye, they're just starting to come through. Now, if we can get on.' The professor turned to face Jo. 'You're not to worry if you can't remember everything, and I'll try and keep it simple.'

Jo just nodded. His mouth was so dry, he could hardly swallow. It was a lot to take in. Apparently, his wing bones had lots of holes in, which was good because that made him light. He also had extra ribs that were growing around his own. 'So, my own rib cage is inside this other one? But why have I got two rib cages?'

'You're not a bird, Jo. Your basic body is how it should be, a perfectly normal teenage boy. This should never have happened.'

'So, I'm a freak?'

'The only freak is the one who did this to you.' The older man leant forward, his eyes glinting angrily. 'You weren't born like this. When you were a baby, someone implanted cells into your spine at the top of your neck. Hoping, I assume, for a pair of embryo wings to form.'

'But what would be the point of doing that?' It made no sense at all to Jo.

'I have my suspicions. At the moment, all I do know is, someone's been messing about with DNA, quite possibly very ancient DNA.'

'Where did they get stuff like that?' Dan interrupted. 'Dad said most of Jurassic Park was rubbish.'

'Aye, and for the most part, he'd be right.' The professor closed his eyes for a moment. 'There's been some success, especially with all the new technology about. But the cretins who put this together...' His voice carried an angry tone. 'The field I work in is pretty small. Chances are I've met the imbecile who did this to you. And when I find out who that is...'

Jo shivered, unnerved by the determination he saw on the man's face.

'Uncle Ian?' Dan whispered.

'Sorry, lads.' He smiled down at the two worried boys. 'Let's finish with what I do know.' He went on to explain that Jo's wings were still very small, and had only just started to develop, and how the wings cleverly folded up because the bones were jointed and slotted over each other. Inside the sacs, each wing rested inside a shallow oval shape, which looked a bit like half an Easter egg. 'Are you with me so far?' he asked.

They nodded, though Jo felt as if his head was about to explode. 'But I take it there's bad news?' Jo said.

'I was hoping the nerve supply that's growing could be easily separated. That's not the case.' The professor took Jo's hand. 'It's attached itself to your spinal cord, very high up at the top of your neck. If I, or anyone else, try to remove those wings, you would end up paralysed from the neck down.'

'So, I haven't got a choice. That's what you're saying?'

'Not really, being paralysed would be the best outcome. The operation would probably kill you.'

'Oh.' Strangely, knowing the truth felt so much better.

'I know it's a bit of shock,' the professor began.

Jo shook his head. 'No, it sort of makes it easier, as long as I'm not going to change altogether, and turn into some sort of bird?'

'Good heavens, lad, no! Is that what's been bugging you?'

'It had crossed my mind. I was worried I might get a tail or... something.'

'I promise you.' The professor playfully ruffled Jo's hair. 'I hope that nephew of mine hasn't been winding you up.'

'No, he told me I was being silly.' Jo looked over at his grinning friend. 'I've been dreading this for days. Now I know the truth, it feels better somehow.' He glanced down at his hands before asking, 'But why did he do it, Professor? What's the point of growing wings inside someone? It's not like I'll ever be able to use them, is it?'

'That is not a question I can answer. At least, not yet. Right now, they're very small and just starting to grow. It's unknown territory, Jo. It's all about weight and wing span. It's going to depend on the rate of growth, your muscle strength, as well as how well you look after them. I can promise you, however, that they won't harm you, if you do what I suggest.'

'Harm me?'

'Your wings are a part of you now, like a leg or an arm. They need care and exercise. Regular exercise, Jo'

'I'm really scared, Professor,' Jo admitted.

'I'm not at all surprised, and I'd think less of you if you weren't. But don't let fear get in the way. Between us, we'll sort this.'

Dan leant in and nudged his arm. 'Too right, and that includes me, don't forget.'

'It's weird, though; if this was such a big experiment, Professor, how come I wasn't locked up all the time? I must have been dumped in at least eight different places.'

'I doubt they expected it to work, or maybe it was about hiding you in plain sight, who knows? I have to say, it's an experience that would push most youngsters over the edge.' He began to tidy the desk. 'Try not to worry. Hopefully, Dan will help keep your mind off things.'

'I need some fresh air,' Jo said, as soon as the office door closed.

They had walked to the pigsty before either of them said anything.

'Did you understand it all?' asked Dan.

'Sort of. The anatomy sounds complicated. I definitely got the bit about not being able to cut them out loud and clear.'

'Yeah. A bummer, that.'

Jo watched a pigeon fly from the roof of the pigsty, its wings driving through the light breeze as it climbed higher and higher. His back gave a sudden twitch. 'I don't think I'll ever have the courage to really do it. Can you imagine me up there trying to do that?' He pointed to the now circling bird and shivered at the thought.

'I can't ever imagine I'll be good enough to do escrima but I'm still going to try,' Dan said firmly. 'Small steps, that's what Dad always says.'

'I like your dad,' Jo said. 'Your uncle's cool too.'

'Being cool runs in the family.'

'Shame it missed you out then,' said Jo, dodging away from Dan's dig in the ribs.

15 Dundee

Mr Fraser woke them early the following morning. 'Seven thirty, that's cruel,' moaned Dan. Ignoring him, Jo rolled out of bed and began to stretch his arms and legs, enjoying the morning chorus as he came to.

'How come you're so cheerful? It's not natural.' Dan continued to grumble as Jo hummed quietly over his bowl of cereal. 'I hate mornings,' he muttered. Rory rubbed his head against Dan's leg as if agreeing.

As soon as the luggage was on the van, Dan slumped onto one of the rear seats and immediately closed his eyes. Jo, in contrast, was wide awake.

'Can I sit up front with you, Uncle Simon?' he asked shyly. It was such a treat being so high up. He wedged a pillow against the door for comfort and watched the miles fly by.

'Can I ask you something?' he said, once they'd been travelling a while.

'Aye, lad.'

'That competition you're judging, is it just judo?'

'It is. Though it's been a few years since I competed. I always try and keep my skill levels up.'

'Do you run lots of judo classes in Leemouth?'

'I do, along with John Brampton and a few others. It's part of the youth centre we run.'

'It'd be so cool to do something like that,' Jo said wistfully.

'Small steps, Jo. Tai chi is a good place to start.'

'I suppose...'

'Jo, there was something I wanted to talk to you about last night, but with everything Ian told you, I thought I'd leave it until today. There's nothing wrong,' he reassured, catching the boy's anxious glance. 'It's just I finally managed to trace that nurse, Julian Trantham.'

'You did? Wow... What did he say? Could he help?'

'Slow down! I found him, I didn't say I'd spoken to the man. He's living and working in Glasgow, which is why he's taken a wee while to find. If it's okay, we'll go and meet him next Sunday.'

'Cool. Does he mind?'

'He doesn't know. I used a nursing agency's website to find him. We'll just turn up. It will be better that way.'

'Did you hack into their files?' As soon as the words left his lips, Jo groaned, embarrassed.

Mr Fraser gave a short laugh, his eyes still on the curving road. 'Not exactly, though preventing anyone entering a secure site or domain without legitimate cause is what I do for a living.'

'Dan said you delivered packages, made sure they arrived safely?'

'That's a good way of describing what I do. Packages aren't always a physical thing. What travels over the internet is often of huge importance and easily sabotaged.'

'So, you stop people trying to track or divert information?' Jo said, after a moment of thought.

'Well put; that's a big part. Needless to say, I don't broadcast what I do. Dan knows, but I trust him not to say anything.'

Jo glanced at his sleeping friend. 'He's good at keeping secrets. He never said a word. Best friend ever.'

'What, even in the mornings, when he's a pain in the backside?' Mr Fraser teased.

'Yeah, I just wind him up more. So, how long before we're in Dundee?'

'We'll get there about one o'clock. I'm not going by the most direct route, and we'll stop somewhere for lunch first. Now, why don't you open that glove compartment in front of you and we'll have a toffee?'

It was nearly two before they reached the city. As they drove around the outskirts, the clouds were slate grey; it made the streets seem bleak and foreboding. The dark skies did nothing to help Jo's mood as he became more and more nervous. He couldn't imagine how he was going to keep his wings a secret. Joining up with the others from Leemouth seemed like a good idea at first. But now it was actually happening, he just wanted to hide - or even better, go back to the professor's house.

'Fabulous place, Dundee, especially when it's fine,' Mr Fraser mused. 'You can see for miles from the top of the city.'

'If you say so, but how much further is it?' Dan grumbled.

'Not far at all. It's just a few miles, on the edge of a village. Have patience.'

Finally, they drove up a long, pebbled driveway and parked outside a large Victorian building. Dan jumped to his feet but Mr Fraser stopped him with a raised hand. 'Stay in the van for just another two minutes, lads.' He jumped out, locking the door after him.

'Does he think we'll do a runner?' asked Jo, trying to quell his jittery nerves.

'He's just being over cautious.'

'Yeah, I suppose. Dan, this morning, when you were snoring your head off...'

'Like I snore!' he scoffed.

'Pigs are quieter, but anyway, after your dad told me about Julian the nurse, he mentioned some of the stuff he does with computers.' Jo watched Dan's expression closely.

'Good. It's been a pain not being able to say anything. I wish he'd hurry up though, I need the loo.'

Relieved, Jo sat back and tried to see if anyone was coming out of the building. 'Do you think the others will mind me not being able to do stuff?' he asked, hoping Dan wouldn't laugh.

'Why would they? Anyway, you can do loads, so stop worrying.'

'It's just…I've never done this sort of thing before.'

'It'll be fine,' Dan promised. 'I've only been to a few of the youth club meetings myself and I'm not even sure who's coming up. John Brampton will be there, only we call him Master Brampton. He's one of the joint leaders with Dad. Darren should be there as well, he's about twenty-three, I think. Then there are two female leaders. Karen's alright, but her son, Liam, is a bit of an idiot. Margaret, the other leader, can be a bit fussy. And then there's about four or five that are our age…'

Before he could say any more the locks on the van clicked open.

'Right, are you ready to meet everyone?' Mr Fraser asked.

Jo nervously stepped inside the large reception hall. To his left came the sound of racing feet and several voices.

'John, why don't you start the introductions?' Mr Fraser smiled at a slim man in his late thirties who stepped forward.

'John Brampton, co-leader of the youth club. And I also teach judo with Simon. It's very nice to meet you, Jo.' He shook Jo's hand, smiling.

A younger man stepped forward. 'I'm Darren Fields. I'm taking part in the competition. I'm a junior leader for the youth club, and a black belt second Dan in judo.'

'Cool. Nice to meet you,' Jo said, impressed.

An older woman stepped forward, long greying hair caught up at the nape of her neck. She looked like an old, bossy school teacher. 'Margret Wilton, co-leader and administrator for the youth club.' She smiled, though Jo noted her eyes immediately travelled over his thick-set shoulders.

The next boy to stretch out his hand was black with spikey cropped hair. He grinned as he shook Jo's hand firmly. 'I'm Adesola Solarin, though everyone calls me Ade. Paul and I are really into rock climbing and cycling.'

'Paul Deacon.' Ade's friend stepped forward to shake hands. 'It's great being in Scotland.' From way down the corridor came the sound of more voices.

'That'll be the girls, late as usual,' Ade said not bothering to hide the smirk.

When the girls turned the corner Jo's jaw dropped. 'LUCY?' He stared at the mass of spiky red hair that framed twinkling green eyes.

'Well, if it isn't Jo Fraser!' She didn't pause. 'Good to see you again, Jo.'

'You know her?' whispered Dan.

'Erm…yeah,' Jo stuttered.

'I'm Lucy Abbot,' she said to Dan. 'I'm so excited to be here. I've only just joined the club. I used to do judo and taekwondo where I lived before. This is Sarah.' She grinned at the girl towering over her.

'Pleased to meet you.' Sarah shook hands. 'I'm here for the senior's, though I'm not seventeen for another couple of months. I'll be going for my black belt in judo in six months.' Jo's fingers tingled from the pressure of her grip.

'And finally,' John Brampton waved forward a petite girl with long, straight blonde hair. She smiled shyly at them.

'Hi, I'm Zoe Rose. This is the best, coming up here. I can't wait to do the canoeing.'

Jo happened to glance in Dan's direction and caught his glazed stare. He nudged him hard.

'Hmm...?'

'Stop drooling,' Jo whispered, trying not to smirk.

'Thanks, everyone. Now these two are my son, Dan Fraser. Dan?' Mr Fraser repeated.

'Hi, everyone,' said Dan, though his eyes were still fixed on Zoe. 'I'm going to be living in Leemouth, so I'll be able to join the club full time.'

'And this is Jo Fraser, my nephew. Jo has recently had some major surgery, so he's not going to be able to do all the activities. Lots he can do, though, and he's learning tai chi as part of his daily therapy. So, unless anyone has any questions, you can all finish unpacking. We'll meet up in the main lounge in, say, half an hour and go and stretch our legs.'

Jo managed to keep his expression still. Surgery? Mr Fraser really should have warned him, he thought.

'Jo, a quick word.' Mr Fraser gently pulled him to the side. 'Sorry, I should have thought about that earlier. I've got to be honest, it was the first thing that came into my head.'

'It's alright, Uncle Simon, only, what surgery did I have?'

'Be vague. If anyone asks, tell them you had heart surgery. That will explain why no one should start jumping all over you, which I will make completely clear.'

Jo followed Dan up the winding, wooden staircase. The room they were to share was right at the back of the large building, well away from the main dormitories. It was pretty basic, with two low beds, a small shower room and toilet. There was a table crammed between the beds, a sash window with a wide sill, and two folding chairs against the wall.

'It's alright, isn't it?' Dan said, flopping straight onto one of the mattresses. 'But I suppose we'd better get sorted or Dad will be after us.' Jo hid a smile as Dan sped through his tasks. 'Hurry it up, Jo,' he called impatiently.

'This urgency, it wouldn't have anything to do with a certain girl with blonde hair?' Jo asked, as he neatly folded some trousers.

'You can talk. What about that Lucy? You could hardly take your eyes off her.'

'Just a shock, that's all. I mean, meeting her in Stetton like that, then she turns up here.' Jo finished putting his socks into a drawer and turned to find Dan staring at him.

'You haven't told me yet how you met her,' he demanded.

It was tempting to wind him up and say nothing. But with a sigh, Jo quickly told him the story of Lucy at the bus stop.

'See. Now, wouldn't you have been surprised?'

'Yeah, I would. Is that why you blushed when she smiled, Jo boy? You were surprised?' Dan's sniggers were cut off by a flying pillow.

They made it downstairs in good time and were soon heading out to explore the village. Jo felt awkward. He'd never been part of a group before, at least not one that didn't treat him as if he was some sort of idiot or freak. Every time someone spoke to him, he could feel the colour rise in his cheeks. It was like his head had been emptied and all that came out of his mouth was a load of gibberish.

'They must think I'm stupid,' he moaned, as he and Dan walked together for a few moments.

'No, just shy. The girls will think that's sweet,' said Dan

'I don't want to be sweet!'

'Stop worrying about it and relax,' muttered Dan. 'You know Lucy and the others all seem fine. It just takes a bit of time.'

'Suppose...'

'Lighten up. If you stopped looking over your shoulder every two seconds it might help.'

'I don't!'

'Want to bet? Look, take this packet of toffee and go ask Ade and Paul if they want one. Ask them about the sports they do. Trust me, you won't be able to shut them up.'

It worked like a dream. By the time they'd completed the circuit of the village, Jo knew more about rock climbing than he ever thought possible.

'I'm starving,' said Ade as the youth hostel finally came into sight.

'Tell me about it,' agreed Jo. 'I can't seem to stop eating at the moment.'

'It's an age thing,' Paul said. 'My dad's taken to locking the fridge at night. Shame he doesn't know I can pick the lock.' Jo sniggered, as did the rest of the group. He suddenly felt much better.

Food was served in the large dining hall at the other end of the building. The hostel provided breakfast from 6-9am and dinner from 5pm until 7pm every day.

'Least we don't have to suffer my campfire cooking,' said Dan, licking his lips. A tray of pork and apple bake landed on the table and he doled himself a healthy serving. 'Eat up, we've no idea how many this is for,' he warned. Jo piled his plate high. It didn't seem to matter how often he ate, his stomach always felt empty.

'Leave some for the rest of us,' Lucy called, hurrying in. 'Let's push the two tables together - the rest are just behind me.'

Once that was done, she settled onto the wooden bench beside Jo. 'So, is that cool black camper van the one you came up in?' she asked, fixing him with her green eyes.

'Yes, we travelled up from Leemouth a couple of weeks ago. Did it in stages.'

'I suppose you'd have to if you'd had surgery recently. Good thing you didn't have to use a tent, wasn't it?' Her expression was deadpan. Then he caught the tiniest of winks.

Managing to tear his gaze away, he looked over at Dan. Fork mid-air, his friend was once again staring at Zoe like a love-sick puppy. She remained oblivious.

'Is your friend always like this?' Lucy whispered.

'No, it's the first time I've seen it. Must be the blonde hair,' said Jo.

'Are you into blondes then?'

Jo shook his head and picked up a forkful of food. 'No, not my type at all,' he said, suddenly uncomfortable. He tried to change the subject. 'So, what's this taekwondo, or whatever you do?'

'You're alright, Jo,' she whispered, touching his arm. 'I'm glad you're safe.' Cheeks scarlet, he began stuffing food into his mouth as fast as he could.

For the rest of the evening they all sat together in the largest lounge, playing cards. 'How come Margaret's here, not Karen?' asked Dan, as Lucy began dealing again.

'Karen had to pull out at the last minute,' Ade explained. 'But at least Liam wouldn't come without his mother to hold his hand, which is always a bonus.'

The others sniggered in agreement.

'The trip almost had to be cancelled until Margaret agreed to step in,' Paul continued. He looked over his shoulder, checking none of the leaders were listening. 'Mind you, all she did on the way up was moan. "I don't know why it can't be Dartmoor,"' he mimicked.

'Careful, she's on the way over,' warned Ade. 'Lucy, let's have a decent hand this time,' he said loudly.

Linda Jones

16 Learning Curve

The following morning Mr Fraser woke them both at 6.45am. 'Exercises first, Jo, then downstairs, both of you, for meditation at half-seven, please. We're using the lounge where we were last night.' He put a thick, white jacket on Jo's bed. 'Wear it when we go to the hall. Everyone else will be wearing their judo kit. I've added some extra padding to yours. There are extra tapes on the inside as well, so you won't have to rely on the belt.'

Jo nodded, blinking sleepily. 'Thanks, Uncle Simon.'

'You're welcome. See you shortly.'

'You get up first,' said Dan, snuggling back under his covers. 'Give me a shout when you're done.'

Reluctantly, Jo rolled out of bed. Ensuring the door was locked he began his exercises. Everything moved much more easily now. Controlling when the wings sprang out was becoming second nature. He practised opening and closing the wings at will then tried to hold them open, as wide as they would go. He managed four minutes before they started to ache. A big improvement, he decided.

Jo glanced over at his friend and something white flickered at the edge of his vision. 'Wow, they've grown!' He twisted from side to side, trying to get a better view.

'What's that?' mumbled Dan.

'Look how much bigger they are!'

Dan rubbed his eyes and slid to the side of the bed to take a closer look. 'Yeah, and some. I can't believe they fold up so small.'

'What happens if they keep growing and they don't fit?'

'That's not going to happen,' Dan said firmly. 'It's not just your wings that are growing. You've sort of expanded around your back and chest as well.'

'Is that supposed to cheer me up?' said Jo. 'I'll end up looking like a barrel with legs.'

'Now you're being stupider than me, and that's hard.'

'What's stupid is to even think they'll ever be any use!' Unsettled, Jo followed Dan to the lounge and sat in a moody silence.

John Brampton called them to order. 'We've decided to start each day with meditation and spend part of each morning practising judo.' He smiled over at Sarah and Darren. 'We'll be using a local school hall, and I'm sure we'll all learn a great deal. Afternoons will be games, canoeing, rock-climbing, with some hill-walking and orienteering as well. Any questions?' With none forthcoming, he rang the small bell to start the session.

The professor had given Jo some deep breathing exercises to practise. He soon found his rhythm and the twenty minutes flew by. When the tiny bell rang out again, he opened his eyes and smiled. His bad mood from earlier had disappeared. He moved to his feet far more easily than even a few days ago.

'Sorry about earlier,' he muttered to Dan as they walked towards the dining room.

'No probs, but I'm starving. Let's try and get there first.'

Breakfast finished, they were soon on the move. The hall they were using was attached to a small primary school a mile outside the village. It was surrounded by open countryside with just a handful of cottages close by. As they clambered out of the vans, Jo looked around nervously. The area looked so exposed, so open.

'Oh!!' Startled, he flinched from the touch on his arm.

'Sorry, I didn't mean to make you jump.' Ade looked concerned.

'It's fine. I'm fine.' Jo smiled, trying to hide his embarrassment.

'Sensei asked me to give you these.' Ade handed over a pair of the thick, white trousers.

'Thanks,' said Jo, wishing his heart would slow down a bit.

As the noise level rose John Brampton called out, 'Everyone help empty the vans, please. It's tai chi first, followed by judo practice.'

The school hall was great, and completely separate to the main school. There was a reception area, with toilets off a corridor, then double doors leading into a huge hall. It had a stage at one end and plenty of room for them to spread out and do whatever they wanted. In the ceiling was a long gap, several feet wide, which went straight into the attic space. Five thick climbing ropes hung down from the rafters in the attic.

It was far more fun doing tai chi in a group Jo thought. To his surprise, he realised he knew almost as many of the moves as the rest of them. At the end of the session, Mr Fraser called him over.

'Yes, Uncle Simon?'

'I'm teaching, Jo.'

'Sorry, Sensei,' he corrected.

'Just to reassure you, the building is kept locked while we're in here, so you can move around freely. Now, if you're up for it, we'll try something a little different this morning. As you're moving so much better, how would you like to try some katas? Remember those practice moves I did with my arms and hands with Dan?'

'That sounds cool,' said Jo, thrilled.

'I'm going to ask Darren to teach you. They should help increase your hand, arm and shoulder strength. Quite a lot of the teaching starts in a kneeling position, so it'll be easy to build you up gradually. Think you're up for it?'

'You bet. Thanks, Sensei.'

Fifteen minutes later he sat on his heels and shook his head in disgust. 'How do you ever learn this?' he moaned, as Darren patiently ran through the routine for the umpteenth time. He watched again as Darren's arms and hands wove the intricate patterns. It reminded him of a playground game he'd seen. Girls sitting opposite each other and clapping alternate hands; only this was far more complicated. Instead of hand clapping, he'd to mimic the thrust of a dagger, or block a stab from an opponent. After forty minutes his shoulders throbbed.

'Don't worry, it was the same for all of us,' Darren assured him.

Jo eyed him doubtfully but managed a smile. 'Thanks for your time, I really appreciate it.'

'Other way round, Jo. This all goes towards my training. Now, let's finish off properly.' Jo bowed and waited to be released. 'Go with the force, young sky-walker,' Darren joked, before he headed off to talk to Mr Fraser.

'You did okay,' said Dan, sinking down beside him. 'First time I had to do that kata, I thought my arms had fallen off.'

'Tell me about it.' Jo rubbed his stiffening shoulders. 'How did you get on?' He'd been so engrossed in his own training he hadn't seen anything else.

'Well enough, I suppose. Lucy's as good as Dad said. She can really move.'

'What about Sarah?'

'She'd tear me up and throw me away,' said Dan. 'She really uses her height and weight well.'

'Does Margaret do any sport?' said Jo.

Dan sniggered. 'No way! Dad keeps trying to get her to do judo. I don't think she approves. She's good at the map reading stuff and walking though.'

'So, how good are Paul and Ade?'

'They're green belts, same as me. Though I reckon Paul's got an advantage with that foot of his.'

'What do you mean? How can a foot be an advantage?'

'Depends what it's made of,' Dan said with a smile.

'You're winding me up, right?'

'Nope.' Dan grinned at Jo's stunned expression. 'Seriously, his whole foot is false. I didn't realise until I tried to take him out with a leg sweep - it damn well hurts!'

'Wow!'

'Yeah, and he's cool about it. Told me he had meningitis and lost it when he was tiny.'

Lucy and Zoe wandered over with drinks, handing down a carton each. 'This'll be interesting,' said Lucy, sliding onto the floor between them. 'Sarah's got Paul and Ade sparring with her. Wait for the fun.'

'What, both at the same time?' said Jo.

'Like that's going to worry her,' scoffed Lucy.

At first it was impossible not to stare at Paul's feet and the soft, black slippers he wore. As the two danced around, trying to catch her out, false limbs were soon forgotten.

'Blimey, she can't half move,' said Dan, as Paul's leg shot out, missing her by a mile. He lost his balance and slipped to the floor. Sarah sprang over him and made a grab for Ade. He was down and out in one quick move.

'Is that the best you've got?' she taunted, stepping away. They were up in seconds and, with a quick bow, formed a pincer movement, trying to grab her between them. She feinted to the left. As Paul made a dive for her, she instantly changed direction and swept her other leg through Ade's. With a smash, he was down. Before he hit the floor, she turned and caught Paul's jacket, spinning him on top of his friend in an untidy heap.

There was a round of applause from the doorway. 'Nice move, Sarah, well fought,' said Mr Fraser. She instantly bowed low.

Between panting and laughing, the boys managed to find their feet and bow.

'Cheers, boys, looking forward to next time,' she said, not even out of breath.

For lunch they devoured the rolls and cake Margaret had organised. John Brampton announced that it was soft ball for an hour, followed by orienteering around the village.

'Can I play, Sensei?' Jo asked, keeping his fingers firmly crossed.

'Of course, just try not to fall over - and if you do, remember to roll properly.'

'I've never played before, though, so I don't know the rules.'

'Not to worry, Dan will explain.'

As Darren and Margaret set out the game, Dan provided a whispered commentary. He pointed out the bases and how scoring worked.

'Sarah, you are captain,' declared John Brampton. 'You've got Dan, Jo, me and Darren. Paul, you captain with Zoe, Ade, Lucy and Sensei. Margaret will referee, her decision is final.'

'Don't forget,' Dan whispered, as their team got ready to field, 'Catch it if you can before it bounces. Throw it straight to the fielder at the base they're running towards. You're on second base, by the looks of it.'

The game was a riot. Dan was better at catching than hitting, although he did manage to score a run. Jo found looking at a moving ball impossible and dropped more than he caught. At least his batting was better; he managed three runs without being called out. A few times during the games he felt his back twitch - he just pulled his belt tighter and hoped the feelings would go away.

'Rematch later in the week,' said John Brampton, as the game finally came to an end. Jo's team had lost by a single point.

They were split into two groups for orienteering. Jo was with Darren, Zoe and Paul, while Dan had Lucy, Sarah and Ade.

'Right, you lot,' Mr Fraser called over the noise. 'Pick up a map and compass each. You should also have a list of reference points and clues. The aim is to reach as many sites as you can, in the order they're set out, by five o'clock. No cheating,' he warned.

'There's no point following each other because each group's trail goes a different way around. When you reach a site, you will need to choose an object to take away with you. If you haven't done things in the right order, you won't know which item you need to pick up.'

'Is it a treasure hunt?' Zoe called.

'Yes. The biggest prize is for the team who covers the most sites, in the correct order, in the best time. Margaret, John, and I will be keeping an eye out. No straying outside the village boundaries, and no talking to strangers. None of the clues involve asking anyone anything.'

At first, Jo found it really difficult concentrating on what the others in his group were saying. Every time a car or anyone walked close, he had the urge to hide or run for the hills.

'Are you alright?' said Zoe. She'd obviously asked him something and he hadn't heard a word.

'Sorry,' he mumbled, feeling daft.

'Do you live in a town? Only it can be weird stuck in the country when you're not used to it.'

'Sort of. Erm…you were good at judo this morning,' he said, desperate to change the subject.

'You think? Mum wanted me to go to this summer ballet school, but it's not like I'm going to take up dance for a career.'

'Oh, I don't know,' said Paul, 'I can see you flapping away in Swan Lake.'

'Like you'd know anything about it, Deacon,' she snorted. 'My foot arches aren't strong enough for one thing, and I can't really see me living in a tutu, can you?'

Gradually, Jo began to relax. Mr Fraser and John Brampton were nearly always somewhere close. Nothing was going to happen. Besides, he thought, orienteering was difficult enough without worrying about being hijacked. He stared down at the map in his hand, trying his best to follow the directions the others were discussing. He couldn't even work out where they were now, let only where to go next. The clues, on the other hand, were much easier to understand.

'What do we reckon this means?' Darren said, frowning at the fourth clue. 'Ex-spire anew.'

'The old church, it has to be,' said Jo. He was surprised to see blank looks from the others.

'How do you get church from that?' asked Zoe.

'Spire, as in steeple…for a church. 'Ex', meaning old, or one that's gone. 'Anew' could mean rebuilt,' he replied.

'Sweet, I'm glad you're on our team,' said Paul.

'Let's check the co-ordinates again,' said Darren, already lining up the compass. 'Yep, looks about right.' It didn't take long to find the neat building tucked away in the corner of the village. The article they eventually chose from the box was a cricket bat.

'Has to be that, to follow on with the other clues,' explained Jo, as the others debated whether to take the tennis ball, badminton racket or rugby shirt.

'Tell us why then,' said Zoe.

'The last clue was: Lord Trent to Head over at Gloucester's behest.'

'Yeah, but that could be the ball,' Paul interjected.

'Wrong sort, it's a tennis ball,' said Jo. 'All those names are cricket grounds: Lord's, Trent Bridge, Headingley…'

'Of course! Am I dumb, or what?!' Paul slapped his forehead. 'How come you're so good at these?' he asked, as the two of them began walking side by side.

'Hours spent in classrooms not being able to do sport. Some of the teachers left me a few quiz books to do.' Jo wanted to ask him about his foot but now the moment had come he felt awkward. 'Paul, I er…'

'It's just from the ankle,' said Paul, obviously used to questions. 'I lost it when I was a baby and I've worn a prosthetic since I was about five. They get changed pretty frequently, especially now, because I'm growing so much. This latest one's the best - it's got a proper moving joint. Great for sports.' He grinned at Jo's embarrassment. 'It's okay, I've got used to it and it's cool watching girls freak out when they see me take it off. Not our lot,' he added. 'They were completely chilled about it.'

'Yeah, they would be. So, do you understand this orienteering stuff?' Jo stared at the squiggly lines that refused to make any sense.

'Pretty much.' Paul lifted the map out of Jo's hands and turned it round. 'It helps if you've got it the right way up.'

Eventually, they arrived at the hostel to find the other group had beaten them back by a few minutes. 'We'll announce the winning team in the lounge after supper,' said John Brampton. 'Go wash up, everyone.'

'First again, I see?' said one of the cooks, as Dan and Jo hurried in after the fastest shower ever. She slid two large dishes of food onto their table.

'Can you blame us? It smells wicked,' said Dan.

'Aye, and I suppose you'll be expecting seconds as well?' she said, though she smiled as she walked away.

'You're so obvious,' said Jo, doling a large spoonful of rice and chicken curry onto his plate.

'Being nice will get us more food. You'll see.'

The rest arrived; soon, everyone was eating and talking through the events of the day.

'What's on tomorrow? Do we know yet?' asked Jo.

'Same in the morning,' said Lucy. 'I heard Darren mention going to Dundee for the afternoon.'

'That'll be cool,' said Ade. 'I need some more batteries.'

Jo and Dan headed straight towards the lounge after dinner, but Darren stopped them at the door. 'Mr Fraser wants to see you in his room,' he said.

'Now what's up,' muttered Dan as they reluctantly climbed the stairs. Jo shrugged, anxiety already gnawing away at his stomach. It was bound to be something bad. Maybe the professor had rung to say he'd found out more about his back?

Mr Fraser's room was similar to theirs just larger, with three beds and chairs. As they walked in, Jo noted his uncle's serious expression. The knot in his stomach tightened.

'Pull up a chair, there's a couple of things I need to talk to you about.' This didn't sound good at all thought Jo.

Mr Fraser continued, 'I've had a phone call from your mother, Dan. As you can imagine, she had a lot to say.'

Dan's face went a deep shade of red. 'Is she trying to make me go back there?'

'No, though I can't say she's happy we're at a tournament. But there isn't a great deal she can do about it.'

'She's always managed to cause problems in the past, why's everything different now?' said Dan.

'Well, let me think. Maybe it has to do with her son threatening to expose some embarrassing moments?'

Dan gasped. 'How'd you know about that?'

Mr Fraser smiled and tapped the side of his nose. 'Moving on. One of the reasons she rang was to say she's going to Spain for the next couple of weeks. The other reason has more to do with you, Jo.'

'Me? But she doesn't know me, Uncle Simon.' Jo looked over at an equally confused Dan.

'Someone purporting to be from the local CID has visited her shop, asking questions about you two. They weren't the police, I'm positive. My guess is, whoever is trying to find you, still hopes to track you via Dan.'

'So, what'll we do, Dad? Mum's useless at keeping secrets. They'll be up here on the next available plane!' Dan twisted in his seat, as if he expected the door to burst open at any moment.

'Stop exaggerating, Daniel. Your mother believes we're in Sweden. There's a judo tournament being held there as well, so I made a double booking. The records will show me as an entrant. They'll realise something's up once they get there, but it gives us a bit of time.'

Jo felt awful. They were supposed to be on holiday, not worrying about him. 'Won't they just have to telephone and check, Uncle Simon?'

'I know the organisers well. They're quite happy to cover my back. Meanwhile, it will give me enough time to put some extra security in place.' He looked at their two worried faces. 'Nothing's going to change, at least for the next few days. John, Margaret and Darren are under the impression there's an issue with security because of my job. That's easier to explain. I don't like to lie but I'm not sure they're ready for the truth.'

'You're right there,' muttered Dan. 'Just imagine Margaret's face if she walked in on Jo.'

'Let's not go there, lads. I've arranged for three security people to join us. Two will arrive tomorrow, and one on Saturday. They'll be in the background but I'll feel much happier knowing they're around. Now, let's talk about sensible precautions.' He eyed them sternly. 'You're both vulnerable. Don't leave this building alone, not for any reason. Ideally, only in the company of at least two other people. Agreed?'

'Agreed,' they chorused.

'If you notice anything unusual, say something. If people in the hostel approach you, or you're asked to take messages to folk in their rooms, just don't, okay? I don't care how rude or ignorant people might think you are, don't be tempted.'

'I promise, Dad.'

'Same here, Uncle Simon.'

'Keep your mobiles handy at all times; take them into bathrooms, showers, everywhere, understood?' Again, they nodded. 'Now go back and enjoy the rest of the evening. And try not to worry.'

'That's easy for him to say,' said Jo as they hurried away.

The others were playing cards when they walked in. 'Everything okay?' asked Lucy, peering at them over the top of her hand.

'Just a phone call from my mum, nothing important. Can we join in, or shall we wait till you finish this hand?' said Dan. Jo kept his head down, wishing he could be as calm and upbeat as his friend.

They had only just started playing again when John Brampton, Margaret and Mr Fraser walked in. 'I expect you'd all like to hear the results of the hunt,' said Margaret, in her usual condescending tone. It made Jo feel about seven years-old. 'Firstly, did you enjoy the hunt?'

'It was great, though we were a bit confused by that fifth clue,' Zoe complained.

'We'll run through the answers in a minute. First, though, I think we should award the honours.' She pulled forward some carrier-bags. 'Second prize goes to...' Everyone waited, eyeing the parcels. - 'Sarah's team.' Over the general uproar she continued, 'Of the eight compass points, you got eight correct but you chose one wrong object. Well done, those clues weren't easy.' She handed a smaller parcel to each of them. 'And to the winning team, congratulations!'

'I've never won anything!' said Jo, taking his larger parcel.

'It's down to you, Jo. We'd never have got some of those clues without you,' said Darren.

Tearing off the paper, Jo smiled at the pocket compass, wind-up torch and box of chocolates. 'Excellent! And they're my favourites,' he said, grinning.

17 Security

Jo's dreams were full of running and dark corners. Every time he tried to escape, Bowden was there. Worse still, the doctor's head kept changing into a vulture's; that wanted to tear him apart. He was glad to finally wake up, though when he did, his shoulders, arms and legs hurt like mad from all the exercise. Despite the aches everywhere else, his wings seemed fine. 'Is it supposed to hurt like this?' he moaned, as he limped down the stairs behind Dan.

'Dad reckons if you can't feel it, then it isn't worth doing, or something like that. The best thing is more of the same.'

'You're kidding, right?'

'You'll probably feel better once you've warmed up. Well, a bit better anyway,' Dan said. 'And what were you dreaming about last night? You woke me up with your shouting.'

'Sorry,' said Jo, trying not to yawn. 'Doc Bowden kept turning into this vicious vulture.'

'Ah, that would definitely do it,' said Dan.

Sitting through meditation was a trial but the large breakfast helped. Dan was right - the warm-up exercises soon loosened everything, and by the time they'd finished tai chi, he could move pretty well.

'Guess you're stiff after yesterday?' Darren asked.

'A bit,' Jo admitted.

'We'll go gently and run through the first set, see how you're shaping up. Don't worry about speed, okay?' As they came to the end, Darren smiled. 'You've a good memory for patterns. How does it feel, could you manage a little more?'

'No problem,' said Jo eagerly.

Darren and Sarah used one end of the hall for judo practice. The others spent the rest of the morning using the climbing ropes and playing relay games. Jo was banned from the climbing but the rest wasn't a problem.

By lunchtime, everyone was hot and panting, ready for some food. Lucy swung down beside Jo and sprawled out on the floor, her face red with exertion. 'I heard we're off around the town this afternoon,' she said.

'As long as it doesn't involve moving my arms, only I got a bit carried away with the katas,' Jo admitted, wincing.

'Have a shower, but make sure you massage your muscles first,' she warned. 'You really don't want cramp.'

Back at the hostel, Jo stood under the stream of water for ages, letting it massage his neck. It felt wonderful. He had only just finished dressing, when Dan came hurrying back into the room they shared.

'Dad said to give you this.' He handed Jo two notes.

'Twenty pounds. What's that for?'

'Duh! What do you think? To spend, of course.' Dan shook his head at him. 'We've both got the same. He said it has to last us until Wednesday, at least, unless there's an emergency.'

'Mega.' Jo couldn't think of a time he'd ever had so much money that he could spend on just anything.

As they arrived in reception everyone was waiting. 'Margaret has decided to stay behind this afternoon,' announced Mr Fraser. 'Ade, Paul and Zoe are with Darren and John in the minibus. Everyone else, with me in the van, please.'

Lucy made a beeline for the long seat at the rear of the van. 'Let's sit back here then we can talk,' she said, with a meaningful glance, to Jo. As soon as the van pulled out onto the road she whispered, 'Right, what's going on? And don't pretend there's nothing.'

'Lucy!' Jo hissed.

'Jo!' she retorted. 'Why's all this security arriving? We overheard Margaret muttering, and she reckoned it's for your uncle. But it's not, is it?'

'We'll be in so much trouble,' Dan murmured.

'Well?' insisted Sarah. 'Do I have to sit on you to get the truth?'

'It's complicated,' said Jo eventually. 'There are some pretty heavy blokes chasing me. Uncle Simon reckons Dan's at risk because we're friends. And that's all I can say.'

Sarah gave a low whistle. 'Have you two been robbing banks?' she began to laugh, stopping when she caught the look on Jo's face.

'This isn't a game, but I promise I'm not in trouble with the police.'

'Well, that's not much to go on, Fraser,' said Lucy

'Look, I can't say any more,' he pleaded. 'Please, Lucy, it's bad enough me being here. If those blokes think you know anything...' Jo sighed. How was he supposed to make them understand?

'So, who are 'they'?' Sarah asked.

'I really can't tell you, and anyway, you wouldn't believe me if I did.' It felt like a brick had dropped into Jo's stomach. The chance of them remaining friends was probably out the window now.

Lucy turned to Dan, her eyes narrowing into green slits. 'Do you know what this is about?'

'Yeah. But I'm not saying a word.'

There was a long silence. Eventually, Lucy turned her gaze back to Jo. 'Fair enough. At least it explains why you're so jumpy. I was beginning to think it was me.'

'Excellent. Now you can help watch our backs,' said Dan.

'Depends whether we think you're worth it, hey Sarah?'

Sarah smirked, smoothing down her thick hair. 'I've always wanted to play bodyguard to two hulking guys, but I suppose you two will have to do.'

Jo felt his whole body relax as Lucy smiled properly. 'Did the rest overhear as well?' he murmured.

'Paul and Ade know because I told them,' she said. 'Zoe...She's a bit of a problem. Her dad's an inspector for the CID in Exeter. Her parents are coming up to Scotland on Monday and they're meeting up with Zoe for the day. I thought we'd wait until they'd gone and tell her then.'

'Makes sense,' said Jo, though Dan didn't look so sure. 'Though I'm not sure Uncle Simon's going to be happy that you know.'

'That's not a problem,' said Lucy. 'We won't tell him.'

They'd been travelling for a few minutes when Sarah nudged Jo hard. 'What now?' he said, rubbing his arm.

'Did you happen to get a look at these men?'

'I could describe one of them pretty well,' he admitted.

Sarah pulled out a sketchbook. 'Okay, describe away.'

As they arrived at Dundee, Jo studied Sarah's drawing

'That's him, almost exactly! Just widen his jaw a bit. He looks different sometimes, because he wears sunglasses and a chauffeur's hat. I've never seen him in anything other than a shirt and tie.' He clamped his lips shut, thinking he'd said far too much, not that anyone seemed to have noticed.

Sarah quickly did another couple of sketches. Dan picked one up, admiring her work. 'These are good. I can't even draw a straight line.'

'I've thought about being one of those police sketch artists,' she said, finishing off the third picture. They were all so absorbed watching her draw that none of them noticed the van had stopped.

'Any chance you could do a copy for me?' Mr Fraser's voice made them all jump. Dan swore. His father instantly held out a hand. 'That'll be fifty pence. The swear box is building up nicely.' Picking up one of Sarah's sketches, he held it up to the light. 'I won't ask for an explanation – yet - but I'm assuming that's a good likeness, Jo?'

'Yes, Uncle Simon,' he muttered, mortified.

'You've a real talent, Sarah. Do you mind if I keep this?' He pointed to the first sketch where the subject had no glasses or cap.

'Sure. I'll copy it, then we'll have a spare,' she said, unfazed.

'And I'm sure I don't need to emphasise that the people after Jo are extremely dangerous. If I think any of you are doing more than just keeping a cautious eye, I'll cancel this trip and have you back in Leemouth within the day. Is that understood?!' He didn't need to raise his voice, they got the message loud and clear.

The subdued group nodded and began to pick up their bags. As soon as Mr Fraser was out of earshot, Lucy whispered, 'Do either of you have any idea what sort of vehicle they drive?'

'A blue Peugeot, and a black BMW,' murmured Jo. 'Dan's got the registration numbers.'

In the car park, John Brampton called them together. 'Right, everyone, it's two o'clock. I want you all to be back here by 4.30pm. Does everyone have their mobiles?' He waited as they checked. 'Any problems, ring Simon, Darren or me. We'll be about, keeping an eye on things. You're welcome to walk with us if you'd prefer.' There was a shuffling of feet and bowed heads. John Brampton chuckled. 'I'll take that as a no. Try to stay together. Be safe, be sensible, and stay out of trouble. High street and various sites of interest are behind you. Take a street map, and have fun.'

Almost as soon as they set off Lucy made a beeline for Ade and Paul. 'Two guesses what she's telling them,' Jo whispered.

'It's better they know,' said Dan. 'It means you won't have to check around all the time. We'll all be on the lookout.'

'But it's not exactly fair, is it? You're all supposed to be on holiday.'

'If it wasn't for you, we'd be stuck on the stupid moor, doing the same stuff we do every year.'

'I suppose,' said Jo, but he wasn't convinced.

A few minutes later Ade and Paul sidled over. 'Lucy's explained,' said Ade. 'It's okay, we won't ask. I knew something was up when you were so spooked all the time.'

'Spooked? Really?'

'Yeah,' Paul said, 'I reckon you'd worked out how many cars, people and dogs lived in that village within a minute of walking in there. And when that car backfired...'

'Give it a rest,' said Ade, nudging him hard.

'Sorry,' Paul grinned. 'My big brother's in the Royal Marines. He's the same when he comes back from a tour. It takes him weeks to sort his head out.'

Jo saw the funny side and began to laugh. 'I'll do my best to chill out a bit. Though you need to know, it's not a joke...'

'Yeah, yeah, we heard the lecture as well.' Ade nodded at Lucy.

Surrounded by his new friends Jo began to relax and enjoy the visit. They trudged through the streets to the Desperate Dan bronze statue and the one of the Dundee Dragon that Paul insisted they should see. Lucy then insisted on dragging them up to the 'Law' - the highest point overlooking the city - so they could look out over the river. She proudly pointed out the two bridges and the fact they were standing on the edge of an extinct volcano.

'Wish the stupid thing would erupt,' Dan muttered. 'I'm frozen.'

'I heard that, you pleb!' she called over the strengthening wind. 'And I thought you Scots were supposed to be weatherproof? Okay, I suppose we could find a café.'

A hot drink later, and a great deal warmer, they walked around the local shops, buying the usual tourist mementos. By the time they got back to the vans, they were glad to clamber inside away from the chill wind.

Dan dumped the dragon-shaped doorknocker he'd bought onto the seat next to him. Sarah immediately picked it up, looking at it in disgust. There was a vivid lime green and red tartan painted across its rump. An odious orange and pink tongue of flame leapt from its purple mouth. 'Just tell me why, Dan? What possessed you to buy such a thing?'

'No need to be rude. Just because I've a keen eye for spotting the unusual.' He grabbed it back, admiring it with a mocking smile. 'It's hideous, isn't it? Thought Uncle Ian would love it. He can put it on his office desk and think of me every time he looks at it.'

Sarah gave his shoulder a reassuring pat. 'Not even you are that hideous, Dan though it's a close-run thing.'

He stuffed the dragon away in a pocket trying not to laugh. 'Let's have a wee look then?' he said, as Jo put down his bag.

Jo pulled out one of the small tissue-wrapped parcels, feeling a bit silly. 'Tell me if you think your dad will like it. 'There's a greenish one for the professor as well.'

It was a keyring with Dundee enamelled in small, gold letters across the centre. Hanging from the short chain was a pair of miniature wings. Each feather, painted with blue enamel, was incredibly detailed. The whole thing was about the length of his small finger. 'Wow, they're cool,' Dan assured him.

As soon as they arrived back, they dumped everything in their room and raced to the dining hall. 'I'm so hungry, I could eat a horse,' Dan declared, sniffing. 'That smells awesome. What do you reckon it is?' he glanced around, hoping to find the place empty.

'You're not first tonight, sweetie,' the cook called out. Jo looked over to the far corner. Two men were ploughing their way through plates of steaming lasagne and chips. One of the men, with pale blonde hair, glanced over and smiled.

'Ya, it's good, Sven, don't you think?'

The man sitting next to him looked up, wincing slightly. 'Very good indeed, Jan.'

Dan caught Jo's eye. 'It has to be security?' he whispered

Despite not being first they couldn't complain as a huge tray appeared in front of them, steaming and bubbling. They didn't say a word for two whole minutes, their mouths full. Zoe appeared next, quickly followed by the rest. Paul heaved food onto his plate and sighed as he took his first mouthful.

'Great stuff, I was starved. Guess what, we've got company in the dorm.' He pointed vaguely at the two men.

Jo was busy talking cycling with Ade when Mr Fraser entered the room and walked directly towards the two men. The blonde rose to his feet smiling in welcome. There was an audible gasp from around Jo's table. The blonde man was easily six foot nine, if not taller. His shoulders were enormous. He stretched out a massive hand, enveloping Mr Fraser's almost to the elbow.

'Oh wow!' said Sarah.

'Looks like we were right,' murmured Dan.

As Jo and the others were scrapping back benches ready to leave for the lounge, Mr Fraser stopped them. 'Before you go, there are a couple of old friends I'd like you to meet. The giant here is Jan Olsen, and this is Sven Milson.'

'Ya, delighted that I am to meet you all.' Jan stood, towering over them all. His pale skin crinkled into deep lines around his eyes as he smiled.

Sven leant forward and shook everyone's hand. 'As I am, but you'll have to forgive my friend, he can sometimes be a little…over the top.'

'Ah, Sven, you say many hurtful things. But Simon explains we may come and join in with your sports, Ya? This, I really look forward to.'

With a practised move, Mr Fraser managed to sidestep Jan's hefty pat on the back. Jan laughed, a deep ringing note.

'So, if it's good with you boys you can show us which beds we are sleeping in?'

'Our pleasure, Mr Olsen,' said Paul, craning his neck to see the man properly.

It was gone seven before Paul and Ade joined everyone in the lounge. 'They're so cool,' said Ade as he flopped into a chair. 'Really funny. Jan's like this giant clown.'

'Margaret's not so keen,' sniggered Paul. 'You should've seen her face just now.' As he said her name, the door opened and she stepped inside, closing it firmly behind her. She kept her hand on the door handle, as if she were afraid they were going to escape.

'Ah, Joseph, there you are. Given the amount of exercise you've had, I thought it might be better if you took it easy tomorrow. I'll be happy to...

The lounge door was thrust open with some force. 'Ow!' Margaret yelped, and staggered a few paces into the room.

'Look at me, I know not my own strength!' Jan's booming voice sounded upset but his eyes as he stepped inside said something very different. 'I think the door is stuck, then 'poof', you are flying.' He began patting the furious Margaret with a huge hand.

'I'm fine, really,' she insisted, trying to push him off.

'Ah, that is good, but you should go check, make sure no splinters.'

'Up to your usual tricks, Jan?' said Sven from the doorway.

'Small accident, this is all,' he said, trying to dust Margaret off a little more.

With a furious shake of her head she succeeded in pushing his hand away. 'Really, I'm quite alright.' She slid past the two men without another word.

Sven waited a moment before turning to the quietly sniggering group. 'Is it something we said?' he asked, his expression a picture of innocence. They burst out laughing.

'Are those two for real?' Jo murmured, much later, as they made their way to their room. 'I don't think I've ever laughed so much.'

'Yeah,' Dan agreed. 'Although I'm pretty sure Jan's accent isn't from any Scandinavian country I've ever heard of.'

'Do you reckon they're only pretending? The voices and everything?'

'Jan is, at least. Not that it matters, I still really like them.'

'Do you think anyone else realises?' asked Jo.

'I don't think so. It's probably because I like mimicking that I picked it up. Jan's over the top. A bit too obvious.'

I suppose you're right.' Jo said, stifling a yawn

.

18 Break In

Jo blinked and smiled up at the familiar face. 'Morning, Uncle Simon.'

'Morning, Jo. Is everything okay?' Mr Fraser sat on the edge of the bed, and glanced over at his snoring son.

'Fine. There's no pain, though they're loads bigger. The exercises the professor gave me must be working.'

'Do you mind if I have a quick look?'

'No, not at all.'

Mr Fraser locked the door whilst Jo stretched and rolled his neck and hips. He let out a low whistle when the two wings flipped out of the sacs to flutter gently. 'Grown quite a bit, haven't they?' He walked from side to side, peering closely. 'Hello, what's this?' He picked up something white from the floor. 'Have you two been having pillow fights?' He held a soft, white feather.

'No, honest.'

'In that case, I think this belongs to you.' Mr Fraser slid the small feather into Jo's palm.

'That's from me?'

'Your wings are full of them, but this is the very first to fall. Like milk teeth.' He grinned as Jo could only stare, speechless.

His exercises finished, Jo woke his friend. Dan grudgingly staggered into the bathroom. 'Was that Dad I heard earlier?' he asked, when he yawned his way back in.

'It was. He wanted to check on my progress.'

'And, what's new?' he asked.

'Just this.' Jo pulled open his drawer and handed him the soft feather. Dan didn't say a word. He stared down at it for a long moment before holding it up to the light.

'It looks mostly white, but in this light, I can see some blue and brown, or green, maybe?' He sounded so excited, Jo wandered over to take another look.

'You want to keep it? Though why the hell you'd want a feather...' The heat rose in Jo's cheeks.

'The first to moult, are you serious?' Dan looked so pleased, Jo immediately felt better.

'I gave that key-ring to your dad this morning.'

'What' did he say?' Dan asked, carefully folding the feather into a tissue.

'I'm pretty sure he liked it. He seemed a bit lost for words.'

'I bet he was.' Dan slid the tiny package into his drawer. 'Thanks for this, Jo. I really appreciate it.'

Meditation was crowded as Sven and Jan decided to join them. 'You're not minding, I hope? Only we are practising the meditation every day. Isn't that so, Sven?'

'Yeah, like I believe that,' Lucy said, rolling her eyes.

John Brampton rang the bell at the end of the session, but it was Margaret who announced the plans for the day. 'You're all going to the hall this morning for judo practice and games. You'll come to the hostel for twelve and change. As soon as you arrive back, put the bags you're taking near the kitchen, so I can put in the rations. We plan to head out to the hills for a walk and have our lunch outside. Okay, everyone, go fill up on breakfast.'

Jo could see she was trying to catch his eye. He ducked behind Sven and almost ran to the dining hall. Last thing he wanted was Margaret clucking over him.

'Why's your dad wearing a red belt with his judo gear?' whispered Jo, as Mr Fraser slid in beside Darren at the front of the van.

'He's an 8th Dan. Black only goes up to 6th. An 8th to 10th wears red. No idea why he's in full rig, though. I guess we'll find out.'

In the school hall tai chi soon loosened everyone up. 'I thought Sven and Jan might have been here,' said Lucy, sidling over to stand next to Jo.

'So did I. Perhaps they'll come along later.' Jo felt a tap on his shoulder and turned to see Mr Fraser and Darren. 'Sensei, is there a problem?'

'Just wanted to say how well you're doing, Jo.'

'Thanks, everything feels loads better,' he admitted.

'I'll leave you with Darren again, if that's okay? Master Brampton and I are going to practise a few moves.' Mr Fraser strode away to the other end of the hall.

'Wow, are they going to fight each other?' asked Jo, as the two men began laying out mats.

'I believe they're planning to have a few rounds. Sensei said something about wanting to loosen up. He's off to meet with a few of the other judges later.'

Despite the distraction the katas went well. Trying to do them at speed was far more difficult. 'Stop trying so hard. Relax,' advised Darren, after Jo fluffed two of the moves for the fourth time in a row. 'It's already in your head. Keep your eyes on me and let your mind and hands do the rest.'

'Can we try again?' Jo willed himself to be steady. Another ten minutes later he leant back, stretching out a kink.

'Much better. You were straight through twice and far more controlled,' said Darren, sounding pleased. 'Now you've got some speed, I'd like you to practise with one of the others. Take a five-minute break then back here.'

Sipping a carton of juice, Jo watched John Brampton supervise Sarah, Paul, Dan and Ade on the mats. He decided to wait for Zoe or Lucy to come back from the toilets and ask one of them to practise with him. He was so absorbed watching the others it took a full second to take in what he was hearing.

'GET OFF! Sensei, Master...Help!'

Jo spun on his heels, but before he could move a step the doors out to reception burst open, crashing against the wall. From out of nowhere Darren leapt, pushing Jo forcefully out of the way.

'What the...?' Jo shouted, bewildered, as a loud thud and a furious shout echoed around the hall.

A menacing figure stood where Jo had been only a moment before, a sneering laugh twisting the stranger's lips. Clutching his injured side, Darren strode in front of Jo. From the back of the room, John Brampton strode forward.

'You want some more?' the man heckled, pointing to Darren.

There wasn't time to say anything before the doors burst open again. Zoe staggered in. Jo only had a moment to take in her white face and eyes wide with fear before Lucy ran in behind her.

There's another, with a knife!' Lucy gasped, shooting a terrified glance over her shoulder.

'You three, get to the back of the hall!' John Brampton ordered.

Like lightning, Darren jumped, blocking the first attacker as he tried to grab Lucy. Jo could hear the others calling out for him to hurry, but he'd only taken a stride when the doors crashed open for the third time. An older man half ran, half limped inside, an evil looking blade clenched in his fist. It was John Brampton who leapt to block the man's way. Jo took his chance and ran for it.

'What are you after?' John Brampton demanded.

'We'll take whatever we want,' sneered the older man. 'There's not much you can do to stop us.' He tried to dodge past Brampton, but a foot stopped him dead.

'I don't think you'll find it that easy,' said John Brampton, shadowing his every move.

Huddled together, all Jo and the others could do was watch. Someone gripped Jo's arm so tight, it went numb.

'Where are the police?' Paul hissed. Jo caught the gasp of horror from Zoe. Mr Fraser had stepped into the hall, he was only yards away from the two men.

It was like watching a film, only in slow motion. The attackers turned, and with a roar, made a dive for the seemingly defenceless man. Jo opened his mouth to yell a warning - but before the words could leave his lips the younger one staggered backwards, clutching his chest. Yelping in pain, he fell, in a groaning heap, to the floor. The older attacker staggered off to the side, swearing loudly.

Eyes like lasers, Mr Fraser glared at him. 'So, you thought you could pick off the ladies? Nice work, Lucy, Zoe,' he called, his gaze not moving from the knife.

'Get out of the way,' The man swore loudly, spittle flying everywhere.

'Darren, phone Sven,' Mr Fraser ordered.

'Sven?' he queried, but dialled anyway.

'Mick, get up!' but his accomplice stayed curled on the floor, groaning in pain.

'Drop the knife or you'll join him,' warned Mr Fraser.

'Like hell I will,' the man snarled. 'Bring it on.'

'Master Brampton, Throw those two bats, please.'

'Rounders bats?' hissed Ade. 'Against a man with a knife. Is he serious?'

'Dad knows what he's doing,' said Dan as two bats sailed through the air. Ade didn't look convinced.

Sarah put herself at the front, arms spread protectively around the group. At one side, Paul hopped from foot to foot. Jo could hear him muttering as he kept glancing at the hall doors, but there was still no sign of Sven or anyone.

'How come he's using two?' Jo whispered to Dan, trying to stop his knees from shaking.

'Using one is called "baston". If you use two in a crisscross style, it's called "sinawali" - and two are always going to be better against a knife.'

Mr Fraser stood with the bats held lightly, his gaze focused on the man. His opponent crouched. Every muscle of his body seemed to twitch.

'Last chance. Give up the knife,' Mr Fraser instructed. The answer was a roaring charge; the man lurched forward, knife raised.

As the man attacked Jo began to worry. He wasn't half bad. It wasn't just the knife - he was really fast on his feet. Worse, Mr Fraser seemed to be nowhere near as quick as Jo remembered. A minute later he began to appreciate the tactic. The stranger was already panting. With hardly any effort, Mr Fraser held the furious attack at bay. His opponent, however, was suffering badly. As he ducked to avoid a clever thrust and sweep of the bats, beads of sweat were clearly visible on his face.

Mr Fraser picked up pace. It was like he'd pressed the next speed setting on a game console. He was so light on his feet; he moved effortlessly around his attacker. With a yelp of frustration, the man tried to dive clear, only to topple backwards. Instantly, Mr Fraser was above him, a bat poised over the man's throat.

'First round, Sensei,' John Brampton called, his voice calm.

'This isn't a competition!' Zoe hissed as Mr Fraser stepped back.

Jo squeezed Lucy's arm, unable to speak. Dan nudged him from the other side. 'Look! Here's Jan and Sven, at last.' The two men peered into the hall, trying to stay out of sight.

'Why don't they come and help?' Ade murmured.

The attacker started to pace again, his face like thunder. 'Not bad,' he jeered. 'Shame you're going to lose a few fingers!'

Mr Fraser didn't react. Cool and focused, he waited for his opponent to make the first move. Once again, the man was like a bull at a gate. The bats twirled faster and faster; the man's yelps grew louder and angrier as they found their mark. This time Mr Fraser raised the pace much sooner. His opponent ducked and weaved, desperately trying to find a way through. Suddenly he darted to the side, making a grab for Zoe. With a hiss, John Brampton was there and kicked him away.

'For the last time, drop the knife,' Mr Fraser demanded.

The man's answer was to spit over his shoulder and make a run for the door. It was hard to understand exactly what was happening. Jo caught the blurred outline of wood; the bats twirled and spun so fast, he couldn't follow them. Mr Fraser leapt into the air, just before the attacker's fist reached Sven. In the next instant, the knife skittered harmlessly across the wooden floor. A bat was held like a noose around the man's stretched neck, a knee lodged firmly into his back. Stunned at the speed of it all, Jo and the others could only stand and gape.

From the door came the slow ripple of applause. 'Very good, Sensei, very good,' called Sven. 'It's nice to know you haven't lost your touch.'

Jan just whistled and cheered. Before anyone could catch their breath, two more men ran forward clutching handcuffs. Mr Fraser, with only a little help, had them trussed up and on their feet within a minute. Jo didn't have time to take things in before they were hustled away.

'Where are they taking them?' asked Zoe, her voice higher in pitch than usual.

'Don't worry, it's all sorted,' said Mr Fraser calmly.

'Yes, but...'

'I promise, Zoe, we just need to ask them a few questions.' Jo went cold as the truth hit like a wall of ice. 'Not now,' Mr Fraser murmured, catching Jo's frantic look.

'Jo, are you alright? 'John Brampton looked anxious. 'He didn't touch you, did he?'

'No, Master. I'm okay, but what about Darren?'

'He'll be fine, lad.'

'I didn't see a thing,' Jo admitted, as he was bombarded with questions from the others. 'Darren shoved me out of the way then I heard a loud thud.'

'That was the guy's foot in Darren's ribs,' said Ade. 'He came charging through those doors - looked like he was heading straight for you until Darren got there. He was quick, mind. That kick came from nowhere. Do you think...?' He broke off after a nudge from Paul.

'Close,' Dan murmured, as the two of them moved away a little. 'Does Dad think this was about you?'

Jo shrugged hopelessly. 'He hasn't said.'

'Don't start thinking the worst,' said Dan. 'They were probably after money and stuff.'

'Bit hard not to. Where's Darren. Is he really alright?'

'He went with Sven, something about checking his ribs.'

'Do you think he'll need to go to hospital?' Jo asked looking anxiously at the door.

'I'm sure he'll be fine, stop worrying.'

It was five long minutes before Darren reappeared. He smiled around, as if nothing had happened.

'I'll be back in a sec, Dan. I just need a quick word,' said Jo. He approached Darren, a little embarrassed. 'I, er, just wanted to say thanks. Are you really okay?'

'I'm fine. Honestly,' Darren promised. 'Sven tells me I'm bruised, not broken.'

'Only if you hadn't pushed me away,' Jo swallowed hard. 'You were amazing.'

'All this extra practising came in handy and there's no real damage. I get worse during training,' he assured him.

'How was he?' asked Dan when Jo reappeared.

'Okay, just bruised. Did Zoe say what happened to them?'

Dan's expression turned bleak. 'They were just coming out of the toilets when those two came barging in. The older one grabbed Zoe but she managed to knee him, hard.' He grinned as Jo winced. 'Lucy got in a good kick as well. They ran into the hall, and the rest you know.'

'How did they get in? I thought the outside doors were supposed to be locked.'

'Margaret,' Sarah hissed over Jo's shoulder. 'She dropped off those drinks. She didn't lock the doors after her, the idiot.'

'Careful, Sensei's back,' Lucy warned.

'Are you lot okay?' He stood beside Zoe and smiled around 'That was certainly an experience.'

'Fine, thanks,' said Sarah. But I'd like to know how they got in.'

'And doubtless that will be one of many questions,' he said without missing a beat. 'You two handled yourselves very well. Your parents will be proud, Zoe. And your gran, Lucy.'

Zoe blushed crimson but she held his eye. 'Are you going to tell them what happened?' she challenged.

'Yes, of course. Trying to attack and rob members of the public is a criminal offence, at least it was last time I checked.'

'Weren't you scared going up against a man with a knife?' asked Paul. 'I mean, you only had a couple of bats.'

'Aye, any sane man would've been. It's what I did about it that matters. Fear's a strange thing, Paul. It can freeze you so that you can hardly move, or you can accept the fear for what it is. An emotion, a warning to the body and mind to get ready, to be prepared.'

'Don't suppose there's any chance you could show us that last move again, is there?' Ade asked.

'Not today.' Mr Fraser smiled. 'Master Brampton and I have talked about starting some escrima classes when we get back. That's if anyone's interested. Now, if there are no more questions, let's spend the last hour playing a game of soft ball. My meeting isn't until one, so I've time.'

Jo looked up at the clock; it was still only eleven. 'It feels more like teatime. I'm knackered,' he admitted. His back ached and tingled; his whole body felt tense.

'It's the excitement,' said Dan. 'Don't worry, once you start running around, you'll soon pick up.'

Paul wandered over, using the pretence of laying out one of the bases as cover. 'Are you alright?' he asked Jo, sounding serious for a change.

'I'm just a bit shaken up, that's all.'

'Sort of makes it real, doesn't it? I don't believe that guff about them being thieves, do you?'

'Not really,' Jo admitted.

'At least we got to see Sensei in action. He's going to take some beating.'

Jo nodded, trying to be positive, though he couldn't stop thinking about what would happen if Darren wasn't there the next time. He didn't have much time to brood. Jan and Sven strode back into the hall.

'Ya, soft ball, this is good,' Jan announced, taking in the bases and bats. 'This way, I won't break the house down.'

They had been playing for forty minutes, and hardly anyone had managed to get a ball past Jan 'This isn't fair!' Ade shouted over the bouts of hysterical laughter. The man's reach was so wide he could just pluck the ball from the air. Sven came up behind Ade to whisper in his ear. Ade grinned then whispered to Lucy, who was attempting to bat.

'Right, once more,' she called. Instead of aiming high, she sent the ball whizzing just above the ground, straight between Jan's legs. Giant arms whirling like a windmill, he lost his balance and crashed to the floor. Pretending to be furious, he started chasing Sven around the room. Jo and the rest fell about laughing. Lucy almost forgot to run.

And then it happened...

Jo's back gave an almighty quiver. He didn't have time to think. Holding his jacket tightly to his chest, he ran, just hoping he could make it to the toilets in time. It was a close call. As soon as he slipped the bolt across in one of the cubicles, he tore off his jacket and T-shirt. The wings snapped out to flutter against his bare skin.

'Jo? Jo?' Dan's frantic whisper echoed through the space.

'It's alright. Are you on your own?' he whispered back.

'Yes, it's just me. Let me in.'

'Is there a lock on the outside door?'

There was a shuffling of feet. 'Locked it. Now let me in!'

'There's not a lot of room, hang on.'

Jo managed to fold his wings just enough to allow him to edge out of the cubicle. For several seconds the two boys stared at their reflection in the mirrors opposite.

'Wow, they look incredible! I'm usually half asleep when you're exercising.' Dan prodded Jo's rippling chest. 'Tell you what, you're really starting to look fit. You've even got muscles.'

'Yeah...? Just the little problem of these muscles back here.' He pointed over his shoulder to the gently flapping wings.

'Hey, careful where you point those!' Dan ducked as a wing- tip whipped past his nose, sending a white flurry into the air.

'Sorry, mate!' Jo tried to move out of the way but only made things worse. He inadvertently gave Dan a sharp dig in the back.

'Those things are lethal,' said Dan.

'Sorry,' Jo repeated, watching as several feathers floated to the floor. Another landed on his friend's head. He looked at the floor then up at Dan. 'Oops!' He couldn't stop the snigger. The floor was now covered with a layer of soft, white down, all the more vivid against the harsh black granite tiles. Beside him, Dan was bent over, desperately trying to stifle his giggles. Jo tried his best not to join in. 'Stop! This isn't funny,' he begged. 'Every time I laugh more feathers fall off.' Another flurry of white settled around them.

Dan turned his back, his shoulders still heaving. 'Sorry, I'll be okay in a minute.'

Jo decided he might as well give the wings a good flutter. 'I think that's all the loose ones off,' he said, relieved.

'We could make a fortune on U-Tube,' said Dan, glancing around at the sea of white.

'Get me locked up in some experimental place, more like. Come on, let's clean up.'

'What are we supposed to do with them?' Dan asked, holding up a fistful of soft, white feathers. Loads more were heaped at their feet.

'We need a bin-bag or something.' Jo looked around for a cleaner's cupboard but there wasn't one.

'We can chuck them out of the window.' Dan pointed to the ones above the sinks. 'I'll take a quick look.' He balanced on the slippery edge and reached up. 'Sweet, the catch on this one is broken. I think it backs straight out onto that school field.'

Folding Jo's jacket over like a bag, they stuffed the feathers inside. Dan shook the jacket out of the window, Jo retrieving the few strays that flew back in.

They were just leaving the toilets when Mr Fraser came hurrying around the corner. 'There you are. I was starting to worry.'

'Sorry, Uncle Simon, only a bit of a 'thing' happened,' Jo began.

Dan snorted and turned away.

Mr Fraser smiled as Jo quietly explained. 'Quick thinking, lads. I'll do a double-check, and make sure you didn't miss any. You go back to the hall.'

'Was it alright to throw them out the window, Dad?'

'They'll degrade, but I think we should have a word with Ian about your exercises. How is your back now, Jo?'

'Fine, all safely stowed away,' Jo ignored Dan's snigger.

'Good. Well, ride up front with me on the way back to the hostel. We need to talk.' Before Jo could ask more, he disappeared into the toilets.

'Sounds serious,' teased Dan.

'Don't. We haven't done anything wrong, have we?'

'Hey, it's you he wants to talk to. Don't pull me into this.'

As soon as Jo climbed into the van he asked, 'Is there something I've done wrong, Uncle Simon?'

'Nothing I'm aware of, but I'm always happy to take confessions, Jo. I just want to talk to you about tomorrow - It's Sunday?' he reminded him gently.

'Oh, Glasgow! I'd completely forgotten.'

'I'm pleased you did. At least you haven't been worrying about it. Hopefully, you're having a good time.'

'Best ever, I wish it could just keep going.'

'We'll head off after breakfast. Say, about nine thirty. You just need to bring your mobile and an iPod, if you want to.'

'If we don't leave until after nine, how are we going to make it there and back in one day? Don't I need to pack something?' He didn't fancy missing more than he had to.

'Nine thirty will be fine, and no, just your mobile and an iPod will do.'

'Is it alright if I still go for the walk this afternoon?' Jo asked, aware of the murmur of voices behind them.

'Why wouldn't it be?'

'I thought, with those men...'

'Sven and Jan will be with you, as well as Master Brampton and Darren. Nothing's going to happen. This morning was a blip. A very annoying one, but it won't happen again.'

'Sorry to be such a nuisance,' Jo mumbled.

'I'll let you know when you are, Joseph. Now stop worrying and enjoy this afternoon, okay?'

'Okay,' he promised.

The boys quickly changed into their hiking gear and were soon heading to the hills. Walking up the rough trails, Jo was surprised how easily he managed. The only dark cloud was Margaret. Every ten minutes she kept wandering over, checking he was alright. 'Wish she'd stop doing that,' he muttered, shooting a furious look as she strode away yet again. 'If she asks me one more time...'

'Maybe she was a nurse or something?' Dan suggested.

'More like a teacher from hell.'

'We'll be stopping to eat in a bit. Have a word with Master Brampton or Dad when he gets back.'

'That seems a bit, you know,' Jo shrugged uncomfortably.

'Sensible?'

'Bog off, Danny boy.'

They found a sheltered spot out of the wind and ate lunch. The view was spectacular. As usual, Jo put his and Dan's backpacks together and lay across them, his chest supported. Contented, he watched the clouds wishing he had a pair of binoculars handy.

'You really shouldn't lie like that, Joseph. It's bad for your spine.' Margaret loomed over him like a storm cloud.

'It helps to relax the muscles,' he said, without looking up. 'My specialist suggested it and it works a treat.'

'What exactly is wrong? I've had a lot of experience with back problems and I've never heard of such a thing.'

'His heart, Margaret.' John Brampton's reply was insistent. 'All sorted now, so Simon tells me. The surgery to correct it left some muscle and skeletal problems, apparently. Fancy another coffee? Sven tells me there's a cup in the flask.'

'Thanks,' Jo mouthed as she was edged away. He caught John's raised thumb behind her back and smiled.

Lucy dropped down beside him. 'What did she want?'

'Just her usual interfering,' Jo muttered irritably.

'It's a great view,' she said, leaning back. 'Look, is that a kestrel?' she pointed eagerly at a bird circling in a thermal of air. 'How cool is that? I can't wait to try hang-gliding. They reckon it's as close as you can get to the real thing. There's a club in Leemouth but you've got to be sixteen. They'll take you up in a micro-glider, but then you've got the buzz of the engine. I think that would do my head in. Would you like to try it?' she asked, still gazing up at the bird.

'Umm...' Jo desperately looked around for Dan.

'You're not afraid of heights, are you?' She turned to look at him.

'No, or at least I don't think so.' Jo shrugged. 'I've never had to try.' Lucy's eyes seemed to bore right through him. 'Toffee?' he fumbled in Dan's backpack for the sweets, anything to stop her staring.

The boys made it into the dining room first, again but only just. Several extra tables had been laid, which made Jo feel uneasy. It was hard not to keep looking around. 'So, what sort of person do you think it'll be?' he asked, trying to concentrate on his food.

'What are you talking about?' Dan bit into a thick, spicy sausage dripping in gravy.

'Security,' he whispered.

'Foreign. Probably Dutch or French,' Dan said confidently.

'Has your dad said something?' Jo said suspiciously.

'No, I'm just guessing. What do you think?' Dan smothered another piece of sausage in a layer of mashed potato before taking an enormous bite.

'Perhaps a woman pretending to be a hiker, or that she's here on business,' Jo said, warming to the possibilities.

'No way, she'd stand out like a sore thumb.'

'Bet you a pound I'm nearer than you?'

'Easy money,' said Dan, shaking his friend's hand.

There were six new people that evening, spread around several tables: two women dressed for hiking, and the rest, middle-aged men.

'None of them look like a bodyguard,' muttered Jo.

'Maybe it's one of the staff?' Dan suggested. 'Or they're keeping out of the way so we don't spot them.'

Later, as they lay in their beds, Dan asked, 'Are you going to ask Dad tomorrow who the third security person is?'

Jo's heart skipped a beat. He'd tried really hard not to think about Glasgow. 'No. That way our little bet will be fairer.'

He changed the subject. 'You get to go canoeing tomorrow, don't you?'

'You mean I'll end up freezing my backside off in the lake,' mourned Dan. 'I'll spend more time in it than the canoe; I usually do.'

'I hope someone takes loads of pictures then. Night, Danny boy.'

It wasn't long before snores emanated from Dan's bed. Jo couldn't sleep for ages. His head was too full of the soaring kestrel, and wondering if he'd ever really be able to fly.

19 Glasgow

There was a lot to do before Glasgow. Making sure he did his exercises thoroughly was first on Jo's list. Unfortunately, as soon as his wings popped out, there was another flurry of white. He and Dan raced round, trying to pick them all up before going downstairs to meditation. After breakfast, Jo watched the rest of the group drive away in the minibus with a heavy heart.

'Are you ready?' asked Mr Fraser, joining him on the gravel drive.

'I suppose.' Jo's stomach twisted with nerves. He automatically turned towards the camper-van.

'We're taking a taxi, Jo.' Mr Fraser nodded to a black cab just pulling to a stop.

'Aren't we going to the train station, Uncle Simon?'

'Not today. Jump in, we need to get going.'

'We can't be going all the way to Glasgow by taxi, surely?' Jo said.

There was a snort from the driver. 'Oh, I wish. It'd pay my wages for a week, lad.'

'Wait and see,' said Mr Fraser, smiling. 'If you can't guess, it should certainly take your mind off things.'

The sign for thc small charter airfield gave it away two minutes before they saw the first plane. 'We're flying? I've never been near a plane, let alone flown.' Jo could hardly contain his excitement.

'A silver lining then, though I hope you don't get air sick. I didn't think to bring any travel sickness pills.'

'It's going to be a problem if I throw up every time I fly,' Jo said, sniggering. Mr Fraser's lips twitched and he had to look away.

'Here we are,' the driver announced. 'You have a good time now. Make sure you have a hard-boiled sweet to suck, it'll stop your ears popping.'

Eyes everywhere, Jo could have happily spent the morning just watching the planes. They boarded a small charter plane with blue stripes running over the wing. Sitting near the front, Jo had the window seat. It wasn't long before a young man in uniform climbed aboard and began explaining the emergency procedures.

'That's the pilot,' Mr Fraser explained. 'We'll soon be taking off.'

A couple of minutes after the pilot climbed into his seat, the plane's engines roared into life. Mr Fraser gave Jo two cushions to put at the base of his back. As the plane rose into the air, they pushed him forward slightly, taking the pressure off his wings.

'Wow, you can really see the curve of the earth! Cool or what?!' Jo was transfixed. He was disappointed when, just twenty minutes later, the plane began its descent towards Glasgow airport.

As soon as they disembarked Mr Fraser headed for the taxi rank. Jo glanced longingly at the huge planes waiting to leave. 'Another time,' the older man promised, catching the boy's sigh. Once they were settled on the back seat of the taxi, Mr Fraser gave directions and they sped off.

'The gentleman we're going to visit lives some distance away.' He held a finger to his lips and gave a small nod towards the driver.

'Are we eating first?' Jo asked. His stomach had started to rumble.

'I'm sure we'll find a café or a pub,' Mr Fraser assured him. Lapsing into silence, Jo gazed out of the window at the strange city. The streets and roads whizzed by in the light Sunday traffic.

The taxi finally dropped them near a parade of shops.

'We'll have lunch and wait around here until nearer the time,' said Mr Fraser. 'He only lives a couple of streets away, so we can follow on foot. Hopefully, he'll head straight home. If he doesn't, - well I'll make it up as we go along.'

'Uncle Simon,' Jo began. 'Those men who broke in yesterday...'

'I haven't spoken to Sven yet,' he said, then changed the subject.

At twenty minutes to two, they walked slowly up the street where the care-home was. Mr Fraser pointed to a shady corner. 'We'll wait here. We should see him leaving without too much of a problem.' As two o'clock chimed from a clock tower, the front door to the care-home opened. Two women walked out and hurried away.

'What if he's already gone?' Jo whispered.

'Patience, he'll be out soon.'

Minutes later, the door opened again. At first Jo didn't recognise Julian; he wore a hat and waistcoat, nothing like his usual uniform.

'It's him, Uncle Simon, I'm positive.'

'Stay where you are until I call.' Mr Fraser walked casually onto the pavement and pretended to tie his shoelace. 'Let's go.' His whisper reached Jo easily. They stayed some distance behind, until Julian walked up to a very smart-looking house and went in.

'We'll give him two minutes,' said Mr Fraser, his eyes scanning the area.

'How much should I tell him?'

'Nothing about your back at all. Just follow my lead.'

He pointed Jo to the side of the green front door. Taking out what looked like a mobile phone, he waved it up and down over the doorframe, before knocking firmly. Seconds later the door swung open.

'Sorry, no salesmen or religious stuff,' said Julian abruptly, the door already beginning to close.

'Mr Trantham? Mr Julian Trantham?'

Jo watched the edge of the door shudder to a halt. There was a definite note of fear when he answered. 'Who are you? What do you want? I demand some identification.'

Mr Fraser waved Jo forward. 'This, Mr Trantham is the only identification I need.' He rested his arm lightly on Jo's trembling shoulders. Julian stared at him, confused.

'I'm sorry, there must be some mistake. I've never seen this boy in my life.'

'Nurse Trantham? Julian, it's me, Jo. Jo Ranson.' Saying his name felt awkward. For a moment he saw confusion before recognition dawned.

'Jo? Little Jo?' He stared, wide-eyed. 'My goodness, boy, what the hell are you doing here?'

'Please, may we come in?' Mr Fraser asked. 'It's probably best not to do this on the doorstep.'

'Of course, yes.' Julian looked up and down the street, before pulling the door firmly closed behind them. 'Go through, the lounge is along on the right.'

'Could I just use a bathroom?' Mr Fraser asked, as they stepped into the light and airy room.

'Of course, I'll make us some coffee. Jo, go on in. I shan't be long.'

Jo stepped into the neat, sunny room, which smelt like flowers on a spring day, but he was far too nervous to do more than perch on the edge of a low footstool.

Mr Fraser arrived back first. Jo jumped to his feet, grateful not to be alone. 'Sorry, I needed to do a quick check,' he murmured.

Julian came hurrying in, the tray clattering. 'Jo, I brought you a juice, is that alright?' Nervously, he fussed over sugar and milk. Wasting time, Jo figured.

'Maybe I should make a start?' said Mr Fraser.

'Yes, yes, you must be in a hurry.' Julian sat back, his brow slick with sweat.

'Can I ask, Mr Trantham...'

'Please, call me Julian,' he interrupted, wiping his brow with a neat blue handkerchief.

'Thank you. Julian. Why are you so afraid?'

Julian fidgeted with his mug. 'I don't know what you mean.'

'Something happened. Something scared you enough to make you pack your bags and move, all the way to Scotland.'

'How do you know I didn't just decide to move here? My partner, Peter…'

'You met your partner after you moved. Please, it's important you tell Jo the truth.'

Jo broke the uncomfortable silence. 'Someone killed the people I'd been staying with. Whoever they are, they've been trying to track me down, and I need to find out why.'

'Killed? You mean…' Julian's eyes were huge.

'Murdered, yes,' said Mr Fraser.

Julian covered his face with shaking hands. Before Jo could speak, Mr Fraser raised a finger to his lips. They watched as the man shuffled and twitched, muttering under his breath, for what felt like ages.

'It's hard to know what to do for the best,' Julian said eventually. 'The answer to your question, Mr…'

'Just call me Simon.'

'It's hard to say what I'm afraid of. You mustn't think any of this is your fault Jo, but it's since I went hunting around at that blasted clinic. Do you remember, when I tried to find out a few things for you? Well, nothing's been the same since. All I did was to ask a few questions, and suddenly, my contract at the clinic was withdrawn. I couldn't find work anywhere locally. I know I sound paranoid, but I felt sure someone was following me.'

'What did you discover at the clinic?' asked Mr Fraser. 'Jo's told me what he can. He remembered a time you were angry about something?'

'There weren't many of us who worked for Bowden; at least, not regularly.' Julian pursed his lips. 'I can understand why; the man was a nightmare.' Jo laughed as Julian began to mimic the doctor's accent. 'Do this, Trantham. Take that, Trantham. Honestly, no respect whatsoever. If it hadn't been for the extra money and the likes of young Jo here, I wouldn't have bothered.'

'I take it Bowden is from South Africa?' Mr Fraser commented.

Jo looked surprised but didn't say anything.

'Definitely, though he's been over here a while. The accent's smoothed out a bit, if you know what I mean. He didn't see many patients, fortunately. Those he did see were all children.'

'Did they come to the clinic at the same time as me?' Jo asked

'Same day, maybe. Bowden always saw his patients' hours apart. It was very strange. I only ever worked for him five or six days a year, if that.'

'Were these other children like me? I mean,' he felt Mr Fraser touch him gently on the shoulder. 'Did they have the same thing wrong with their necks?'

'All I was ever told was that you all suffered with some sort of cyst that couldn't be removed. Now, let me think.' He drummed his fingers on his knees for a moment.

'Susan Richards, she'd have been fourteen or fifteen. Very sad. She'd never been particularly well, but she died, recently, about two months ago. Maggie called to tell me. She'd overheard Bowden on the telephone talking to someone about it. He was furious, apparently. The last time I saw Susan, which was fourteen months ago now, the swelling was large. Maggie told me it had suddenly grown a lot bigger, and then she'd gone.'

He looked more closely at Jo, his eyes travelling over his neck and shoulders. 'I'd never have recognised you on the street, Jo. Your shape has changed so much. You look positively normal, if I may say so.'

'Surgery,' interjected Mr Fraser, before Jo could say a word. 'A colleague of mine managed to sort the problem before it did any more damage.'

Julian nodded, seemingly accepting the explanation. 'There were other children when I first started,' he continued. 'But whatever his speciality was, Bowden's patients didn't survive very long. Susan was one of the oldest. Sorry, Jo, I don't mean to be so blunt. By the time I left, there were only the three of you remaining. The other is a younger girl - Amy Smith I think they called her. Frail little thing, looked like a pixie. She must be ten or eleven now. That's if she's still with us, of course.'

Jo shuddered. Images of the bathroom at the Bigwells and the cave flashed into his head. Amy had been so scared. It wasn't fair.

'What did you find out when you went hunting for information?' Mr Fraser asked again, trying to bring Julian back on track.

'Well, that's the thing, hardly anything. I mean, Jo's file should have been inches thick. Instead, all I found were four pages and a birth certificate, and that was stuffed in a brown envelope.' He paused, his brow furrowed as he tried to remember. 'Only one of the pages was about you, Jo. There was a woman's name, Rachel - but the surname had been scribbled out. It started with a 'C', I could make that out. Then birth weight; you were a tiny thing, only four and half pounds. There was something about, Rig-stock? I remember that because it puzzled me. It wasn't anybody's name; there was no Mr or Mrs, just the words: Rig-stock.' He sat back and took a swig of coffee.

'Rachel Ranson was on that birth certificate you sent me,' said Jo. 'Does that mean Ranson wasn't her real name?'

'We'll find out,' Mr Fraser said quietly. 'Let's hear what else he found when he read those papers. You did read them, I assume?'

'I tried, but hardly any of it made sense. 'Full procedure' was all I could make out. I managed a copy of the certificate, but I didn't see the point in copying the rest.'

'What was the name of the clinic? Only, I never saw the name and no one ever told me.' Jo was suddenly desperate to know.

'Crosslands.' Julian smiled. 'Parklands was the name of the main hospital but that closed years ago. Mostly it was just called 'The Clinic'. As far as I remember there wasn't even a sign. Very odd, now I come to think on it. Lots of different consultants used the place though, and it was pretty busy.'

The two men talked quietly as they drank their coffee. Jo sat fiddling with the straw in his juice, his mind racing, until once again Mr Fraser squeezed his shoulder, bringing him back to the present.

The next question had Julian squirming in his seat.

'I asked why you were scared; are you worried that Bowden or someone connected to the clinic has tracked you to Glasgow?'

Julian's cheeks went white. 'Pete thinks I'm stupid, and maybe I am. It's ever since Maggie. I haven't known what to think.'

'Maggie?' Jo blurted. 'What's wrong with her?'

'I'm sorry, Jo, but she was killed about five weeks ago. Hit and run. She phoned me just two days before it happened. She sounded really scared. She was sure someone was following her. Then her phone started to ring and no one would answer. She'd been asking questions about Susan, you see. My fault, I should have told her to keep her head down but I thought it was me being stupid.'

'I'm so sorry, Julian. I really liked her, she was so kind.' They sat in silence for a moment.

'I take it you think you're being followed again?' said Mr Fraser.

'Yes,' he admitted. 'It started just over a week ago. Phone calls as well. I pick up, or Pete does, and there's nothing. I've tried the phone company but they're worse than useless. They can't trace a thing.'

Jo saw a flicker of sympathy from Mr Fraser as he leant forward. He spoke in a low, urgent voice. 'I believe you're in danger, Julian. Once young Jo here set things in motion, I'm afraid you became a loose end, which they really can't afford to have. Unfortunately, you're also an easy man to find.'

'I don't understand.'

'Jo ran away from Doctor Bowden. Very fortunately he found his way to me. If he hadn't, I've no doubt that he'd be dead or maimed for life by now. Those children in Bowden's care were deliberately experimented on. For what sick reasons, I've no idea. But what I do know is that you and Jo are in serious danger.'

Jo swallowed hard. Mr Fraser's words were hard to hear.

'But that's preposterous,' said Julian. You can't seriously think I'm in any real danger?'

Mr Fraser dropped his hand onto Jo's shoulder. 'I'm so sorry you have to find out like this, Jo, but I'm afraid the news gets worse. Jo told me about several of the people who cared for him over the past five or six years. Of the sixteen adults I've managed to track, all have died recently, and none from natural causes.'

'What?! You mean the Camberwells? The Suttons, - all of them, gone?' Jo froze on his stool. He couldn't take it in.

'I'm so sorry, Jo.'

'What am I supposed to do?' Julian pleaded.

'Leave. Preferably, the country. Get as far away as you can. I can arrange everything, but you have to go now.'

'What about Peter? What if they attack him while trying to find me?'

'Both of you go. But I need you gone as soon as you can pack.'

'Please, Julian, take your friend and just go,' Jo begged.

'He's back in an hour or so. I don't know, I really don't,' he said, flustered.

Mr Fraser stood and looked down at the worried man. 'Jo and I need to leave now. This is a contact number, for a colleague. Just tell the person on the other end you're the package for Simon. They'll understand and arrange everything.' He made Julian repeat what he'd said and look at the paper he handed him. 'Someone will telephone you regularly, either here or at work to check you're okay. Please take this seriously and get out.'

There was nothing else they could do. Jo hugged Julian tightly and headed for the door. 'Be safe, Jo. I'll always remember you,' Julian called.

As the door shut behind them, Jo shivered. 'Why do I feel so afraid?' he whispered, wishing they were already in the air.

They walked to the end of the street, Jo struggling to shake off the sense of doom that had descended like a thick fog.

'Well, at least our lift has turned up and on time for a change.' Mr Fraser sounded far more cheerful. Jo dragged his eyes from the pavement to see a grey car parked just ahead of them, a familiar figure leaning against the bonnet.

'It's about time, Simon. I've been kicking my heels for the last twenty minutes.'

'Professor!' Jo ran the few steps to his side and buried his head against the older man's shoulder. His back was throbbing like mad.

'Do you need to have a stretch Jo?' Mr Fraser asked, noticing the wince when he slid into the car.

'If we could, but it's going to be messy,' said Jo, thinking of all the feathers.

'That's no problem,' the professor assured him. 'We'll just go back to the flat. It's only ten minutes away.'

The flat was on the second floor of a pretty tree-lined street. As soon as the door closed, the professor drew the curtains and turned on the lights. In a daze, Jo pulled off his jacket and shirt, easing the stiffness from his neck and shoulders. As the wings snapped out onto his back he groaned with relief. It felt so good. He made them flutter and sweep, gradually allowing them to move faster, the movement becoming stronger. 'Oh, that's so much better,' he muttered, his eyes closed.

The professor gave a low, soft whistle. 'Pretty impressive, Jo, if I may say.'

'Sorry,' he opened his eyes. He'd almost forgotten they were there.

Pushing up the tiny glasses he wore for close work, the professor stepped closer. 'Don't be silly. I can quite understand the need to let them out. I think Simon was right - we might need to rethink your exercise plan.' He studied Jo for a few moments. 'Very good muscle definition. He said you'd been working hard and it shows.'

'I hate to hurry you both,' Mr Fraser interrupted. 'But we do have a plane to catch.'

They made it to the airport by the skin of their teeth. 'Are you coming back with us?' Jo asked hopefully, as the professor dragged a couple of cases from the boot of the car.

'I wouldn't miss it. It's ages since I've spent so much time with my younger brother.'

'Did he tell you about the attempted robbery yesterday?' Jo asked, as they fastened their seat harnesses and waited for the roar of the engines to kick in.

'No. Did someone finally manage to get the better of him?' the professor teased.

'Can I tell him, Uncle Simon?' he pleaded. 'I'll do it really quietly.' By the time the plane landed Jo felt in a much better mood.

'I'm looking forward to meeting our Scandinavian friends again,' the professor said blandly. 'They were keen to help then, Simon?'

'We'll talk later,' Mr Fraser muttered. Jo caught his guarded tone.

Dan and the others were still unloading the canoeing gear from the van as the taxi pulled up. 'Hey, Jo,' Dan threw open the taxi's door before Jo had a chance to move. 'At least you made it back in time for food.'

'Good to see your ugly face as well,' said Jo, managing a smile.

With a hug for his uncle, Dan pulled his friend to the side. 'Are you alright?' he asked, 'You don't look happy.'

'I suppose...'

'Let's go on up. The rest can finish off here, they won't mind.' They hurried upstairs and locked the door after them. Jo flopped onto his stomach, not sure where to start.

'So,' Dan asked. 'What did Trantham tell you about Bowden?'

By the time Jo finished telling him everything, Dan looked as upset as he felt. 'What a crappy thing to hear.'

'It's just...I know what those kids must have felt. They must have been terrified, in agony. I feel sick just thinking about it. And all those people I stayed with, just wiped out.' He shut his eyes, trying to blot out the images. The bed creaked as his friend slid next to him. 'Don't know what I'd have done without you and your dad,' he mumbled.

'You've been there for me as well, Jo, don't forget. I haven't forgotten all those times you stood up for me, got me through all that stuff with Mum. Bowden's not going to get away with this,' Dan promised. 'And who knows, maybe we can track down this Amy. Give her a fighting chance.'

He sounded so determined, Jo managed a weak smile. 'I still don't get why this has happened. I mean, what's the point of it all?'

'Uncle Ian will find out, and when he does, he'll make Bowden pay!'

'And I'm going to be there when it happens,' Jo said fiercely.

'Oh, Bowden won't stand a chance. Uncle Ian reckons you and me make a great team. - Only, we'd better get downstairs because this half of the team is starving, and I work so much better on a full stomach.'

At first it helped being back in the hostel, listening to the others talk about their day's canoeing. Jo even managed to laugh at the video of Dan being thrown in the water by Darren. But the brutal images kept creeping back. As he listened to the chatter, it made Glasgow and everything he had heard more terrifying than ever. Bowden had killed at least sixteen people he knew of. He may not have liked the Bigwells, or been particularly fond of the other people, but none of them deserved to die like that. Maggie had been warm and kind, always ready with a smile and a story, and now she was dead too.

Hearing Dan's laugh in the background, Lucy's sharp retorts, and more giggles from the rest, he shivered. Had he put them all in danger? Maybe if he just left now, whoever was after him would leave the rest alone. Let them live?

The thought of being alone again cut like a knife. What did that matter, at least his friends would be safe? Jo pushed aside his chair. He needed to find some air, to think.

'I'm going to walk about a bit, Dan. I'm really stiff. I'll see you in the lounge later.' Deep in thought, he didn't see Jan until the tall figure stepped out in front of him near the main doors. 'Sorry, wasn't looking where I was going,' he apologised.

'Heading for some fresh air?' asked Jan.

'I was just going to stretch my legs. I've been a bit cramped up all day, that's all.' Jan's startling blue eyes continued to gaze at him until Jo turned his head away.

'A man alone with his thoughts is one thing. A man alone with fear is quite another, Jo. Come on, it's a pleasant evening. I'll let Sven know.'

Without waiting for a reply, he ushered Jo outside then spoke briefly on his mobile, in a language Jo guessed was Norwegian. His flamboyant accent had disappeared.

'I heard from your uncle,' said Jan. 'He tells me you were given...' He paused, searching for the right phrase. 'Heart breaking – yes, that was the word he used, heart-breaking, troubling news.'

Jo could only nod. It took a moment to find his voice again. 'Jan, if someone was after you, and they didn't care who they hurt trying to find you, wouldn't you get as far away as possible?' He stopped, trying to frame his thoughts more clearly. 'I mean, if the person they were after left, then those other people, his friends, would be safe, wouldn't they?'

Jan's expression didn't change. 'Do you really believe that if you run away, your friends would be left alone? What of this man in Glasgow? Why bother with him?'

Jo tore his eyes away and looked at his feet. 'Loose ends,' he said bleakly. 'They aren't going to leave anyone alone who knows about me, are they?'

'No, they won't. They must believe there's too much to lose.'

'But what do I do? I'm terrified. Not for me, or, at least, not just for me. There's Dan, and Uncle Simon, Lucy, all of them.'

'Don't divert all the energy and goodwill. If you run away, maybe you buy your friends a short breathing space.' He shrugged those massive shoulders. 'Or maybe not. I do know those who care about you will come after you. They're good men, they could do nothing less. Then the energy is divided and the whole is weaker because of it. If you stay and accept the fear - face it - you can prepare and help defend yourself and these others.'

Jo swallowed. The knot inside eased; his head felt clearer. 'What you're telling me is we're safer together.'

'No, what I'm saying is we're all stronger together, that's what will make the difference.'

'Yeah, that makes sense. It's been a crappy day. That's helped a lot.'

Jan frowned, his blue eyes almost disappearing under furrows. He flipped back into his outlandish accent. 'This 'crappy'. I know not this word?'

'Why the accent?' Jo asked, beginning to smile. 'Is there a reason for it?'

'It's called winding my partner up. Truly, he can be like a stuffed fish. I like to lighten the mood, you know?' Jo burst out laughing; he sounded so absurd.

20 Hill Run

Monday morning, Jo woke to brilliant sunshine and a smiling professor leaning over his bed. 'Morning! I'm your early call. I thought I'd stay and watch, if you don't mind?' He cocked an eye at his sleeping nephew. 'I see he's still not a morning person.'

'It gives me more room, and I get to feel smug,' said Jo.

He stretched and yawned his way out of bed. It was some twenty minutes later before Dan decided to surface. Jo and the professor were still deep in conversation.

'Morning,' Dan grunted. He staggered to the bathroom.

The professor stopped mid-sentence to watch the spectacle before turning back with a heavy sigh. 'It's a good thing I know he'll grow out of it. Imagine any poor lass or lad having to wake up to that every morning.'

'How'd you know he'll grow out of it?' Jo asked.

'Because he looks and sounds just like his father did at his age. Simon was a terror in the mornings.' He winked. 'Now, do you understand the exercise well enough?'

'Concentrate on the sweeping motion: lifting and downward.'

'Aye, and make sure you up those exercises to three times a day. That should stop any unwanted interruptions.'

'But what about all the feathers? Am I supposed to lose so many at once?'

'You've a big wing span. Try and remember to take a bag or something for any strays. I think, though, if you're exercising more regularly the problem should ease.'

The question Jo really wanted to ask hovered on the tip of his tongue.

'What is it, Joseph?'

'Will I ever be able to fly?' he blurted.

'I'd say there's a good chance you'll have some flight, the way your wings are developing. However,' the professor cautioned, raising a warning hand, 'that is a long way off. If you attempt to lift your body weight with your wings as they are now, you'll cause so much damage, flight may never happen. Do I make myself clear?'

'Yes, Professor,' Jo said. 'But you really think...'

'Laddie, there's much we don't know. Each day is a discovery, so patience, yes?'

'Okay.' Jo smiled. It felt so reassuring to have him there.

'Morning, Uncle Ian. Jo's looking good, isn't he?' A different boy, awake and washed, walked out of the bathroom.

'Like Jekyll and Hyde. Just like his father,' the professor muttered.

After the usual meditation, Mr Fraser stood up to make the day's announcements. 'Darren and Sarah's first rounds start on Friday. This morning we're at the hall for a couple of hours of judo practice. Midday, you have a choice: orienteering or cycling. I need your preferences now, please?'

'Are you orienteering?' Dan asked as they got to their feet.

'Think I'd better. I've never ridden a bike in my life,' Jo admitted.

'Excellent. I don't mean about you not being able to ride. Only, I'm rubbish. I can't balance for toffee.'

'Are you sure? You're not just saying that?'

'Dad,' Dan called. 'What if I said I wanted to go on a bike?'

'Well, the route we've planned is pretty steep,' his father said, eyeing him doubtfully. 'I could probably arrange for you to go a different way, I suppose.'

'See, told you. Orienteering it is.'

Jo rushed through his breakfast, desperate to pack a bag for later. 'I'll need to exercise before we go orienteering,' he explained when Dan looked surprised. 'I don't want to hold everyone up. I'll see you down in reception.'

Bag packed, exercises done, he hurried downstairs. Margaret was stood at the door, a clipboard in hand.

'Joseph, you're down for orienteering, yes?'

'And me,' said Dan. She gave him a withering look and ticked something on her sheet.

'Make sure you've a compass, Daniel. Joseph, don't worry, I'll make sure we don't go too fast.'

Jo scowled at her retreating back. 'Maybe we should go cycling after all,' he grumbled.

'It'll be fine. It won't just be her,' Dan assured him.

'Where's Zoe?' Jo asked, looking round.

'She's gone out with her mum and dad. She was really miffed about missing out. I was there when they phoned.'

'Oh yeah? And what else were you and her doing, Danny boy?'

'Like I'd tell you.'

'Nothing then, or you'd be full of it,' Jo teased.

'What are you doing?' Dan asked Paul, as the van drove out of the gates.

'We're both cycling,' he replied. 'Ade does BMX trial stuff, but I'm not that good. What about you and Jo?'

'We're orienteering,' said Dan. 'I'm about as good on a bike as I am in a canoe.'

'You weren't that bad,' said Ade. 'No worse than me. Four times I ended up soaked.'

'What about you, Lucy?' Jo asked.

'Orienteering, and Sarah is as well. I don't mind cycling, but not up and down mountains.'

'Sound.' Jo grinned, the afternoon was definitely looking up. 'Are we eating before we go, or taking it with us again?'

'Taking it,' said Sarah. 'Hope Margaret's done something better than that ham we had yesterday. It was gross.'

'It isn't just her going with us, is it?' Jo whispered.

'I doubt it,' said Sarah. 'I know Darren's off cycling with Mr Fraser, but there's Master Brampton, Sven and Jan. Your uncle's not likely to leave security in the hands of just Margaret, is he?'

'Maybe Uncle Ian will come. He likes a good walk,' Dan added.

Tai chi and katas out of the way, Jo sat on a bench, watching Sarah and Master Brampton practising some moves. Despite his obvious experience, Sarah was more than holding her own. The rest were taking advantage of the other mats and extra judo tuition. A telephone rang, its piercing ring coming from the small office in the hallway. He got to his feet and was just going to answer it when Mr Fraser caught him.

'Don't, let it ring,' he said. 'Just a precaution. No one I know would call on this number.'

'Uncle Simon, those men on Saturday…' Jo started to ask.

'They were local thugs, known to the police,' he said and immediately hurried away. Jo watched him go, not at all convinced by the explanation.

As soon as they arrived back at the hostel, he and Dan ran up to their bedroom and locked the door. With the curtains firmly closed Jo let out his wings.

He ran through the new exercises for almost fifteen minutes. 'The moult seems to have slowed down a bit,' he said, pleased to see only a few loose feathers.

Dan looked over from zipping up his bag. 'I'll start hunting them down if you like, while you get changed.'

Five minutes later, they headed to reception. 'At last!' Margaret came bustling over. 'Pick up your lunch pack, Daniel. You don't need to worry, Joseph. I'm sure one of the others will be happy to carry yours.'

'No, thanks,' he said. 'I'm used to carrying things and it's not heavy.' He looked around. The girls were nowhere in sight.

'We three can leave in one of the cars,' she said. 'It will give you a head start. Jo. Jan can bring the girls in the van.'

'I don't need...' he began, but Jan's booming voice interrupted from the doorway.

'Margaret, a moment. Only the kitchen lady wishes to see you. Something about liver…or was it deliver? I am not so sure.' The boys hid their sniggers as best they could.

'Oh really, she could have waited.' She bustled away, her nose in the air. As she disappeared around the corner, Paul and Ade came hurrying down the stairs, looking the part in cycling shorts and helmets.

'Thought you'd gone,' said Ade, helping himself to a food parcel.

'I heard Margaret tell the girls not to rush,' added Paul. 'She told them you two were having a twenty-minute head start, or something like that?'

'What? I don't believe her!' said Jo.

'I'll go and tell them that's a load of bull,' said Dan, and immediately headed off down the corridor.

'Who does Margaret think she is? Do I look like an invalid?'

'Didn't she tell you then?' Ade asked.

'No, she bloody well didn't,' fumed Jo.

'Keep it down,' whispered Paul, pulling him to the side.

'I don't care. She treats me like I'm soft in the head.'

'I'm trying to save you money,' whispered Paul.

Jo paused, trying to work out what he meant.

'The swear box,' Paul explained. 'Say what you like, but I'm sure these walls have ears. It's costing me a packet.'

Dan came hurrying back down the corridor just as Margaret reappeared.

'Bags up and we'll be off, boys' she announced.

'The girls are just on the way,' said Dan. 'They should be here any second.'

Margaret opened her mouth to argue but the girls were already turning the corner.

'We've just seen the professor, Margaret,' Lucy said. 'He'll be out in a minute. It'll be so much better all going together.'

'Very well.' Her back rigid, Margaret strode towards the door and the hulking form of Jan. 'The cook had already left for her break,' she said huffily. 'Now, if you wouldn't mind, we need to pass.'

'We're leaving together? This is good. I'll bring the extra food and drinks in my pack,' he offered, his blue eyes flashing.

'Lucy, is it me, or does she seem really put out?' asked Jo as they climbed into the van.

'Sarah says she's always a bit strange. Want a toffee? I bought them in Dundee.' She slid into the seat on the aisle opposite and handed him the bag. The van suddenly tilted wildly to the left, as Jan pulled himself on board.

'I'll ride with you, more fun I think,' he announced. 'Maybe I teach you some Norwegian drinking songs, ya?'

They drove for half an hour, parking at the bottom of a sparsely wooded hill. Jo surveyed the steep hillside ahead of them. 'It, should be cool under the trees at least,' he said.

'As long as we stop and eat soon. I'm starving,' said Dan.

Sarah gave a snort. 'What's new? You never stop eating. Oh, here she comes - stand to attention!'

'Everyone got your bags? Good. There are eight different climbs, and as we all have such differing abilities...' Margaret paused, her eyes fixed on Jo. 'I think it best we split into groups.'

He opened his mouth to argue but the professor spoke before he had chance. 'Aye, well, Jo, Dan and the lasses are probably as fit as I am, so we'll head off together,' he said smoothly.

'That wasn't exactly what...only I thought, with his disability...'

'What disability? Jo was hill-walking with us in the two weeks before we arrived here. He'll do just fine. Have you decided which route we'll take?'

'Very well,' Margaret sniffed. 'I suggest we take the path that goes up near the small loch. Maps out, everyone; let's take our bearings. I'll be relying on you four to give directions. First bearing-point is this large boulder. We'll eat there. It should take roughly an hour.'

'An hour?' Dan grumbled. 'My stomach's hurting already.'

They walked steadily through the shaded, lower slopes. Jan stayed to the rear, some distance behind. With the professor, Sven and Margaret walking just in front, it was impossible to talk about anything personal. Surrounded by friends and the big Norwegians, Jo soon began to relax and enjoy the trek. Slowly, he got his head round the map reading, although he still thought the contours looked more like a heap of spaghetti.

They'd walked for almost fifty minutes when Sarah frowned at her compass. 'I reckon if we turn a couple of degrees west, we should reach that large boulder in about five minutes.' Jo did the compass bearing along with the others and, for once, understood what she meant.

'Then lead on, Mac-Duffy,' said Dan.

'It's Macduff, you ignoramus,' Sarah corrected.

'Mac-Duffy's his cousin twice removed who went into catering. Big Mac's his son. Don't you know anything?' Dan quipped. Everyone laughed.

'How'd you come up with those?' Lucy asked.

'It's hunger. I hope Sarah's right about this. I need to eat.'

The boulder appeared on cue. Sarah beamed, patting the huge stone fondly as if she'd won a prize. She pulled out her mobile and took a selfie, standing next to it.

'Nice, Sarah,' Dan called. 'Though it'll be hard to tell which is which. You carry on snapping, we'll eat.'

'These are so good,' said Jo, tucking into a second cheese and salad roll.

'I know,' Dan agreed, crumbs spraying everywhere.

'We'll sit for fifteen minutes then continue,' Margaret called. 'Boys, use the bushes up to the left, girls to the right.'

'So which side are you using, Dan?' Sarah teased.

'Yeah, yeah.' He stretched out on the grass, refusing to bite.

'Well, I'm off to find a handy bush,' Jo said a few minutes later.

'May as well,' Dan agreed, jumping up beside him.

They made their way past the boulder and turned left. The trees thinned out rapidly but there were still some thick bushes ahead.

'Do you think we'll be going down a different way?' Jo asked, as they headed towards a particularly large shrub.

'Not a clue.' Dan stopped, frowning at something on the floor. 'What the...?' He lurched back, pulling a bewildered Jo with him.

'Dan?' Jo couldn't work out what was wrong.

'RUN!' Grabbing his sleeve, Dan pulled him hard.

Jo caught a glimpse of something slithering away under the blanket of leaves. For a moment he stood, transfixed.

'RUN!' Dan yelled again, still dragging at his arm.

It was like being in a dream. Jo's feet were moving but he had no idea why. Something whizzed through the air near his ear. His eye caught something small, bouncing crazily on the collar of Dan's shirt. He continued to run; the rough ground under his boots crackled like ice. Within seconds they were back in the clearing but they didn't stop.

'IT'S A TRAP! MEN!' Dan shouted as they hurtled towards Jan.

The huge man jumped into action. 'Ian, get Sven. Take the girls. You know what to do,' he roared. 'You two keep running,' he ordered, steering them away from the track. 'Stay together; it's going to get steep.'

For a big man, Jan moved like a mountain lion. As he fought to keep up, Jo had to admire the way he swept down the hillside. He just wished he'd slow down a bit but there wasn't time to think. Stray branches whipped across his arms and face but he hardly felt it, too busy trying not to fall. Beside him, Dan had his eyes fixed on the ground, concentrating on staying upright.

Jan finally slowed a little. Some distance behind and to the right, Jo could hear heavy footsteps. he just hoped it was the professor with the girls.

Whoever it was snorted, cleared their throat and spat.

Just ahead, Jan swerved sharply to the left. Weaving between thick bushes, he dived behind a larger one. Jan's thick arm snaked out grabbing Dan. Jo quickly followed. They crouched, desperately trying to muffle their laboured breathing. Two sets of footsteps rushed on down the hill. Jan held a finger to his lips, keeping them silent for what felt like ages. 'Gone. Now, we wait,' he whispered. 'Sven will send someone up to us.'

'Are you okay?' Dan panted, still breathing hard.

'I need another set of lungs,' gasped Jo, 'But yeah. I've never gone so fast, ever,'

'Didn't think Jan could move like that,' Dan wheezed.

'Maybe we should've gone cycling,' Jo panted. 'Riding up the side of a mountain sounds pretty easy in comparison.' He cocked his head; more footsteps were coming.

'It's just the girls,' Dan assured him, sneaking a quick look around the bush.

'You ran, all the way down here?' Lucy said for the third time. 'Are you crazy? It's, like, mega steep.'

'We sort of ran, but blame Jan, not me. We were being chased, you know,' Jo added for good measure.

'Margaret was being such a prat.' Lucy lowered her voice. 'Talk about slow. I really thought the professor was going to leave her behind.'

'Wish he had,' Sarah glowered over her shoulder. 'She only told Sven he was jumping at shadows. As if!'

Margaret stood at the edge of the group, out of earshot. She looked furious.

'What the hell happened up there?' asked Sarah.

'There was this rope thing under the leaves,' said Dan. 'A trap, I suppose. I saw it moving, so we just ran.'

'I didn't see a thing,' Jo admitted. 'Next thing, he's dragging me by my arm and we're running, like the hounds of hell were after us.'

'Well, they were,' Dan reasoned.

'How long do we have to stay here?' asked Lucy, looking nervously around.

'No idea,' said Dan. 'We've got to wait for reinforcements, I suppose. Anyone fancy a bit of chocolate? I brought a couple of extra bars.' Despite the bravado, his hands were trembling as he fumbled open the button on his trouser leg pocket. He pulled out a large bar of soft, almost-melting chocolate.

'What's this?' Sarah frowned, pulling something from the back of Jo's jacket. She held it up to the light.

Jan's deep voice made them all jump. 'Don't touch the tip, Sarah!'. He took it from her, and carefully tucking it into his top pocket

'They tried to dart you!' Lucy's eyes were enormous.

'Both of us,' said Jo. 'I'm sure something like that landed on Dan's collar. It must have fallen out as we were running.' The horror of it was finally sinking in. 'I should've stayed behind. Sorry,' he mumbled. 'I put you all in danger.'

'Stop it, Jo,' said Lucy. She snapped off a piece of the chocolate and handed it to him. 'Anyway, it beats one of Margaret's field trips hands down.'

'I'll second that,' Sarah agreed. 'Besides, I don't think it would've made any difference. They'd still have tried to nab you, wherever you were.'

'Cheers, Sarah!'

'Well, it's true,' she said, biting into a chunk of chocolate. 'And I'm not down-playing the danger, Jo. It's a warning for all of us to keep up our guard. If we stick together, things will work out, you'll see.' She took out her mobile and began sweeping it in a wide arc above her head.

'Photos,' she announced cheerfully. 'There's nothing like woodland for some great atmospheric shots.'

The extra help came in the form of three large men, 'security' printed across their jumpers. 'Afternoon, boss,' the tallest said to Jan. 'Mr Milson said you can head down now.'

'Bit of an anti-climax, really,' Jo muttered.

'We could run off into the woods and see how long it takes them to catch us?' Dan suggested.

'I want to eat for the rest of the week, thanks. And anyway, I've got a blister on my toe,' Jo complained.

'You've two huge slits running down your back and you're complaining about one tiny blister,' Dan hissed. 'What are you like?'

'I was only saying.'

'What were you saying?' The professor was suddenly beside them, carrying his and Dan's backpacks on his shoulder.

'I've a blister on my big toe, Professor. Must've been from going downhill so fast. It was a bit of a buzz,' Jo admitted.

'I'll tell Margaret, she could add hill-running to the agenda for next year,' the professor said dryly. 'Any pains in your back?'

'It's fine, but what was hidden under those leaves?'

'A nasty trap, designed to catch a foot. They'd have zapped both of you then hauled you away, Jo.'

'Dan saw it first. If I'd been on my own...' Jo felt sick at the thought.

'Yeah, well, you weren't, so that's okay,' Dan said.

'The men were spotted near the stream,' said the professor. They'll pick them up shortly.'

'That's something, I suppose.'

'It's more than something, Jo. Wait until they've been interrogated. You both reacted brilliantly, by the way. That pace down the hill would've tested the best of us, and I've done several runs with the big man.'

'How did they know where we were, Uncle Ian?' asked Dan. The professor sighed and pulled a small plastic container from his pocket. Something small rattled inside. 'I found a basic tracker in the toggle of your backpack, Jo.'

'How did that get there?!'

'Has your bag been out of your sight at any time?' asked the professor.

'No...'

'Yes, it has!' said Dan. 'On Saturday, before we went for that walk. Margaret told us to leave our bags by the kitchen.'

'I'd forgotten that,' Jo said, feeling foolish. 'Sorry, Professor.'

'It's not your fault,' he reassured. 'But in future, both of you must keep your bags with you. Now, I need to check you over, just to be sure there aren't any more.' He pulled out a similar looking device to the one Mr Fraser had used in Glasgow.

'Checks for bugs,' said Dan. He held up his arms as the professor moved the item over him. 'This is so cool. It's just like being in a James Bond movie.'

'Can't you take anything seriously, Daniel? Okay, you're both clear.' The professor slipped the scanner back into his pocket. Now, do you need me to take a look at your foot, Jo, stick a plaster on?'

'I'm fine, it'll keep.'

When they arrived back at the hostel, they found Zoe pacing anxiously on the driveway.

'What's wrong?' asked Sarah.

'Mum and Dad, that's what. They only thought I was going to leave and stay with them. As if! They thought I'd hate the sports. They can go stuff it. And they made me miss the cycling.'

'Good for you; us girls have to stand together,' said Lucy.

Zoe glared at her. 'I would if I knew what we were supposed to be standing against!' Her eyes narrowed. 'I know something's going on. Why don't you trust me?'

Sarah cut in. 'We do, and now you're back, we can fill you in.'

'Sorry, Zoe,' said Jo. 'Only with your dad coming and everything...' Jo heard a collective groan and immediately wished he'd kept his mouth shut.

'What?' Zoe's eyes were like daggers.

'I, umm, - What I mean is,' he blustered, looking desperately at his friend for help but Dan's eyes were fixed firmly on the ground.

'You think I'd go running to my dad? Is that why you didn't tell me?' With her hands on her hips, she took a furious step towards him. She may have been several inches shorter but right at that moment all Jo wanted to do was turn and run.

'It was just we, - I mean, I didn't want to put you in a difficult position,' he stuttered. 'If the police got involved, my life would be impossible.'

'That doesn't mean anything!' she spat. She glared at one uncomfortable face to another. 'Well?' she demanded.

Jo glanced at the door. Someone would be out any second. 'I'm sorry, Zoe, I got it completely wrong. I should have told you with the rest.' He quickly repeated what he'd told the others.

'Though we've no idea why these men are chasing him, but I suppose he'll tell us one day?' Lucy added. 'Anyway, I'll tell you all about this afternoon's narrow escape when we get up to the dorm.'

Jo waited for an explosion but Zoe just nodded. 'That's why Sven and Jan are here,' she said, putting two and two together. 'And why they carted those two off on Saturday. I knew something was up.' She gave a tentative smile. Jo began to breathe more easily. 'Okay, I suppose you're forgiven. I love my dad; I respect what he does, but I'm my own damn person. I don't have to check with him every time I breathe. Understood?'

'Fair enough,' Jo agreed. 'Sarah's got some sketches for you to look at, as well as two sets of number plates. I promise, when it's safe, I'll tell you everything. For now, you'll just have to trust me.'

'Thanks, Jo,' Lucy murmured, as she brushed past him.

'I would not want to be on the wrong side of either of those two,' said Dan as they watched them leave.

'I didn't notice you jumping in to help,' said Jo.

'Well, if you will open your mouth and put your foot in it.'

They'd only just stepped inside the door when Mr Fraser called them over. 'Before you go up, lads, you'll need these.' He handed them both a blue wristband. Each had a small, metal logo on one side. 'I've scanned your room, just in case, but you'll need to wear these all the time. They're to do with a sensor in your room. If anyone else goes in, an alarm goes off on my watch.'

'Wicked,' said Jo, slipping it on. 'Did the professor tell you about us running down the hill?'

'In detail. Are you both okay?'

Dan shrugged, fingering the wristband, 'Got a few blisters between us. Have they caught those men yet?'

'They've picked them both up, so you can relax,' said Mr Fraser. 'Go get changed, you don't want to be last to dinner, do you?'

'What's up?' asked Jo, noticing Dan's frown as his father left.

'I know those men had the tracker, but they still had to get ahead of us and guess where we'd stop,' said Dan quietly.

'What are you saying?'

'Nothing.' He clammed up as another guest came towards them. 'Let's get a shower. We can talk later.'

Washed and changed, they were downstairs within ten minutes.

Ade and Paul had beaten them to it, their plates already piled high. 'That woman's still here,' whispered Jo, heaving mashed potatoes onto his plate.

'So are a couple of the men. You haven't won yet.'

Jo tried to study the woman without making it obvious. He had to admit, she didn't look much of a candidate for a bodyguard; a bit prim and proper, he thought. Maybe Dan was right.

'How did the cycling go, Ade?' asked Dan.

'We got down and dirty,' he said, grinning. 'I'm going to have a whopper of a scab on my hip.'

'You want to see the ones on my knees,' said Paul. 'Going up was hard, but back down, - man, I thought I was going over the top at one point. Heard you had a bit of a close one too,' he whispered.

'Just a bit,' said Jo.

'Sarah collared us,' said Ade. 'Told us about Zoe. ...Anytime you want help, just shout,' he added, with a pointed nod at Jo's shoulder.

In the next second, the professor strode over. 'Lounge as usual, lads and lasses. Any injuries need sorting, come and find me.'

That night, as Jo clambered into bed, his friend looked at him thoughtfully. 'You know you got Sarah to sketch that bloke who's been following you? Do you think you could get her to do the same for Doctor Bowden?'

Jo glanced over at his friend, guessing the truth. 'I should think so. Was it your dad's or your uncle's idea?'

'Can't I have a good one occasionally?' Jo waited his friend out. 'Dad's,' he finally admitted.

'Ask her at breakfast, I don't mind,' said Jo, yawning.

'Excellent! And I'll get the credit for persuading you; neat.'

Dan was soon snoring. Jo tried to ignore the anxiety wrapping round him like a blanket. He was safe, he reminded himself. The men had been caught, and hadn't Mr Fraser said they could relax?

So, why was he feeling so edgy? In the bed opposite his friend turned over in his sleep.

'I'm really scared, Dan,' he whispered, 'Scared you and all this will just disappear...' But the night swallowed Jo's words, without offering a crumb of comfort.

Hill Run

21 Watertight

The following morning, Dan was up and dressed before Jo had finished his exercises. 'What's got into you?' Jo asked as he threw on some clothes.

'I kept waking up, probably because I was so stiff from all that running downhill. Have you had a look outside? It's a bit bleak.'

Jo thought it far more likely that like him, he'd had nightmares about being chased. 'Maybe it'll clear up later,' he said trying to sound up-beat.

Downstairs, they found everyone else stiff and sore. Zoe eyed Paul's grazed knees and winced. 'Ouch! Bet that hurts.'

'There's going to be a cool scab, though, plenty of pickings,' he said, inspecting them closely.

'Gross, Deacon.' She turned away, disgusted.

'What, like you never pick a scab?' he mocked. 'You should see Ade's hip, that'll keep him going for days.'

'Don't! I've still got to eat breakfast.'

'Any idea what's on today?' Lucy asked Jo, sliding onto the floor next to him.

'No. It would be nice to do more walking, we missed out yesterday.'

'Are you serious?!' She began to laugh. 'Aren't you worried they'll come after you again?'

'A bit,' Jo shrugged. 'They've caught those two, so that'll slow them down, don't you think?'

'I do,' she said. 'What I'd really like to do is go for a swim.'

'That's another thing I've never done,' he admitted. 'Not sure I'd be allowed.'

'Rubbish, swimming's great for back problems. My gran goes all the time.'

'I can safely say my back problem's different. Though it wouldn't stop me paddling?' he added, hoping to see her smile.

They didn't have to wait long to find out. After the session, John Brampton shared the day's plans. 'Straight after breakfast, everyone has an hour to pack their kit for a night's camping. You heard right,' he added, as the whispering began, 'we're off into the hills.

Please bring a swimsuit or shorts, and a couple of towels. You'll only need to take a water bottle, the tents, etc. are provided. Put in a change of clothes, torches, compass and basic first-aid kit. Treat it as part of your Duke of Edinburgh, and you won't go far wrong. I've got a map of the area for everyone and I'll hand them out later.'

'Looks like you'll get your wish, Lucy,' said Jo.

'Yeah. Sounds like it'll be a mountain stream, though. It's going to be icy. But you'll be able to relax, because we'll be miles away from everywhere.'

Sarah made a point of sitting next to him at breakfast. 'Dan had a word,' she said. 'I'll bring my sketchbook with me on the bus.'

'Thanks, that'll be great. Ow! Ade, do you mind?' he said rubbing his shin.

Ade pointed over Jo's shoulder. He turned to see the woman he'd noticed the previous day staring right at him. Jo felt the hair on his neck rise at least an inch.

'What's up?' whispered Dan.

'That woman, she's staring.'

'You reckon she's been spying on you?' said Zoe.

'I didn't think so, but who knows? I'll catch Uncle Simon later.'

'No, you do it now, don't put it off,' urged Lucy.

Grudgingly, he finished his last spoonful and grabbed a piece of toast. 'I'll see you upstairs, this won't take long.'

The professor intercepted him in the reception area. 'Jo! I was just coming to see you. Is everything alright?'

'I'm not sure.' He checked no-one was close and told him about the woman.

'You're safe, I promise,' the professor assured him.

'She's one of ours?'

'Sheila most definitely is. Let's go to your room, there's something I want you to try on.'

When Dan finally arrived, Jo was peering into the small mirror, admiring a black swimming vest. 'What'd you reckon? I don't look too stupid, do I?'

'Not at all.' Dan circled him, nodding approval. 'It looks like a vest the Navy Seals use. He ran a finger over the smooth, rubbery surface. 'This is clever stuff, Jo boy.'

'Yeah, it feels good. Not much chance of anything popping out.' He ignored Dan's snigger. 'All I've got to do now is not drown. Is it hard - swimming?' His nerves were already bubbling.

'No, it's a pinch of salt. Well, sort of. You'll be fine. Anyway, Dad says I've to help you pack.' Jo continued to strut around. 'Are you planning on keeping that on?' asked Dan.

'Better not. The professor said there's quite a walk and I don't want to overheat.' Reluctantly he unzipped the side of the garment. 'By the way, you owe me a quid. The woman in the dining room is one of ours, Danny boy.'

Vans loaded, they set off. Sarah sat next to Jo, listening intently as he described Bowden. The likeness she produced was close enough to give him goose bumps.

'A very shifty-looking man,' she muttered. 'I'll give it to your uncle when we stop and see if he wants another copy. Did I tell you he had a quick word?'

'About you lot knowing everything?' Jo guessed.

'What else? Unsurprisingly, he told me, not to going looking for trouble, and a few other choice phrases, but that about sums it up. He was very tight-lipped when he heard how we found out.'

'Oh, I know that look very well,' said Dan.

'And,' she continued, 'he told me they've sent a decoy van, as well as taking a couple of cars to follow us, so we don't pick up a tail.'

'How come he tells you?' said Dan, looking put out.

'I asked,' she said. 'It's quite nice being almost seventeen. Most of the time I get treated as an adult.'

When they finally arrived the cloud-cover had started to lift, the temperature with it. 'Right, everyone, listen up,' Mr Fraser called. 'Make sure your water bottles are full. If anyone needs a comfort break, you stop in groups of three, minimum. No one wanders off, and any problems phone or use your whistle. Reception's likely to be patchy once we start to climb. Sven's bringing up the rear with Margaret, and they'll be following on ten minutes after the rest of us. Are there any questions?' Everyone shook their heads. 'Then we're off. It's a steep climb, so we'll take a steady pace.'

'Did you see Margaret's face?' Sarah muttered. 'I don't think she's keen on our Norwegian friends.'

'She's not keen on anyone, unless they're wearing a Brownies' uniform,' said Zoe.

'I reckon yesterday was her fault,' blurted Dan. 'I mean, who else knew where we were going? She was the one who'd got it all planned out.'

'Margaret?' Lucy didn't look convinced. 'Why would she want to hurt Jo?'

'I didn't say that. But she wouldn't think twice about telling someone if they happened to ask. She's always talking to those hikers. Haven't you noticed?'

'Can't say I had, though it would make sense,' Jo admitted.

'Only if there's a contact at the hostel,' Lucy pointed out.

'Yeah. But it fits with that tracker and them knowing which route,' said Jo.

'Are you lot planning on joining us anytime today?' the professor called. 'Or is walking and talking too much to ask?'

'Sorry, on the way,' Sarah called back. 'We'd better get a move on. We definitely don't want Margaret catching us up.'

The climb was steep, in parts narrow, but well worth the effort. Two hours later, they reached a path leading down to a sheltered glen. The sound of water was everywhere.

'Must be a waterfall,' said Dan.

'Wow,' said Jo, open-mouthed. The butterflies in his stomach were in full flight as he caught sight of the spectacle. The water streamed over several piles of boulders. In-between each fall were various sized pools. The largest looked enormous.

'We're camping beyond that bank of trees,' John Brampton shouted over the noise of the water. 'We'll drop off our kit and come back.'

It was all Jo could do to drag his eyes away from the crystal-clear water. 'We really get to swim in that?' he said. 'What if I just sink?'

'You'll learn fast, don't worry,' Dan assured him.

'But...'

'It's going to be freezing,' Ade interrupted with a shiver.

'Icy,' Paul agreed.

'And you lot will be doing the camp's washing up, if you don't move your backsides.' Sven had crept up, his eyes flashing with amusement.

'We're just looking,' said Lucy. 'You're lucky, you get to see this sort of thing all the time in Norway.'

'Do I indeed? Move,' he instructed, 'or should I ask Margaret to have a word?'

'There's no need to be nasty,' said Zoe. 'We get the message.'

'I could just watch,' Jo murmured, not at all sure he fancied the idea now.

'It's fun, honest,' said Lucy. 'I can't believe you've never swum before.'

'Do you reckon we'll be able to touch the bottom?' asked Paul.

'No. Mr Fraser said they're deep. Sorry,' Ade added, catching Jo's panicked expression. 'It's going to be fine, you'll see.'

Not sure he believed any of them, Jo hurried towards the tent that Mr Fraser pointed out. It was definitely one of the largest. He and Dan both whistled, impressed as they stepped inside. There were two camp beds set up, with a small table to one side.

'Wow, Uncle Simon, you could fit six or seven people in here, easily,' said Jo.

'But they might have something to say about your, additions,' Dan pointed out.

'I've given you one of the largest for obvious reasons, lads. Though all the tents are pretty big.'

'How come they're here at all, Uncle Simon?'

'They belong to an outward-bound centre a friend of mine runs. They get used for parties on team-building weekends. If you stand in the centre, you should have enough room to flap. A word of warning though: don't try it with the lights on. Your silhouette will cause a bit of a stir. Ian's going to wait outside while you have a quick flutter, Jo. I'll see you later.'

'I'll wait, Dad. I want to make sure Jo doesn't do a runner.'

'Are you alright, Jo?' Mr Fraser asked, sounding concerned.

'Fine,' he replied, grimacing at his friend. 'I'm just a bit nervous.'

'Of course you are, it's to be expected.'

'Uncle Simon, that sketch Sarah did, will it help?' Jo asked, as Mr Fraser turned to leave.

'It already has, she does good work. Don't be too long now.' He'd ducked out of the tent before either of them could say a word.

'So, what's that supposed to mean?' said Jo turning to his friend.

'I've no idea, and he isn't likely to tell us, is he?'

'Suppose not.' Resigned, Jo pulled off his top and let the wings out. The tent was only just high enough; a couple of times he brushed the top, pushing it upwards.

'Never mind, it's only for a day,' he said, as they hunted for lost feathers.

With the black vest on under his T-shirt and towels under his arm, Jo nervously followed Dan outside. The professor was sitting on a deckchair reading a newspaper.

'Vest alright?' he asked, folding the paper neatly.

'Great, thanks, but I've never even attempted to swim before.' His butterflies were now doing cartwheels.

'There's always a first time, laddie. It took Dan here a while to find his fins but he now swims like a fish. There's a smaller pool we'll use to begin with. Get you used to the water.'

They heard the shouts of laughter long before they saw anyone. Jo felt his heart race. 'Is it really that cold?' he asked, catching sight of a shivering Paul, balancing on one foot. A second later he'd hopped in, sending a spray of water shooting up.

'Colder, probably. The trick is to keep moving. There's a smaller pool that's slightly warmer. Dan, you go with the others and leave us to it for a bit,' the professor ordered.

Jo watched his friend walk away. 'Do I have to do this?' he whispered.

'Do you trust me?'

'Yes, but...'

'Then face the fear, Joseph. Thinking is far worse than the doing.'

The smaller pool was some distance away from the others. Self-consciously, Jo stripped off until he stood in his trunks and swimming vest. He looked nervously at the gently lapping water. It wouldn't have been quite so bad if he could've seen the bottom.

'Sit on the edge, and I'll get in first,' the professor instructed.

'I-It's like ice!' Jo stuttered, pulling out the toe he'd dipped in.

The professor jumped straight in, disappearing briefly below the clear surface. 'Not bad once you're in,' he said, slicking the water from his face. 'Don't think about it, Jo, just get in. Here, hold my hands. Worst that'll happen is you'll swallow a mouthful of water.'

'Are you sure?' he pleaded.

'Just do it.'

Gritting his teeth, Jo slid in.

'Oh, mmm…my,' he spluttered, as he bobbed up and down. His skin felt like it was on fire, it was so cold.

'Now, gently kick your feet; it's called treading water. That's it, well done,' he said, as Jo, desperately clinging to him, tried to do as he asked. 'I think you'll find if you let go that you'll float. I'm right here. I won't let you sink.'

'P-p-promise?' Jo stuttered.

'On the count of three.' As his hands slid away from the professor's, Jo felt a moment of sheer panic. 'Just keep those feet going, but not too fast,' the professor encouraged.

'I'm doing it, I'm floating!' He couldn't believe it. Despite everything, there he was, in the middle of the pool, bobbing up and down like a cork.

'Aye, you are, and the air in the sacs is helping,' the professor whispered. 'Now, you need to get used to getting your face wet.'

When John Brampton appeared forty minutes later, Jo was lying on his front, attempting his first ever solo swim.

'We won't be long. He's just going across to the side and back,' the professor called.

Jo knew he was splashing a lot and his legs could've been a whole lot stronger but he didn't care. 'I did it! All the way across and back!' he called. John Brampton cheered from the bank.

'Now towel off and we'll give those feathers a quick shake,' the professor whispered. 'I'm not sure you're completely watertight. After lunch, you can have a dip in the big pool with everyone else, if you'd like.'

Jo had never felt so free before. Messing about in the large pool with the others that afternoon was the best. By the time Mr Fraser called them all out to change, his legs felt like jelly.

'I'm exhausted,' he said, grinning at his friend as they arrived back at their tent.

Dan flopped onto his camp bed and looked just as shattered. 'It was wicked, though,' he murmured. 'Sweet, the way you just kept bobbing back up. I heard Sven talking about it to Dad, trying to work it out. He was enjoying having one over on them. I heard him telling Uncle Ian.'

'You heard a lot, Danny boy.'

'Yeah, sometimes it pays to keep your ears open. I learned bad habits at Mum's, I suppose.'

Jo shrugged his shoulders a few times and heard a squelch. 'I think I'm a bit soggy. I'd better have another shake-out.'

'Hang on, just let me cover the bedding up. Uncle Ian said he'd left us a couple of large plastic sheets somewhere.'

'After what happened at lunchtime, I'm not surprised.' Jo began to laugh. 'It was funny, Dan. You should've seen his face. I didn't know I was able to shake my feathers like that. The professor said it was like being hit by a shower of hailstones!'

Dan sniggered at the thought. 'Then I'll keep watch outside.

You don't want to drown your best friend, do you?'

They ate around a huge campfire. Food, Jo decided, had never tasted so good.

'You want another hot-dog, Jo?' asked Sven.

'No, I've had four. Might have one of those kebabs, though.' he said, eyeing up the skewered fruit and meat. They told silly stories and sang into the night, until they were hoarse. Even Margaret relaxed enough to smile.

'Best time ever,' Jo grunted, as he and Dan finally turned in.

'Yeah, I love camping,' Dan agreed.

It wasn't easy to get comfortable. With memories of the cave, Jo piled up his and Dan's backpack and slept stretched over the top. If he woke, he didn't remember.

It was the professor's quiet voice that roused him the following morning. 'I'm sorry, Jo, I should have thought about padding for your bed. Did you manage to get much sleep?'

'It was fine. It's how I slept in the cave.'

'The cave? I'd forgotten you were so resourceful. Have a flutter, then you can help me cook breakfast.'

Being the first up felt great; the campsite was so still, it could have been just the two of them. 'You want me to butter the rolls?' asked Jo, searching for a knife.

'Please. I think we'll have sausage and tomato this morning. The others will probably go swimming again for an hour. But, if you don't mind, I think it best you leave it.'

'What, no soggy wings?' Jo said, laughing.

'Aye, we can't exactly stop for you to have a shake-out today.'

'That's okay. Are we going back the same way we came?'

'No, we'll follow that stream downwards. We should be back at the vans for about two.'

'Wish we could stay longer,' Jo said wistfully. 'I could stay here for weeks.'

'It's a good place,' the professor agreed. 'Though I know several that can match it.'

'Bet you've been to loads of places. Dan said you lived in China for a while?'

'I did. Simon was not much older than you. It's a huge country, beautiful and terrible. In parts, it's not so different to here.'

'Will you ever go back there, Professor?'

'Now, there's a question,' his lips curved into a smile. 'The authorities would probably still throw me in prison, or worse. But that's definitely a story for another time. How many sausages each, - three, do you think?' He busied himself with the fire, leaving Jo to wonder.

It was an uneventful trip back down the mountain. Most were too tired to do anything more than stare out of the van's windows or talk quietly. Jo nudged his friend, the conversation with the professor still buzzing in his head.

'Has your uncle ever told you about what happened to him in China?' he asked.

'He got married, I know that much.'

'I know, but did he tell you anything else?' Dan paused then shook his head. Jo told him about the conversation that morning.

'Wonder what that was about? He must've been doing the sneaky stuff, I suppose.'

'I thought that was your dad?' Jo said, confused.

'Both of them. Uncle Ian stopped a few years ago. Least he that's what Dad said.'

'You reckon they worked for Sven?' Jo murmured.

'Not sure how it worked because they never told me anything,' Dan shrugged and looked away.

It felt as if they had been away from the hostel for days. 'Dinner's in an hour,' John Brampton called, as they piled out of the van. 'Make sure you all put your towels on the radiators to dry.'

'Got your wristband on?' asked Dan, as they trudged upstairs.

'Yep, and bags me the first shower.'

'Yeah, like you'll get there first, slow coach.' It was close but Jo won by a shove of an elbow.

After dinner they met up with the others to play cards. Sarah and Darren were nowhere to be seen.

'Any idea what's on tomorrow?' asked Paul.

'I heard climbing, but I could be wrong,' Lucy said.

'What about you, Jo?' said Ade. 'Would you be allowed?'

'Doubt it, but I can always watch you lot fall off. Have Sarah and Darren gone to check the sports centre out this evening?' Jo asked wondering where they were.

Zoe slapped her cards down with a pleased grin. 'A full house! No, Sarah told me they're going tomorrow. I doubt they'd want to risk climbing before the big event.'

'Is this competition really important then?' said Jo.

'Where have you been these last few days?' Zoe shook her head at him. 'Honestly, it's an open senior's!'

'What she's trying to say,' Lucy interrupted, 'is that the best in the country will be taking part, and the British Judo scouts will be there. They were both due to go to a contest in Bristol later in the year, but Mr Fraser managed to wangle them into this event.'

'So, do they stand a good chance?' asked Jo.

'Definitely,' replied Lucy. 'Darren especially, but Sarah's improving all the time. I think she'd have preferred to wait until Bristol, but she's doing okay.'

'Jo?' the professor called from the doorway. 'Just a quick word. It will only take a minute.' Jo followed him into the hall. 'Tomorrow, the others are going climbing, so how would you feel about coming into Dundee with me? I need to do a spot of shopping and we can go to the sports centre with Sarah and Darren after.'

'Fine. But I don't mind just watching them if it's easier?'

'It isn't about ease, Jo, I enjoy your company. And it has to be better than sitting at the bottom of a rock-face all day.'

'Okay then, shopping and sports centre it is.'

22 Families

The following morning Jo watched the van pull away and tried not to mind too much. It didn't matter that he couldn't climb, loads of people couldn't. It still left an empty feeling in the pit of his stomach as his friends disappeared from sight. A dark green Range Rover pulled up alongside him, the window slipping silently down.

'Transport's arrived!' The professor smiled from the driver's seat.

'Nice,' said Jo, clambering into the sleek interior. 'Is it rented?'

'Not exactly, it's one of Sven's. Buckle up and we can go. There's a cushion to put against your lower back if you need it.'

There was hardly any traffic, though Jo noticed a car pull out behind them as soon as they set off. 'Is he supposed to be trailing us?' he asked.

'If they want to get paid. Don't worry, they won't intrude.'

'Do Sven and Jan know everything about me, Professor?'

'Not all, Jo. Enough to keep them interested, and less than they'd like.' The professor raised a finger to his lips and winked. 'They have big ears. Better safe than sorry.'

'But those men they caught, didn't they talk about me?'

'Much to Sven's disgust they knew nothing of interest. Only that they were paid a lot of money to pick you up.'

'So, do you trust them?' Jo asked, watching the professor's expression.

'That's another interesting question, but yes, I suppose I do. It's more a matter of what they might want to do with any information once they get it.' He shook his head not wanting to say more. 'I'm being vague on purpose, sorry. Right now, all they need to do is keep you safe.'

'Fair enough. So, do you think Bowden's men will try to nab me again in the next few days?'

'I wouldn't have thought so, but it's better to be safe than sorry. Why don't you put the radio on, see what the local news has to say?'

Smiling, Jo stopped asking questions and did as he asked. He knew how to take a hint.

They left the car in the same car park they'd used before and walked into the centre. Jo shivered a little in the biting wind.

'We'll get you a warmer jacket, lad, and some thicker trousers. There's a decent shop just around the corner.'

'But Uncle Simon bought me loads,' Jo objected.

'Good, now I'm buying you more. We'll do that first then go find a cafe. There's something you and I need to talk about.'

Irritated, Jo frowned. He could have just told him when they were driving. Now he'd spend half the morning worrying.

'I can hear you thinking, Jo. I promise it's nothing to fret about.'

Easy for him to say, thought Jo but managed a smile instead.

It was almost an hour before they left the shop. Jo wore the new warm jacket and trousers he'd been bought, carrying another pair and a couple of new shirts in a bag. He couldn't help checking his reflection in windows as they walked along.

'Looking good,' the professor teased.

'Yeah, cool jacket,' he murmured, feeling foolish.

'Clothes help make the man, or so they say. They certainly help keep you warm, especially up here. There's a bonny cafe I know near the waterfront; we'll go in there. We need a hot drink and something sweet to ward off this chill. I can't believe it's still August.'

As they walked through the streets Jo was aware of Sven's men trailing behind. It was a weird sensation knowing they were being watched.

The cafe the professor chose was fairly busy. A few families with young children were in the seats near the windows. Leading Jo to the back of the room, the professor went off to order.

Several groups of teenagers were huddled around tables, chatting easily about nothing in particular. What must it be like, he wondered wistfully, to just go and sit in a cafe with a bunch of friends?

Loneliness rose up out of nowhere, twisting his gut. That was never going to happen, not for him. In a few days it would all be over, and then what? Maybe Mr Fraser would find him a family not too far away from Dan, but it would still be another faceless couple, tedious hours of nothingness.

'Jo! I said, do you want marshmallows with your hot chocolate?'

'Sorry... I suppose.' He pulled his gaze back from the laughing group. A tall glass, topped with cream, was put in front of him. 'Thanks,' he managed, trying to shake off the black mood.

The professor said nothing as he sipped his coffee, though Jo could feel him watching. 'What is it, Jo? Why the sudden gloom?'

He shrugged, his eyes on his drink. 'Just, you know...things,'

'Like?'

'Everything's going to be over,' he blurted. 'It's freaking me out, not knowing what's going to happen.'

'I can understand that. Is it okay if I make a suggestion?'

Jo nodded, stirring the swirling chocolate into a caramel haze.

'Simon and I want to become your legal guardians.'

For a moment the words didn't click. Sorry, what?' He must have heard wrong.

'It means going through a legal process. I've already taken advice, Jo, but it's up to you, of course. We won't proceed unless it's what you want.'

'I-I don't believe it. Really? I...' He couldn't speak.

'Do I take it that's a yes then?' the professor asked speaking softly.

Jo could only manage a nod as he wiped his eyes with the back of his hand.

'We'll talk in more detail once you've absorbed the idea, but you'll spend term time with Dan and Simon, as that makes the most sense.'

'I-I can't believe it,' he stuttered. 'What about Dan, doesn't he mind?'

The professor began to laugh. 'Are you serious? He's thrilled! He reckons he wins because you'll get to do half the chores.' Jo laughed along with the professor. 'So, how about calling me Uncle Ian? After all, you'll soon be an official member of the Fraser clan.'

'Cool, Uncle Ian it is.' Grinning he raised his chocolate, tapping the side of the professor's mug. 'And this is really for real?'

'Aye, laddie, not a dream, I promise.'

Jo sat in a haze for a few minutes, trying to take it in. 'Can I ask you something, Uncle Ian?' he said shyly. 'It's about the stuff I heard in Glasgow.'

'I'll try and answer if I can,' said the professor.

'It's about the little girl, Amy. I know her, and if things go the same as they did for the rest...' He shivered, he couldn't help it.

'We've already started to search for her. We'll make more headway now we know who Doctor Bowden really is. That sketch was good enough to name him.'

Jo gasped. 'Who?!'

'Edward Steiner. Does that name mean anything?' Jo shook his head. 'No reason why it should, but I promise, he's being hunted as we speak.'

'And what about my name? It isn't Ranson, is it?'

'You're an astute lad but nothing is known for certain, yet. Just remember, you're officially a Fraser now, which gives Simon and me the right to order you to have haircuts and peel carrots.'

'Oh, I think I'll manage, Uncle Ian. I've had worse.'

'That I'm sure of. Joseph Fraser happened to be the name of my grandfather's brother you know.'

'That's cool by me. Wait till I see Dan. I can't believe I've really got a family!'

The professor drove them the short distance to the sports centre. Jo kept glancing over at the quiet man at his side, hardly daring to believe it was true. It felt as if he had a permanent grin stuck to his face.

'What time will they be back from canoeing, Uncle Ian?' he asked, as they walked towards the large building.

'Four, I should think; it's a good hour's drive away. I said we'd meet John and the others here just after midday.'

As soon as Jo stepped inside, he wrinkled his nose in disgust. It stank of chlorine, and the place was packed. The queues snaked around the large reception area.

'Didn't you have a pool at one of your schools?' the professor asked, catching Jo's reaction.

'No, they always had to travel by bus, so I never bothered going.'

'Public baths aren't for you, I'm afraid, not until we work out any side-effects of the chlorine. I'll give you a tour, if you like. The place is pretty big. Let's start with the main hall where the competition takes place.'

'Huge, or what?' Jo hung over the balcony, amazed at the amount of space. There were two badminton courts set up and there was still plenty of room left. 'Do people watch from up here?'

'For the early part of the competition. There are usually two or more bouts taking place at a time. There will probably be seating downstairs as well for the latter stages.'

They wandered through the rest of complex, ending up back in the main reception. The queues for swimming were still huge and the noise was incredible.

John Brampton and the others were standing near the main doors, trying to avoid the crush. 'Shall we go straight through, John. The hall's a lot quieter,' suggested the professor.

'Nice jacket,' said Sarah, as soon as she could make herself heard.

'I got new shirts as well, and guess what?'

'I've no idea,' she said. 'Did you get voted teenager of the year?'

'Funny,' He was bursting to tell someone. He pulled her to the side and whispered, 'Promise you won't say I told you?'

'Depends what it is.'

'My name, it's not really Fraser...'

'I'd sort of guessed that, Jo.'

'Oh...' Surprised, he hesitated.

'It wasn't hard to work out. So, what's the big news?'

'I'm going to live with Uncle Simon and Dan in Leemouth - officially and everything. How cool is that?! Uncle Ian gets to be my other guardian and, well, I can't believe it.' She grinned as he rambled on. 'I'll be Joseph Fraser for real, but I've got to wait a bit for the official paperwork.'

'That's fantastic news. Now I'll get to rough you up regularly in judo practice!' She grinned, slipping an arm through his. 'Don't worry, I won't say a word. I'm really happy for you. It couldn't have happened to a nicer bloke.'

Walking around the vast hall, she hardly said two words. Jo put it down to nerves. Darren talked quietly with John Brampton, his eyes darting everywhere.

'Is this place lots bigger than you're used to?' Jo asked her.

'A little. It's more about trying to imagine it tomorrow. It always feels different on a competition day.'

'You'll do great,' he said confidently. 'I've watched you practise - you're amazing. You're so strong.'

'Being strong isn't everything. I used to think I could throw people around the floor with sheer force. It doesn't work like that.'

'What made the difference?'

'Working with Master Brampton and your uncle. I learnt how to respect myself and use meditation to focus. It sounds soft when you say it, but it really works.'

'I'll be cheering you on, big time,' Jo promised. 'Though I still haven't got my head around why the competition takes two whole days.'

'The preliminary and quarter-final rounds in the light and middle weight sections are on tomorrow morning. The heavy weight preliminaries and quarters, in the afternoon. Saturday, it's semis and finals day for everyone. Darren and I are both on tomorrow morning.'

They heard the professor calling, 'Are you two ready for lunch?'

'Think I can squeeze something in. How about you, Sarah?'

'I'll try. I'm always nervous the day before. Still, I've got you to wind up, so that might help a bit.'

At five minutes to four, Jo stood outside the hostel, waiting impatiently for the minibus to arrive. The professor leant nonchalantly against the edge of the door, his arms folded. 'We could wait in the warm, Jo,' he suggested, checking his watch.

'But they won't be long now. You said five minutes.'

'Aye, I should've kept my mouth shut,' the professor muttered.

'There they are at last,' Jo said, grateful to see the minibus finally appear.

'Did he tell you?' Dan called, as soon as his feet touched the ground.

'Yeah!' Jo grinned, suddenly shy. 'I get to live with you.'

'Dad wouldn't let me ring or anything. He told me on the way there that Uncle Ian was about to tell you. It's alright, isn't it?'

'Are you kidding? It's the best news ever.' They stood grinning foolishly at each other until Lucy sidled up.

'Are you going to shut up now, Dan? Honest, Jo, that's all he's been rattling on about all day.'

'Have not!'

'You have too.' She made a face then turned to grin at Jo. 'Your uncle told us all that you're moving down. So that means you'll be just up the road?'

'Suppose I will,' said Jo, suddenly lost in those deep green eyes.

Nothing and everything had changed, Jo thought, as he sat in the lounge with the others after dinner. It was belonging, he decided. Knowing there was someone who cared, and not just about how big his neck was or how much blood they needed to take. As the others talked over plans for the coming weeks, it felt amazing to think he'd be a part of it all.

'Hey, have you seen my elbow?' Zoe pulled up her sleeve to show him. 'I caught it as I swung off to abseil down the cliff face. You think it'll scar?'

Jo studied the graze, trying to keep his lips from twitching. 'No, just enough scab to keep you busy.'

'You're as bad as the rest,' she muttered, twisting her arm to take a closer look.

'So, no one came a cropper then?' Jo asked.

'Not even close,' said Ade. 'Wicked, though, especially down that zip-wire. It went straight across this gorge with about twenty foot of water at the bottom.'

'Cool,' Jo admitted, taking a look at Paul's video on his mobile.

'I've got some of the best shots,' Lucy said, smirking at Dan. 'Him at the top of the abseil, before he finally let go of the instructor.'

'I'm not good with heights,' Dan said, laughing with the rest. 'I'm amazed I did it at all. I climbed up, no problem. But throwing yourself off a cliff…'

'You had great big ropes all over you,' said Zoe.

'Don't care, no way am I bungee-jumping or parachuting in this lifetime.'

'Bet you'd change your mind if Margaret said you couldn't do it,' teased Zoe.

'Why, what's that about?' asked Jo.

'She tried to mollycoddle me,' Dan muttered crossly. 'Only reason I abseiled was because I heard her prattling on to the instructor about me.'

'Reckon she did it on purpose to make you have a go?' said Lucy.

'Doubt it. I think she gets a kick out of making people feel bad, and don't look at me like that, Zoe. You didn't have to listen to her. Anyway, you were cool, you did it like a pro.'

'Weird, it doesn't bother me. I was more freaked out by that pool.' She shivered, pulling her sleeve back down. 'All those fish touching my legs, yuck.'

John Brampton came in, followed by Sarah and Darren. 'I just want to let you know what's happening tomorrow.'

He outlined the times of the matches and what they needed to take with them in the morning. 'So,' he said, 'once the matches are done, Darren will drive you back to the hostel to change, as I've booked a couple of hours of archery.' He smiled at the cries of approval. 'I'll follow with Ian once I've finished all the paperwork. Any questions?' Everyone shook their heads.

'Moving on then. Margaret is going into the supermarket near Dundee, straight from the sports centre. She's going to need two of you to help.' Ignoring the groans, he held out a hat. 'All names are in here, apart from Darren, Sarah, and Jo's, for obvious reasons. Lucy, do you want to pick the first one?'

'Not really, but if I must.'

She took a slip of paper and handed it to John Brampton. 'Paul, it's you,' he said. 'Do you want to pull the next one?'

'Don't bother,' Ade said with a sigh. 'I'll go with you.

23 Competition'

There was a definite air of tension at breakfast the following morning. Sarah kept her eyes on her food. Darren sat, grim-faced, not saying a word.

'You'd think they were going to court,' Dan murmured.

'It must be nerve-wracking,' Jo muttered back. 'Especially when they might get chosen for the British team.'

'Suppose, but I can't ever remember being that nervous.'

'Me neither, closest was going to that poxy clinic.'

'Yeah, but never again,' Dan whispered backed.

They'd only just climbed into the van when Sven put his head in and called for silence. 'A quick word,' he said seriously. 'No one is to walk around that sports centre on their own. If you can, please stay on the balcony or on the benches in the main hall where you can be seen. If you are going to one of the food outlets, tell one of us. If you're approached by anyone you don't know, tell either Jan or me. If it's one of my security people, they'll have a password: 'red-head'. Does everyone understand?' He gazed around until everyone nodded. 'Good, enjoy,' he said with a smile.

They pulled into the sports centre just before 8.30am. The car park was already half full. 'Big place,' said Dan as they walked inside.

'Wait till you see the hall. It's huge.' Jo dodged a huddle of excited little girls.

'Hell! What're they doing here?' Lucy's muted exclamation had him spinning on the spot.

'Who? What's up?'

Before she could answer, a heavily built man with a pot-belly pushed his way towards them. His face creased into an unpleasant smile.

'Well, well! If it isn't Lu. Aren't you going to say hello?'

Dan and Jo instantly stepped in front of her. 'Sorry, we're running late,' said Dan.

'I see you've got some new friends, Lu,' the man sneered. 'You've not seen your old dad for a while though, have you?'

Lucy strode away. Her knuckles were white as she clenched the stair rail. Jo could sense her rage even though he was a few feet away. No one said a word until they were safely installed in the small warm-up room. She threw down her bag, kicking it savagely.

'I don't want to talk about it!' she said when Jo walked over.

'Okay.' He bent down to unroll one of the mats.

'If you think I'm going to splurge it all out, forget it,' she said a few minutes later.

'Yeah, I understand,' he said, looking up from the pamphlet he was thumbing through. Opening a first-aid box, he made a show of checking the contents. No one else came anywhere near.

'What do you think you're doing?' she demanded angrily.

'Sorting stuff.' Jo watched her cheeks flame then turn icy white.

'Why are you treating me like this?' she hissed.

'Because when you're ready, you'll talk to me. You're so angry right now we'd probably end up having a fight.'

'Why do you have to be so nice all the time? I - I could kick you!'

'Let's make a deal. When Sarah and Darren have won convincingly, you and I'll have a long talk?' He stared at her, watching the fire inside slowly die.

'Okay. Hang about with me though? I can't face having to talk to any of those morons.'

He hated seeing her so upset. 'No problem.' He glanced around, checking where everyone was. 'It looks like it's time for tai chi. You go in with the others. I just need to ask Jan something.'

He found him leaning over the balcony, apparently talking to thin air.

'I know you're busy, Jan, but a little problem has turned up for Lucy.' He quickly explained, pointing out the man and the small group in the far corner.

'Don't let it worry you, I'll make sure I'm around. Are you going to be in the room doing tai chi with everyone?'

Jo nodded. 'Yes, and I promise not to do anything silly.'

'I think Ian's just being over-cautious.' He shrugged his massive shoulders. 'These men must think you are valuable, ya?'

'No accounting for taste, hey, Jan?'

'You go and I'll make enquiries about these people who bother our Lucy. I like to know the fools I must deal with.'

With tai chi over, they all went out to the balcony. Lucy had no sooner stepped out of the room when the pot-bellied man strutted towards her. His path was instantly blocked by Jan.

'Did you tell?' she accused Jo, her eyes flashing.

'Yes. But just look at the idiot. It's really messing with his head.' The man was pacing angrily, his cheeks scarlet.

'He's a creep and a liar, and a lot worse besides,' she muttered.

'Where are they from? Not Devon?'

'Norfolk. And I'm not saying any more.'

'No problem. Can you talk me through what's happening down there?' He pointed to the two arenas that had been set up.

Dan came and stood at the other side of Zoe, effectively blocking Lucy's view of the Norfolk group. He held out a bag of chips. 'I bought these to keep us going.'

'It's not even half nine, Dan,' Lucy said, though she still took one.

'It was this or popcorn, but you should see how much that costs.'

Jo found the bouts fascinating. Each one consisted of three rounds lasting three minutes, with a bell signalling the start of each round. With two contests taking place at the same time, it did get a bit confusing.

'There she is!' said Zoe.

'Where?' Jo narrowed his eyes, searching. None of the women looked remotely like Sarah.

'She's wet her hair and pinned it back,' Lucy told him. 'Her opponent's a brown belt as well, so that's good.'

The nerves of earlier had obviously disappeared. Sarah was poised and ready for action. Opposite, her opponent was bouncing all over the place. As the bell rang, the other woman charged, but she may as well have hit her with a pillow for all the effect it had. Sarah weathered the attack and grabbed the woman's belt. Within seconds she had her up and over her hip. The woman landed with a thump on her back.

'That's called an 'uki goshi',' explained Darren. 'She's using a scarf hold called 'kesa gatame' to keep her down. If she stays down for 25 seconds, it's over.' The count seemed to go on forever. 'Nice one!' he shouted, as Sarah stepped back. Straightening her jacket, she waited for her opponent to find her feet.

'Did she do it then?' Jo asked, bewildered. Darren shook his head.

'She didn't pin her down for long enough, but Sarah's well in the lead.' The two scrabbled around each other for a couple of minutes before Sarah suddenly had her chance. With a quick whip of her feet, her opponent was once again flat on her back, shoulders pinned to the floor. This time the 25 seconds passed without a hitch.

'She's done it, she's through,' said Lucy, hugging Zoe.

'That move was as clean as a whistle,' said Ade.

'Is that it?' Jo said, astonished it was over so quickly.

'She's got another round then the quarters to go,' said Dan. 'Her next bout's in about half an hour, I think.'

'All that work and it's over in less than five minutes.' Jo shook his head, baffled.

'Yeah, but what about the 100 metres sprint?' said Ade. 'They practice for months and run for less than 11 seconds,'

Sarah's next bout lasted into the third round. It was halfway through that when she managed to pull off another hip throw and hold, to clinch the win. Paul and Ade went to find John Brampton, to check when the next round was. 'Master Brampton says she has half an hour before her quarter-final bout,' Paul told them. 'Good news for Darren - he's got a 'bye' in the first round. A few have pulled out, apparently.'

Lucy leant over the balcony to watch the end of the other women's contest. She turned to face them, her expression grim.

'Problem?' Zoe asked.

'Sarah will be fighting a girl called Chris from that lot. Hope they do a drugs test.' She scowled across at the excited Norfolk group.

'I'm going to grab some food. You lot coming?' asked Paul.

'Yeah, I'll have a wander,' said Zoe.

'No, I'd better stay,' said Jo, nodding towards Jan and another security guard hovering near the door.

'No problem, I'll bring you something back.' Ade held out his hand for the money. 'Lucy, what about you?'

'I'll stay. Make mine an ice-cream, and some crisps.'

'Dan, could you do me a favour?' whispered Jo. 'Ask Uncle Ian where I'm supposed to exercise?'

'Understood.' Dan hurried away after the others, leaving Jo alone with Lucy. He couldn't think of a thing to say. He could feel the heat from her hand as it rested next to his on the rail. She smelt faintly of flowers and honey, and he suddenly had a ridiculous urge to sniff her neck.

'What are you thinking?' she asked.

Fire flashed into his cheeks. 'Not much. Just - things.'

'You do a lot of thinking, Jo Fraser. I like that.' She grinned and lightly touched his hand. A pulsing heat raced up his arm. 'You wouldn't have been thinking about me and my little 'Norfolk' problem, would you?'

'Umm, well...' He just nodded. It was safer.

Her cheerful veneer fell away as she began to talk. 'My dad isn't the nicest of people. Right now, he's in prison. Doing time for armed robbery.'

Jo's jaw dropped. He couldn't help it, that was the last thing he expected to hear. 'Hell, Lucy!'

'Yeah, but even worse - if that's possible - he tried to make me a part of it. I've always been fit, into sports and stuff. About eighteen months ago, he tried to persuade me to climb over this wall and break into a jeweller's shop for him.' Horrified, Jo put his hand over hers. Her skin felt icy. 'When I said 'no way', he beat me then locked me in my room. He told me he'd leave me there until I changed my mind.' She shrugged but Jo could hear the bitterness in her voice as she continued. 'It took three days but I finally managed to force the hinges off my door. And then I ran, got away to my gran's. I was so scared.' She shivered and stared into the distance.

'That's terrible. So, who's that bloke over there - a friend of your dad?'

'He used to fence the stuff for them. Not that I could prove it, mind.' Her usually bright emerald eyes clouded. 'Dad's convinced I was the one who ratted on them. I suppose in a way I did. But it was actually Gran. As soon as she got the story out of me, she went straight to the police in Exeter.'

'Good! Sorry, but how could he, to his own daughter? What about your mum?'

'She died when I was seven. At least I've got Gran.'

'I don't know what to say,' Jo admitted, a little shaken.

'Nothing you can say. It's not going to make it right, is it? I'm just glad I told you. Zoe and the others already know; so does your Uncle Simon, and Master Brampton as well.' A glimmer of a smile returned. 'I don't mind you telling Dan, it's probably best. Only not when I'm about, yeah?'

'Sure. And Lucy, I was thinking about you, but it had nothing to do with that idiot,' he admitted, before he realised what he was saying.

'Is that right?' She smiled properly, her eyes dancing with light. 'I love it when you blush, Fraser. You do that a lot too.'

He was saved from answering as Dan came hurrying back. 'Uncle Ian wants a quick word, Jo.'

The disabled shower-room the professor showed him was just large enough to stretch out one wing at a time. Jo spent ten minutes doing what he could. Sarah's next round would be starting soon, he needed to hurry.

'Here you go, chicken bites and chips.' Paul handed Jo his box of goodies.

'Cheers. Have I missed much?'

'Sarah's up after this next round,' Paul assured him. 'Was there a problem?'

'I just needed to stretch my back a bit that's all.'

Dan had to hide the snort of laughter with a cough.

Sarah's quarter-final bout was a scrappy match. Lucy kept up a furious running commentary. 'It's a good thing no one else can hear you, Lu,' said Dan. 'You'd be paying at least two quid into the swear box.'

'Did you see that?' she hissed. 'She tried to bite her, and she's pulling her hair. The ref must be blind!'

'Lucy!' hissed Zoe. 'Keep it down. The judges have noticed. Sarah's well up on points.'

'Yeah, well, her opponent should be disqualified,' Lucy growled.

Sarah didn't wait for a referee's decision. Swerving away from darting hands, she crouched slightly; suddenly, the Norfolk woman was flying through the air. Smack! She hit the floor so hard, Jo winced. Sarah pinned her down before she could even think of moving.

'Yes, yes, yes!' Lucy grabbed Zoe in a bear hug then turned and did the same to Jo.

He closed his eyes, breathing in her delicate scent. 'Is she through to the semis?' he finally managed to stutter.

'Yes. Now all we need is for Darren to do the same,' said Dan.

They had to wait another half an hour before Darren had his first bout. Jo glanced along the line as they leant over the rail. The anticipation was almost painful.

'He looks so serious,' said Zoe.

'He's going to need to be against this guy,' warned Paul. 'He won his regional final last year.'

The two men bowed and immediately began to move towards each other. Whether a slip or a mistake, in the fastest move Jo had seen so far, Darren picked up his opponent and threw him in a high shoulder throw. The slap, as the man landed, vibrated around the silent hall. Darren dropped to pin him down, though the judge had already rung the bell. There was an explosion of noise.

'It can't be over!' said Jo, as everyone hooted and cheered.

'It is,' said Dan over the din. 'You've just witnessed an "ippon". He won because he threw him down with enough force to end the contest. Wow, that was mega cool! Bet the bloke he's got in the quarters is freaking out.'

Darren's quarter-final bout was an anti-climax in comparison. The contest went for two rounds, but in the end, he won without any real difficulty.

'He's really good.' Jo applauded emphatically like everyone else.

'He's got to be up for the gold medal,' agreed Dan.

'Paul? Ade?' the professor's shout carried easily from the doorway. 'Sorry, lads, but Margaret's arrived to go shopping.'

'Great,' Paul said, his shoulders sagging.

'Maybe she'll buy you an ice-cream,' teased Lucy.

'Yeah, right. We'll see you later,' said Ade.

John Brampton came through the doors, beaming. 'What a great morning! Darren's gone to shower and change but he'll only be ten minutes or so. Go and buy yourselves something to keep you going.' He held out a few notes. 'Make it sandwiches, and get something for him as well while you're at it.'

'Sure,' said Sarah, taking the money. 'What about Jan and Sven?'

'Sven's already left, and Jan will sort himself,' he assured her.

'Good. We'd need twice as much otherwise,' she said with grin.

24 Distraction

They had driven just a couple of miles from the sports centre when there was an ominous, metallic clunking sound. Steam began to spill out from under the bonnet of the minibus. 'I don't believe this!' Darren hissed. 'Sarah, give Jan or someone a ring, will you? I'm going to take a quick look.'

Dan jumped to his feet. 'I'll give you a hand, Darren.'

'Can you believe there's no stupid signal?' said Sarah. 'I'll have to get out. I might have more luck.'

'Shouldn't one of the security cars have caught up with us by now?' Zoe said, staring through the rear window.

'Definitely. Something's up,' said Jo, his stomach beginning to churn.

He looked over to the door as Sarah clambered back in. Her expression was bleak. 'Still no signal and Darren say's the radiator has blown.

'We need to get the mini-bus off the road, now,' called Darren. 'Jo, open the gate to that field opposite then steer for me. Everyone else, push.'

Jo ran to the gate, his heart thudding. He glanced up and down the road, listening for the roar of an engine. All was quiet. It took a lot of huffing and puffing; finally, the minibus slid into the field against the hedge.

'At least it's not immediately visible,' said Darren, wiping his dirty hands on the grass.

'What now?' asked Sarah. 'Shall we sit with our backs to the hedge or...?'

'No.' Darren peered over their heads to glance up the road. 'There's not enough cover. You lot need to get right away from here.'

'Couldn't we just have broken down?' said Zoe.

Darren's expression was bleak. 'Sven and I checked all the vehicles last night and this was fine. Someone must have tampered with it. Whoever it was, they won't know exactly where we've broken down – but, it's not going to take them long to find us. There's no point walking back to the sports centre, they're bound to be searching those roads. And anyway, there's no cover to speak of, we'd be spotted in an instant.'

'They'll probably have the roads and fields near the hostel covered as well,' added Sarah. 'They'll guess we'll try to head back there.'

'I think you're right,' agreed Darren. 'In that case, Sarah, take Jo and the others and head for the cottages near the school. There should be someone home who can help. If you stick to the edges of those fields opposite and keep your heads down, no one will see you. That route keeps you well away from the roads, and those hedges are much higher. You should be fine.'

'So, you know they're after me?' Jo said.

'Your uncle thought it safer to take me into his confidence, Jo. Now, I'm going to wait here, see who turns up, but I've got a bad feeling about this.' He held up a hand to stop their protests. 'If no one arrives in the next ten minutes, I'll follow. That way, if you have run into trouble, I'll be able to dig you out.'

'That's just plain stupid, we should stick together,' said Sarah.

'And they could be armed,' said Jo.

'They won't even know I'm around. If I can take out whoever turns up here, there'll be fewer to worry about later.' He picked up a hefty metal spanner. 'I found this with the spare tyre. It might come in handy. Make sure your phones are on silent but keep trying to ring for help. The signal might be better a few yards further on. There's no time to argue,' he insisted, when no one moved. 'Remember, keep close to the hedge and cross over the road at the next gate. Don't stop until you get to those cottages. Go!'

They made a dash across the road and along the edge of the field. Sarah took the lead with Zoe bringing up the rear. A few minutes later they all heard Zoe's frantic hiss of warning. 'Stop. There's a car!' They crouched instinctively; Jo caught a fleeting glimpse of red through a gap in the hedge.

'What did you see?' Dan whispered as Zoe crept closer.

'It was a red car going slow,' she whispered. 'They've probably ditched the blue Peugeot.'

'Still no signal!' Sarah held her phone at all angles. 'Anyone got lucky?' she asked, but nobody else's phone was faring any better.

'We'd better keep moving,' Lucy warned. 'We can be spotted too easily here.'

The field, thankfully, had deep, curving sides, making it easier to run. They were almost at the gate when Lucy suddenly dashed ahead. Instead of crossing over the road, she ran in front of the gate, waving the others to follow.

'Shouldn't we be crossing over?' whispered Zoe.

'That's the easiest route to the hostel,' said Lucy 'They're bound to be keeping watch. We can still get to the cottages this way, it'll just take a bit longer.'

They had only moved a few yards when Dan gave a low whistle. 'Hide! There's a car coming back towards us.' Just ahead of them was a large clump of nettle and briar. They made a dive for the meagre cover, crouching as the noise of the engine grew louder.

'It's stopping!' Zoe whispered. Her eyes were wide with terror. Jo felt as if his heart was in his mouth. He rubbed clammy hands on his trousers. Beside him, Dan was crouched like a sprinter, ready to run. At the sound of a car door clicking open, no one moved a muscle There was a muffled exclamation as metal hit wood.

'Bloody kids! No, it's Frank. Speak up Paolo, I can hardly hear you.'

Jo's mouth went dry. His knees felt like jelly as he recognised the driver's voice.

'Nah, we missed them,' Frank continued. 'I'm checking the smaller roads but they've probably headed across the fields to the hostel. All I found was that van of theirs. I've left Rand there in case the kids go back.' His tone changed. 'How do I know? Nev's rung to say no sign as yet. Those security idiots went chasing their tails, like I said they would. Yeah, yeah. The others are busy working their way across, so we'll just keep looking.'

The one-sided conversation they were privy to seemed to go on forever. Jo's knees were trembling with the effort as he crouched, too scared to move a muscle.

'There's not a lot of cover apart from hedges and I've got Ed and the others coming this way. They should be trawling the fields around here in about five.' Frank paused for a few moments before talking loudly again. 'Have they picked off the other two at that ruddy supermarket yet? As soon as you hear anything, you tell him to get them to me. That'll shake Ranson out of cover when he hears them squealing.' They heard cruel laughter. 'I'll be there shortly. Stay sharp.' There was another metallic crunch before the car accelerated away.

'He was talking about Ade and Paul!' Jo exclaimed as the truth finally hit.

He tried to stand but someone gripped his arm. 'Stop it, or it'll be all of us,' Dan urged. 'And we don't know for sure if they've got them, do we. Listen to me,' he pleaded.

'They're going to kill them! Let me go!' Jo couldn't think, couldn't see straight.

'I'm going to try ringing again,' said Zoe. Bent double, she scurried to the gate and disappeared from view. The seconds ticked away endlessly. Dan and Lucy held on tight to Jo's arm, trying their best to calm him. All Jo could think about was what those men might do to his two friends.

Making barely a sound, Zoe came hurrying back. 'I got through to Ade,' she said breathlessly. 'Two men tried to grab them at the petrol pumps but they got away. They're both in the security guard's office at the store, safe and sound.'

'But what about Jan, or the police?' Sarah whispered.

'I told Ade as much as I could. He said there's another problem at the sports centre and the hostel. He'll do what he can; I didn't want to hang around.'

Standing as tall as he dared, Jo looked down at the others. 'Let me go on ahead. You lot go back the other way and raise the alarm.'

'Are you dense?' said Sarah. 'Not happening. Sit down, we need to plan.'

Guilt mixed with fear was hard for Jo to swallow. 'But if you stay with me, you'll be in far more danger.'

'I said sit. Does anyone else think differently?' Sarah demanded.

'Stop it, Jo. It's really not helping,' said Zoe. 'This isn't your fault. And anyway, we're all in this together.'

'Look, let's just get to the cottages like Darren suggested,' said Sarah. 'We'll decide what to do once we've got some decent cover.'

'Agreed,' said Lucy. And it has to be better than sitting here, waiting to be found.'

Running behind Dan, all Jo could do was concentrate on putting one foot in front of the other. His mind felt as if it was full of a swarm of angry bees, buzzing loudly; he just couldn't think straight.

Lucy took the lead again, warning them all to stay low. It felt like an eternity, but only a few minutes later the school and cottages were within sight. 'We need to crawl to those trees,' she ordered, pointing to a narrow band of woodland. Beyond it was a low hedge that separated the cottages and school. 'We'll stop there and make sure it's clear before we try for the buildings. Stay as low as you can.'

Zoe had only moved a couple of feet when she groaned in disgust. 'Ugh, a stinking cow pat!' She tried to wipe it off on a tuft of grass.

'Just keep going,' Lucy urged, 'Unless you want to get caught?'

Those few yards seemed to stretch on forever. Jo wanted to kiss the tree as he finally slid behind the wide trunk, he felt so relieved.

'Sarah!' Lucy hissed. 'What the hell is she doing?'

Ignoring Lucy, Sarah had crawled along the hedge until she was opposite the front of the school. On her stomach, she pushed her camera-phone through a gap in the hedge.

Jo desperately listened for the sound of sirens. Surely help would come soon, he thought. He pulled out his phone. There was still no signal.

Sarah came scuttling back. Even from a distance, Jo could tell the news wasn't good.

'You'd better take a look,' she muttered. Jo groaned out loud when he saw what she'd filmed. Leaning against the open door of the school was Frank, the driver. As the video played on, it was obvious he was talking to someone inside.

'Now we've had it,' moaned Zoe. 'What the hell do we do now?'

'We get to those cottages,' Sarah hissed. 'There's hardly any cover out here, and these trees aren't going to hide us for long. Let's hope someone's home and they let us in.'

'We could bury ourselves,' suggested Dan.

'And how do you plan to dig a hole in this ground?' Lucy scoffed. 'It's like iron.'

Jo sighed, knowing she was right. He looked up, perhaps they could climb? But the nearest branch was easily fifteen feet above his head.

'We've got to do....' Zoe broke off. She stared over Jo's shoulder, her face chalk white. Everyone turned to look through the swaying branches and froze.

Lucy was the first to react. 'Down, and start moving!' She threw herself to the ground. No one argued. They began to crawl towards the hedge, keeping the trees between them and the group of men fast approaching.

Jo's head was in turmoil. If there were men lying in wait at the school, wouldn't they be at the cottages as well? But the truth was they were out of options.

It was the hardest thing in the world to crawl slowly when all he wanted to do was get up and run. It didn't help that his back was twitching like mad. Bending over was not easy.

Dan turned to whisper, 'Lucy reckons the cottages are clear. Just round the back of this one and we can take a breather.'

They sank in a line against the wall of the cottage. Jo groaned with pleasure as he straightened his aching back against the warm stone. He didn't know about the rest but his chest and back were throbbing with the strain. Above his head he could hear chattering sparrows. Everything seemed so normal.

'Stay put. I'm going to check if anyone's home,' said Dan. Lucy began to object but he was almost at the first door. It took less than two minutes for him to come scurrying back. 'Guess what?' he hissed, slipping down beside Jo. 'There's not so much as a dog in any of those cottages. I've checked every one!'

'Of course! There's that big festival in Dundee,' Lucy said, smacking her forehead. 'The posters were all over the sports centre. Either that or they're at work.'

'Those men are bound to come soon and check the cottages,' Sarah warned.

Jo wanted to scream with frustration. They were sitting ducks.

'We don't have a choice, do we?' said Lucy. 'It's got to be the school.'

'They're bound to have put someone at the back of the place,' said Sarah. 'How the hell do you expect us to get in?'

'What if I draw them all to the front?' suggested Lucy.

'Right, and we do what?' said Zoe in a sarcastic tone. 'We break a window, except they'd hear it and we can't exactly jemmy the back door open, can we?' Lucy ignored her and chewed thoughtfully on a nail.

'But that's mad,' said Jo. 'We might as well just give in.'

'They won't have a clue once we're in there,' Lucy insisted. 'But it's how to get you in.'

Jo couldn't believe they were even considering it.

'Jo, take a look.' Dan pointed to the floor and a grey feather caught in the gravel. 'Are you thinking what I'm thinking?'

It took a little while for the penny to drop. 'The toilets. It might work,' Jo admitted.

'There's a window with a broken catch in the men's toilet,' Dan announced.

'Perfect!' Lucy beamed at him. 'All we have to do is get to the end cottage and we're almost opposite the toilet block. Dan, stay at the back and keep checking where the men are, but stay low!'

'How does she know all this stuff?' muttered Jo, as Lucy began to edge her way towards the corner of the building.

'Her dad,' Zoe shrugged. 'He taught her some really dodgy stuff. I don't care, as long as she saves our necks.'

'Uncle Simon's not going to be happy about us going in there,' whispered Jo.

'I don't like it either, but Lucy's right,' Zoe conceded. 'If we stay put, they're definitely going to find us. But I tell you, my dad's going to go ape when he finds out.'

They made it to the corner. Lucy held up a hand and waited for Dan to catch up.

'What if Uncle Simon, or Sven, arrive...' Jo began.

'And if they come too late? Do you want to risk it?' said Lucy.

'We're out of time, they're almost here' Dan warned. 'We've less than five minutes, six at the most.'

'Right,' Lucy was all business. 'My dad had his uses. He taught me how to pick almost any lock by the time I was ten. Not something I'm proud of, but if it saves us, I'm sure your dad will forgive me.' She gave Zoe a tight smile.

'If you can do that, why not break into a cottage?' hissed Jo.

'Alarms, wally, take a look! The men must've already disabled the school.'

Jo glanced up at the nearest cottage and saw a large yellow alarm box flickering at him. 'Sorry,' he murmured.

'I need hair-pins. Zoe?' Lucy asked. With a sigh, Zoe pulled some from her hair. She opened her mouth to say something but obviously thought better of it. 'You lot get ready to make for that window as soon as you hear the diversion. And make sure your phones are on silent, just in case.'

'Wait!' Dan grabbed Lucy's arm as she began to move away.

'What should we do once we're in?'

'Head up to that attic space. I'm sure your dad left the gap open with the climbing ropes down. You should be able to see and hear everything?'

'Great idea,' said Dan. 'There's no reason for them to go up there.

How will we know it's safe to move? Will you send us a text?'

Lucy laughed, a low, wicked sound that made Jo smile, despite his nerves. 'Trust me, you won't need a text,' she promised.

'I guess this is where we synchronise our watches,' Jo said, trying to lighten the mood.

'Two minutes and I'll be ready,' said Lucy. 'Once you're in, get up to that attic.' She was gone before anyone could ask questions.

'Your dad's really not going to like this,' Jo whispered to Dan as they waited with their backs flat against the wall.

'If we get out alive, he'll forgive us, I hope.'

With every second ticking by, Jo assumed they'd be discovered. He glanced at his friends' nervous faces. He'd never forgive himself if anyone got hurt. Next to him, Zoe muttered under her breath. Sarah was like a rock: impassive, her eyes everywhere. He couldn't imagine anything fazing her.

'Ten seconds!' whispered Dan. Jo wasn't sure if it was his own thudding heart he heard or his friend's.

Lucy was thirty seconds late. They heard a house alarm then a noise that was so farcical, it was impossible to believe.

'Is that what I think it is?' muttered Dan. Jo nodded, grinning.

Zoe stared in disbelief. 'That's an ice cream van! Where the hell did she find one of those?'

'A bloke in one of the cottages,' Sarah whispered. 'We saw him cleaning it the other day. I think it's safe to say Lucy's dad taught her a lot more than picking locks. Come on, let's not waste the opportunity.' With a last glance over her shoulder, she ran the short distance to the back of the school.

At least finding the right window proved easy. 'Poor bird,' whispered Zoe, looking sadly at the small pile of soggy, white feathers.

Jo heard Dan's snigger; he didn't dare catch his eye.

Sarah pointed to several large wooden pallets near a doorway. 'Give me a hand,' she whispered. It took seconds to carry one over and lay it up against the wall. 'It's enough to give you lot a boost. I'll go last. I can manage without.'

Dan almost ran up the side of the wall. At the top, he leant against the window, checking it was clear, before sliding inside. His hand reappeared a second later, waving them on. Zoe went next, swiftly followed by Jo. The wooden pallet creaked a little, but he pulled himself up quickly, managing to squeeze his shoulders and back through the opening. Careful not to make a sound, he dropped onto the sink and waited for Sarah to appear. He and Dan had to help her through. Red faced and ruffled, she slid soundlessly to the floor.

'I put the pallet back,' she said, straightening up. 'We'd better get out of here before that music stops.'

Dan carefully cracked the door open an inch. The toilets were a third of the way down a long corridor, with a set of stairs at each end. The door leading into the reception area was at the far end, to the left.

Sarah and Zoe went first. The boys gave them a twenty second start before making a run for the stairs. As Jo put his foot on the first step, he knew it creaked, but the din of 'I'll take the high road' was more than enough to drown it out.

It was dark at the bottom of the stairs, and impossible to see much. The light improved a little the higher they climbed. There was a single arched window in the gable end wall, but the attic was still gloomy. As they reached the top, Jo saw a flicker of movement in the shadows and grabbed Dan's arm. His heart was hammering like mad.

'It's just the girls,' whispered Dan, picking up the pace.

They found Sarah and Zoe kneeling beside a slumped figure on the floor. 'W-we almost fell over her.' Even in the gloom Jo could see Sarah was trembling. 'She's been shot in the leg.'

Jo bent a little closer and knew instantly who it was. 'It's Sheila,' he muttered. 'She works for Sven. Is she...?' He couldn't say the word.

'She's alive, but drifting in and out of consciousness,' said Sarah. A sob escaped but was quickly gone. 'They, um, missed her artery, but she's still lost a lot of blood. I need to put a strap on to stop the bleeding.' She fought to hold back tears.

Shaken, Jo could only nod. Beside Sarah, Zoe was ashen. She held her mobile in a shaking hand with the screen's light pointing down. Her other hand pressed hard on the woman's leg, her fingers coated in something dark. Jo had to turn away as the bile rose in his throat.

'We'll check out the gap,' said Dan. Jo followed him automatically. He really didn't want to look too closely at that dark stain on the floor or Sarah's anguished expression.

With the noise from the van still echoing, they inched forward on their bellies and stared down into the school hall. 'Watch out!' hissed Dan, grabbing Jo's arm. A man walked across the hall, right underneath them. He paused and suddenly looked up. It was a good thing the attic was so dark and they were in shadow, thought Jo. Even so, he held his breath, too terrified to even blink.

The hall doors opened and the noise from the ice-cream van was instantly louder. Frank, the driver, walked in. He looked to one of the ceiling beams near the door and began shaking his head. He said something but they couldn't hear what. The other man grabbed a stepladder that leant against the wall, climbed two steps, and stretched towards the wooden beam to pick something up. Jo couldn't for the life of him work out what it was. Intrigued, he watched as the man got down, picked up the stepladder, and began to walk towards them.

'Duck!' hissed Dan.

Jo's forehead hit the dusty attic floor. He squeezed his eyes shut, praying he wouldn't sneeze. He counted slowly to sixty before he dared look. When he did, the hall was empty, apart from a small, winking light on top of a beam roughly six feet below them.

'Hell fire!' muttered Dan.

25 Show Time

Jo couldn't drag his eyes away. His heart was racing like never before. 'That's a - a bomb!'

'I'd guessed that,' Dan said between clenched teeth.

'A bloody bomb?' Zoe hissed when they quickly explained.

'You need to get out; now,' Jo urged.

'I'm not leaving,' Sarah said so calmly. The tears were gone; the rock was back. 'Sheila could die if I don't stay and help her.'

'But it's a bomb!' Jo hissed again.

'We could carry Sheila down between us,' said Zoe.

'Maybe so, but how do we get her out?' said Dan. 'There's no way she'll fit through that window.'

'No! You'll kill her if you try and move her without a stretcher,' Sarah said flatly. 'She's barely alive as it is.'

'Hang on, Jo. We saw him move the bomb, didn't we?' said Dan.

'Yes, but...'

'If he picked it up then it can't be motion sensitive. As long as we can get it outside, even if they trigger it, we should be okay.'

Jo ran a shaking hand through his hair, wondering how much worse things could get. Then a memory stirred. 'There's the fire escape. The key is hanging on a chain to the side. I watched Master Brampton open it the other day.'

'Then lower me down,' said Zoe. 'I'll grab the bomb, unlock the fire escape, problem over!' She made it sound like the easiest thing in the world, though her hands were stuffed under her armpits as she tried to control the shakes.

Jo couldn't believe what she was suggesting. 'You can't,' he said.

'Well, you can't do it, you're far too heavy to lower down,' she reasoned. 'It has to be me.'

'Are you sure about this?' Dan muttered.

'No, but do you have a better idea?' No one said a word. 'Look, they'll set that bomb off soon,' she said, a note of panic creeping in. 'They put it there ready to kill us once they'd got hold of Jo. Well, they haven't got him, have they? Now they need to cover their tracks, and what better than a big explosion? We've no choice but to get rid of that bomb.'

Jo didn't like the idea one little bit but he knew she was right. 'We can't just hang on to your legs,' he said. 'Just give me a minute and I'll find some rope.'

The attic space ran the whole length of the hall. It was full of scenery, and bits and pieces the school used for plays and sports. He found the longest length of climbing rope he could and hurried back.

Zoe took out her mobile and slipped it into a pocket that had a button. 'I, um, I can't do the button up,' she mumbled, close to tears.

Without a word Sarah knelt down and did it for her. 'You don't have to do this,' she murmured.

'Yes, I do. Let's just get on with it.' Blinking hard, she held up her arms. Jo tied one end around her and the other around Dan's waist.

He could hardly watch as they lowered her slowly towards the flying saucer-shaped object, balanced precariously on the edge of the beam. He saw her fingers stretch out but she suddenly started to sway. Her knuckle caught the edge of the device.

It was like everything happened in slow motion. Jo saw the bomb begin to topple, heard Zoe's frantic - 'No!' as she lunged toward it. Caught Dan and Sarah's desperate groans as the rope raced through their burning fingers. SNAP! With only inches to spare, the rope went taut. Zoe swung at the end, the bomb gripped in her fingertips. Her long ponytail swept the floor as she swayed back and forth.

'Hell on wheels!' grunted Dan. 'We'd better pull her up or put her on the floor.'

'Don't you dare move or I'll drop the stupid thing!' Zoe shouted 'Think of something, and quickly!' Her frantic call reached them loud and clear, even over the noise of the ice cream van.

'Bloody hell!' Sarah gasped. 'What do we do now?'

'I'll slide down and...' Jo began.

'NO!' they yelled in unison.

'I'll have to find something. Just, - hang on!'

Jo began rummaging. He scrabbled through piles of discarded bits and pieces. Grabbing a couple of poles, he lashed them together with string, making them as long as possible. Noticing a length of sheeting, he tore off a large square, folding it into a makeshift basket. Securing the sheeting to the end of the poles, Jo slotted the end through the gap. Lying down, he stretched as far as he could. It was only just long enough. Praying the whole thing wouldn't fall apart, he called to Zoe, 'Put it in the sheet!'

Slowly, she manoeuvred her hands toward the pole. Jo felt a tug and saw her lift her arms to show they were empty. He tried to stop the tip of the pole from dipping down; there was one terrifying moment when the whole bundle began to slide towards the floor. Frantically, he raised the tip, praying the knots would hold firm.

Several sweaty minutes later, the bomb was safe in the attic.

'Listen!' Sarah urged. 'The music's stopped. Get her up, NOW!'

With the three of them heaving, Zoe flew up from the floor in seconds. As Dan grabbed her arms to pull her away from the edge, they all froze in horror. Someone walked into the hall, dragging Lucy with them.

Sarah tugged at Jo's arm. 'Get away from the gap!'

Jo felt cold. His hands trembling, he could hardly move.

'We'll think of something,' hissed Dan. 'Just move!'

Sarah crept over to her patient. Jo in a daze could only follow Dan's insistent tug.

'Sheila, can you hear me?' Sarah gently shook the woman awake. Sheila opened her eyes and tried to focus on the unfamiliar faces. 'We've found this bomb they planted,' Sarah told her. Even in the shadowy light, Jo swore Sheila went two shades paler.

'Dear heavens,' the woman murmured. She tried to lift her hand but she was too weak. She waved Sarah close and whispered something in her ear.

Sarah listened for a moment and then waved the others closer. 'She says, there's a switch on the front? We have to move it from left to right to deactivate it.'

Jo could just make out a tiny plastic knob that jutted out. 'Are you sure about this, Sheila?' asked Jo.

'Yes,' the injured woman managed.

His back was soaked with sweat. He didn't dare look at any of the others. With trembling fingers, he grasped the switch.

'Just do it!' Zoe hissed as she tensed, waiting for the worst.

'Left to right,' he repeated. For a moment the light stayed green.

'It's off,' said Sarah. Jo sank to the floor, holding his head in shaking hands.

'Nice one.' Dan patted him with a trembling hand. 'I'm going to listen,' he murmured and crawled off. Thirty seconds later, he came scuttling back. 'I've got a signal at last, Dad's sent me a message. Make sure your phones are all on silent.'

Jo checked his. There were various missed calls from Mr Fraser and the professor. They're probably worried sick, thought Jo.

He turned to Dan. 'What's happening down there?'

'We need to take a look,' Dan replied. 'But it's not good.'

Laying on their bellies, Zoe, Dan and Jo cautiously peered over the edge. Below, Lucy, her red hair defiantly poker straight, sat bolt upright. She was gagged. Her hands were behind her back and tied firmly to a chair.

The driver was by her side, busy typing into a phone. Jo felt his own mobile vibrate. He read the message. Where are you? I'm really worried. Ring and tell me where you are. I'll come and meet you. It was supposed to be from Lucy.

'They must think you're an idiot,' Dan said when he showed him.

And that, Jo thought, was why Bowden was going to lose. He and his men had no idea how he'd changed or what he was capable of.

'He's leaving,' whispered Dan. Jo wanted to lean over the edge and call to Lucy, but Dan shook his head. 'Let's get back to Sarah. We don't know how far sound will carry in a space like this. We can at least send messages to Dad at last. Come on.'

'What about the police?' said Sarah, tapping away on her mobile.

'Not until we've got Lucy free,' Jo insisted. 'They'd use her as a hostage for definite.'

'I could swing down and cut her loose, then you two hoist her back up here,' Zoe suggested.

'There's nowhere else to go other than up here,' whispered Sarah. 'When they realise, we'll all be trapped.'

'Don't forget the fire escape,' said Zoe.

'And there's another small door that leads to the back of the stage,' said Jo. But I've got an idea.' Jo talked fast. As far as he could see, his plan was the only logical way out.

'I'm not sure,' muttered Dan. 'Why not just make a run for it through the fire escape? It makes no sense to hang around now we've taken out the bomb.'

'The moment they see Lucy's gone they'll just come up here to finish off Sheila,' said Jo. 'They'd have to - she can identify them. But whatever we decide, we have to get to Lucy, we're running out of time!'

Dan looked at the other anxious faces. 'I suppose your idea could work,' he said slowly. 'As long as there are only a few of them, and they don't all come running into the hall at once.'

'I'll make sure whoever comes in is looking straight at me,' Jo assured him.

'What do you mean...?' Dan began, but Sarah hushed them into silence.

'Hide! Someone's coming,' she whispered. Grabbing his arm, she pulled Jo towards the shadows near the stairs. A few seconds later they heard the creaking of the wooden steps.

'I'm ready,' Jo mouthed, raising an old cricket bat above his head.

Beside him, Sarah stooped, ready to pounce.

Jo saw a shadow spread across the wall. Any second now, he thought, bracing himself. 'Stop!' Sarah hissed. She jerked her head forward and sniffed the air. 'I'd recognise that sweat anywhere.' Bewildered, Jo stared at her.

Then Darren stepped out of the shadows.

'It's us!' Sarah whispered.

Jo saw him hesitate, arm raised, ready for battle. 'It's me,' Sarah, said again, and slid out so he could see her.

Jo hugged him hard. He had never felt such relief.

'We thought that man had caught you, 'Zoe whispered. 'How on earth did you get in?

'Let's just say Lucy gave me a great opportunity.' They saw a flash of white as he grinned.

'Where's Uncle Simon?' Jo asked.

Darren shook his head. 'There's a problem. They're on the way and the police, but it's going to be at least another ten minutes. I've managed to take out three men who were near the cottages, which only leaves two here in the school. Sven's got his hands full stopping the other group from getting here.'

Jo's heart sank and Zoe groaned in despair. 'They've got Lucy,' Jo muttered, 'If they hear the police coming, they'll kill her…or take her away as hostage, which is as good as.'

'Jo's got this idea about picking them off,' said Dan. 'If there really are only two of them left, and you're here, we might stand a chance.'

As Jo finished explaining Darren didn't look convinced. 'And how are you planning to keep his eyes fixed on you?' He's going to realise it's a set-up as soon as he sees you.'

'Trust me, he'll be watching,' said Jo.

Pulling his friend out of earshot, Dan whispered, 'Jo, you can't. Remember what Uncle Ian said…you mustn't!'

'I'm not going to try and lift off or anything.'

Zoe interrupted them. 'There's no time to argue, that's our friend down there!'

'It'll be okay,' Jo whispered to Dan before turning to Darren. 'He'll take notice, I promise. But it would be better if we only have to deal with one at a time. The tension was palpable. Jo dug his nails into his palms, trying not to look at the gap.

Reluctantly, Darren nodded. 'I think you may be right. We have to get Lucy, and that device out of here. But you have to let me get to the front of the building first, understood? I need two minutes.' He was gone before they could argue, leaving the four of them alone.

Dan immediately grabbed Jo's arm again. 'Don't!' he pleaded.

'Only if I have to, I promise.'

White-faced but determined, Zoe was already at the ropes, ready to descend.

'I'll send the parcel down once you reach the floor,' whispered Jo.

'Just get rid of it well away from here, then go hide,' urged Dan. She nodded, tight-lipped.

Hand over hand Zoe climbed down. Lucy almost toppled backwards as she ran past her. Dan went next. Jo had never seen his friend more agile.

'Will you be alright on your own, Sarah?' asked Jo.

'Just let them try anything. I'm here if anyone comes up, and I'm only a second away if you need help down there. Now get on with it.' She sounded so grim. Sarah was one person he would never want to cross, thought Jo.

His attempt on the rope was less than elegant. He made it without falling but his hands stung from rope-burn. By the time his feet touched the floor, Lucy was free. She hugged Dan then walked to Jo and kissed him on the cheek.

He noticed a large swelling on her chin that was already turning a nasty shade of purple. Just one more thing to add to the payback list, he thought. He felt something touch his head. Sarah had lowered down two lumps of wood. Quickly, Jo untied them, handing one to Dan.

'Get out, Lucy,' he whispered, pointing to the now-open fire exit.

'Not a chance. I'll take that cricket bat.'

'Please go,' Jo begged. How was he supposed to flip out his wings with her watching? She just stood there, waiting. With a mournful sigh, Jo gave in.

'What the hell are we supposed to say to her?' whispered Dan.

'I don't know. Maybe I won't need to…you know,' Jo hissed back.

Lucy and Dan hid behind the long red curtain closest to the doors. If the plan was going to work, thought Jo, whoever came in would need to walk a good third of the way into the hall. He had to make that happen and keep their attention focused on him.

His fingers were shaking so badly it was all he could do to unfasten the top few buttons of his shirt. In the end, he just pulled it over his head and slipped his jacket back on. Now all he needed was someone to appear. Even from the far end of the hall, Jo could hear Darren's yells. He checked one last time that his escape route was clear. If the two men came into the hall at once, it would be close.

The doors began to move. Time was up. Every muscle in his body tensed.

It was Frank who came blustering through. 'She'll tell me all right, just sort out that imbecile,' he yelled over his shoulder. 'When you catch him, bring him in here. I want to put a bullet through his head.' He kicked the doors closed. Muttering furiously, he walked just three paces.

'What the...?' His eyes wide, he stared at the empty chair before his gaze moved to fix on Jo. He snarled, his face twisting into a vicious scowl. 'You! I'll make you wish you'd never been born.'

Jo cowered. He let his arms hang by his side. 'Quasimodo, eat your heart out,' he muttered. He pretended to tremble and shake. 'Just leave my friends alone!' he called, trying to make his voice sound weak and feeble.

'You call that rabble 'friends'? Monstrosities like you don't have any friends. Now, come here.' The noise from the fight outside grew louder. Frank's face was red with rage. He took two more steps into the hall and stopped again.

Silently, Jo urged him on. Just another few steps. 'Leave me alone! I don't understand...' Jo wiped away an imaginary tear.

'Leave you alone, freak? I don't think so. There's too much money invested in you. But don't worry, Ranson. They're not interested in how you arrive, as long as you're breathing.'

Jo felt his stomach churn. Freak? Monster? He couldn't allow himself to think. Frank took another couple of steps forward, his hand moving to a back pocket.

'Maybe I'll give you something to cry about, huh? A little hole somewhere?'

He couldn't allow Frank to pull out a gun. Kicking the chair to one side, Jo stood tall and straight. Frank gazed, dumbstruck.

'Now, now, Frank,' Jo mocked. 'I'm sure Steiner, or whatever he's called today, wouldn't want you to damage his prize experiment.'

Sensing a trap, Frank glanced at the red curtain, his hand moving towards his gun once again. Jo's jacket slipped to the floor. In one slick, easy motion he dropped his head and rolled his shoulders. The air pulsated as the wings flipped out and began to beat faster and faster. He'd never flapped so hard, ever. For a single moment, he swore his feet began to lift from the floor.

'Impossible...' Frank was gobsmacked. From somewhere above his head Jo thought he heard a scream.

'I never dreamed... The boss will love this!' Frank was laughing, a cruel, callous sound that echoed around the hall. Unable to take his eyes from the fluttering wings, he forgot about the red curtain. 'I'm in for a bonus if I get you back in one piece. Shame, and I was so going to make you pay for the weeks of extra work and earache you put me through. Now get here, freak, before I beat you to a pulp. I said now, weirdo!'

Crack The wood landed sending him reeling. Frank yelped in pain before collapsing in a heap on the floor. He tried to roll away, only to be met by a wild-eyed Lucy.

She kicked him in the knee - hard. 'Monster!? The only freaking monster is YOU!!' she kicked again even harder.

'Jo, put them away!' Dan shouted, diving to the floor. Heaving the gun and a knife from Frank's belt, Dan sent them sliding out of reach.

In a daze, Jo realised he was still flapping. He drew in a breath and concentrated for a second. The muscles in his chest burned as the wings folded away.

'Where have they gone?' Lucy stared at him.

'Not now!' Dan hissed urgently. 'Come and help.'

Between them they dragged the groaning man to the side of the hall. 'You two go, I'll keep an eye on this weirdo,' she promised, her green eyes flashing.

They positioned themselves on both sides of the door. Jo quickly pulled his clothes back on. 'Did she say much?' he gasped, as the noise from outside grew more intense.

'Are you serious?' Dan spluttered. 'She almost had a heart attack.'

'I'm sorry, okay…but he was going for his gun.'

'I know, but she isn't the problem. Zoe saw as well,' blurted Dan.

'What?!'

'Later,' warned Dan, as the door started to move. It flew open and Darren came charging in.

'No, Paolo!' But Frank's warning came too late. Jo reached around the door to grab the startled man's arm, pulling him in. As he toppled forward, Dan stuck out his leg. Paolo fell heavily, head-butting the floor at Jo's feet. Dan and Darren were on him in a flash. Seconds later, a large knife joined the other weapons at the far side of the room.

Lucy's scream cut the air. Frank was back on his feet, a hand firmly around her throat. 'Get over here, Ranson. Unless you want to watch her eyes pop out.' He dragged her towards the open fire exit. Paolo staggered to his feet, disorientated. Dan and Jo looked helplessly at each other.

'Now! Or I'll make sure she suffers,' he laughed, tightening his grip. Lucy pulled desperately at his thick fingers, her lips already blue. 'I mean it,' hissed Frank. 'Hurry up, I've still got an 'accident' to check up on in Glasgow.'

Jo took a step. His legs felt like lead.

'Don't you move another inch, Jo,' Darren ordered. He grabbed Paolo in a vicious arm lock. 'First and only warning. I swear I'll break his neck and then yours, before you can get one foot out of that door. Let her go!' He twisted harder and Paolo squealed in pain.

'You're all dead, you hear me? You've only got that piece of trash to blame,' shouted Frank.

'Not interested. Let her go now, or I'll do exactly what I said.' Darren twisted again. Paolo yelped like a wounded animal. The two men stared at each other. Darren didn't blink. Beside him, Jo felt Dan gripping his arm. All he could see was Lucy's terror.

With a snarl, Frank threw Lucy across the floor. Arms flailing wildly, she went skidding into Darren's legs. Taking his chance, Frank grabbed Paolo's arm and pulled him roughly through the fire exit.

'Damn! Damn! Damn!' Darren slapped the wall in frustration.

'Shouldn't we go after them?' Lucy cried, already clambering to her feet. As she spoke, Zoe appeared through the fire exit. She took one look at Jo and instantly looked away. It felt like a pile of bricks dropping into his stomach.

'No need,' she said in a subdued voice. 'They won't get far.'

Darren looked at her as if she was a ghost. 'Where did you come from? Have the police arrived? I didn't hear anything.'

'I found the car, that BMW you were telling me about. It's not far, just behind some large metal bins.'

'What did you do to the car?' Lucy asked, frowning.

'I used a nail to let down the tyres. It should slow them enough so the police can catch them.' She smoothed her crumpled jacket with trembling hands. She still wouldn't look at Jo. He hung his head. His stupid plan had ruined everything.

'But what about the package?' asked Dan, hurrying to her side.

'It's next to the blue metal bin, hidden under some cardboard. Don't worry, they won't be able to see it but I know where it is.'

Dan began to whisper urgently in her ear. Jo turned away, unable to watch, to find Lucy staring at him. Her green eyes were like slits.

Not her as well? His whole world was collapsing. 'Lucy, please, I'm...' he began.

Darren suddenly spun away from the fire door. 'Zoe, did you say a blue bin?' he barked.

'Yes, but...'

'EVERYONE, DOWN!'

There wasn't time to think. Pulling a bewildered Lucy to the floor, Jo dropped down, sheltering her with his body. Even as he did so, the muscles in his chest burned.

Whoomph... A huge explosion ripped through the yard outside. The hall began to shake and tremble. It felt like the air was being pulled from his lungs then punched back into him. Windows rattled in their frames.

Even when the noise stopped Jo stayed where he was, reluctant to move. He watched as dust particles floated down, dancing in the light. It hurt when he breathed in, but at least they were still alive. Lucy coughed and pushed her hand against his chest. He winced at the pain and tried to cover it up with a smile.

'Promise you'll never, ever do that again,' she rasped, her throat full of dust.

'Which bit?' he managed.

She began to laugh. 'You scared me, Jo but we're okay, you and me, I promise.' There wasn't time to say more. Darren came rushing over.

'Jo, Lucy, are you alright?'

Jo managed to struggle to his feet. Holding onto his arm, Lucy scrambled up beside him.

'We're fine,' she said. 'Just a bit dusty and shaken up.'

'I'm not so sure about Zoe,' said Jo. She sat with her head in her hands, Dan next to her.

'Give her time,' said Lucy, before hurrying over to her friend.

'The stupid men must have reversed over the bomb,' he heard Zoe say. She kept shaking her head, as if trying to dislodge something. Jo sighed heavily. He knew it wasn't just the explosion that was making her so upset.

Darren knelt to check her over. 'She's just a bit deaf from the noise,' he called. 'It'll pass.'

On unsteady legs Dan walked towards him. 'Are you hurt?' he asked, noting Jo's wince.

'I've just pulled my chest muscles a bit. I'll be fine.'

'Dad's going to be hacked off with us, what with the damage and everything.' He looked at the dust-filled space and groaned.

'They'll just be pleased that you're alive,' said Darren.

'What about Sarah and Sheila?' asked Jo.

'They're both fine. I heard Sarah shout down,' said Dan, sounding as weary as Jo felt.

'I killed those men,' Zoe sobbed into Lucy's shoulder. 'I should've taken it right away from here!'

'They killed themselves,' Darren told her firmly. 'You weren't to know they'd reverse into that bin. If they'd escaped, how many more would they have murdered? They certainly had no qualms about finishing us off.'

'How am I going to explain the 'wing thing' to Uncle Simon and Uncle Ian,' muttered Jo. He rubbed his chest, trying to ease the pain.

'Zoe won't say a word.' Dan managed a small smile. 'It'll be funny in about twenty years or so.'

'Yeah, but there's Sarah,' said Jo. 'She saw as well.'

Dan groaned and then shrugged. 'I'll ask her not to say anything. It'll be fine.' He sounded far more confident than Jo felt.

Dusty and bedraggled, the five watched as police and ambulances rushed to a halt. The first car had hardly pulled to a stop before the rear doors flew open. Mr Fraser and the professor swept out of the car, descending on them without a word. Opening their arms, they enfolded all five in an enormous hug.

'Mr Fraser, Sarah's upstairs tending to Sheila. She's been shot,' Darren explained.

Jo couldn't hide his discomfort as a pain shot through his shoulder. He began to squirm under his uncle's intense gaze. 'I, um, I've hurt my ribs,' he stuttered. 'I think it must have happened when I dived on top of Lucy. Sorry.'

'How bad is it?'

'I can manage, Uncle Simon. Honest.'

'I'll send Ian to you. Wait here,' he ordered. Taking Darren with him he hurried away.

The professor came over and spoke quietly to the rest of them. 'Just play dumb. Tell the officers you didn't arrive until just before the explosion and let Simon handle the rest. Jo, I want you to sit in the back of the other car with Dan and stay well away from the medics.'

'So far, so good,' Dan muttered, as they slid onto the seat.

'Yeah, well, if I don't take them out again soon there's going to be a few more surprises,' whispered Jo. His chest and back were fit to burst. 'What did you say to Zoe before the blast?'

'Not much, I didn't exactly have the time, did I.'

Jo watched the police officers scurrying around. The bricks in his stomach doubled in weight. 'I'm sorry if I've messed it up between you and her,' he murmured, feeling worse than ever.

Dan's sigh said it all. Jo sat in silence, wondering how he was ever going to make things right again.

'Dad's on the way back,' Dan said finally. 'I wonder what fairy story he's managed to come up with. Roll your window down a bit more, we might hear something.'

With the window open, they could just make out what was being said. 'It seems Inspector, when Miss Corden arrived to open the hall ready for our activities, she saw two men acting suspiciously,' Mr Fraser began. 'Unfortunately, before she could raise the alarm, she was seen and chased into the attic, which is when she was shot. She couldn't understand what they were saying, and thought one of them had some sort of middle-eastern dialect. It could well be they were using the place to hand over weapons or even prepare for a terrorist attack. They must have seen the youngsters arriving back and decided to run for it. I suppose, in their rush to get away...' He shrugged. 'Accidents happen.'

'Do you think the inspector's going to swallow that?' said Jo as the men walked away.

'They might believe this was a possible terrorist attack. Although it does mean no one will ever know what we did.'

'At least we won't have to explain our bit of bomb disposal in the hall,' said Jo.

Dan laughed. 'You really think Dad won't find out?'

To their relief, the police seemed happy enough to believe Sarah and Darren's statements. All they asked Jo and Dan was if they'd arrived with the others just before the car exploded.

'I'm glad that's over,' said Dan as the officer walked away.

'Do you think I should own up about the stunt with my wings?' Jo suggested, rubbing his aching side.

'Are you serious?! Look, no one's going to say anything.'

'If you say so.' Jo wasn't sure if he should believe him.

Sheila was finally brought down on a stretcher, Sarah following close behind. With the window down, they had managed to learn quite a lot. Frank and Paolo had not survived. According to the fire officer, the car, and everything in it, had been burnt beyond recognition.

'I thought that explosion was a bit much for one bomb,' whispered Dan. 'Did you hear them - at least two devices, maybe more? They must have been in the boot of the car. Idiots.'

'But why so many?' muttered Jo. 'Who drives around with high explosives in their car?'

'You two alright?' The professor slid into the front seat and turned to face them.

'My back's a bit tight,' admitted Jo. 'Did they pick those men up at the hostel? What about Ade, Paul and Margaret, and where's Jan and...'

'Wow!' The professor raised a hand to ward off the verbal attack. 'Sven managed to collar a few, once he realised he'd been sent on a wild goose chase. Unfortunately, they'd only been recruited fairly recently and knew nothing. We could have done with at least one of this lot alive, but never mind.'

'Is Zoe okay?' Jo asked. 'Her hearing seems to have been affected.'

'She's more upset than anything, but I think that has a lot to do with her impromptu bomb disposal.' He fixed the boys with a cool stare. Jo kept his head down. 'As for Jan, he and John went hurtling into Dundee to rescue the two lads. They'd already managed to extricate themselves from a tight spot. We've got several of Sven's men hunting down those perpetrators. As for the rest, whoever organised this attempt was much cleverer. They set up a diversion at the sports centre, and another on the main road near the hostel. Made the sports centre diversion look like a gas explosion at first. Don't worry,' he assured them as they gasped in horror, 'no one was hurt. Just lots of noise and smoke. They had to evacuate the building, but there's no damage. They've put it down to a smoke-bomb. It did mean we were trapped there, however, until we convinced the police we weren't responsible.'

'So, have the police connected that with the school and us?' asked Dan.

'The inspector seems to believe the terrorist theory. He thinks they were using the sports centre and the accident near the hostel as diversions while they set up a meeting with local terror cells. He'll be too busy chasing leads to start worrying about us. With luck, the bomb parts will lead back to Steiner, which wouldn't be a bad thing. Now, you two stay put. I'll chivvy things along.'

'Notice he didn't say anything about Margaret,' muttered Dan as they watched him stride away.

'Suppose they weren't interested in her.'

'Maybe.' Dan didn't look convinced.

Most of the police vehicles, along with the last of the ambulances, finally began to leave. 'I've got to get out for a bit,' Jo insisted. Supporting his back against the door frame, he was startled when Darren came hurtling past him.

Mr Fraser stopped him before he could run down the road after the cars. 'Darren, what's the problem?'

'I can't believe... How could I forget?' spluttered Darren.

'Just tell me,' Mr Fraser insisted.

'There's another one, I left him tied up under a hedge! I completely forgot. He was sent to watch the van. I need to tell the police.'

'Not to worry,' said the professor. 'As it happens, I know just the people to sort the problem for us. No need to bother the local constabulary.'

'Right.' Confused, Darren looked to Mr Fraser who was already on his mobile. 'You'll take care of him?'

'Definitely. We'll take care of him, you have my word,' he replied

26 Telling All

Sven, they were told, would drive them back to the hostel. He arrived at the school in a newly-rented minibus. 'Everyone on board,' he ordered, taking his place in the driving seat, stern-faced and tight lipped.

Before she slid into her seat, Sarah whispered in Jo's ear, 'Don't worry. I won't say anything.'

Jo just nodded, too tired and sore to do more than feel a glimmer of relief. He glanced across to where Zoe sat next to Lucy. Her eyes were fixed on the road outside.

'What's the time?' asked Dan, shaking his watch and frowning.

'Ten minutes to two. Why?'

'I just thought my watch had stopped.'

Nodding, Jo knew exactly what he meant. How could so much have happened in such a short time? His mind still refused to think clearly. There was no sense of victory or even relief, just a bone-deep weariness. Worse, was the growing fear that he'd thrown away any chance of friendship. Lucy might say she was alright at the moment, but if Zoe thought he was a freak, was she really going to be okay with him? Jo tried to shut off the swirling thoughts, but it was impossible.

Sven stopped them all before they headed into reception, warning them not to talk to anyone in the hostel about what had happened. Wearily, they all nodded, no one spoke a word. Jo and Dan had only just started climbing the stairs when Sven called the two of them back. 'You've got twenty minutes, lads, then up to your dad's room. Both of you.'

Dan groaned loudly. 'Now we're for it.'

'At least tell me what to expect,' Jo pleaded.

Dan nodded towards Jo's back. 'Just be careful what you say. Dad can sniff out a fib at a hundred paces. Trust me, I've tried. Oh, hi, Uncle Ian,' he said quickly as their room door swung open.

'Lads. Jo, go take a shower, the water's already running. Do you need a hand?'

'No, I should be able to manage,' he said, self-consciously. He came out to find Dan busily sorting clothes and the professor staring moodily out of the window.

'Right, let's take a look at the damage,' the professor ordered. 'Dan, go and shower.'

The relief as his wings slipped out was amazing. 'I've wanted to do that forever,' groaned Jo, allowing them to flap gently. The pain in his chest lessened immediately.

'While they're out, I need to feel your ribs. Put your hands against the wall and try not to stab me in the head.' The professor's searching fingers dug gently into his chest, sides and back, easing knots of tension as they went.

'Just a few torn chest muscles, thankfully. I can't wait to hear how you managed that, and no, I'll wait,' he added, as Jo opened his mouth, ready to confess.

'I'm sorry, Uncle Ian.'

'Aye, lad, I'm sure you are. Let's see if you can slide them back in without too much pain.' There was some discomfort, but nowhere near as much as before. Jo shrugged a few times to settle everything into place. 'I'll go to the kitchen and get a couple of ice bags. You two, finish dressing and I'll meet you in our room. No hanging about.'

Grudgingly, they did as they were told. They were halfway up the back stairs when they met Darren. He still hadn't showered; streaks of dust lined his face.

'Just knock and go in, lads,' he said, managing a smile.

'He didn't look like they'd given him too hard a time,' Jo whispered hopefully.

'Yeah, well, he's not us,' said Dan.

When they finally reached the door, Dan raised his hand to knock. 'I hate this,' he moaned. 'Are you ready?' Jo shook his head.

They went in anyway.

Mr Fraser, his back to the door, was looking out of the window. It took a moment for Jo to realise he wasn't alone. Jan was sitting on a chair in the shadows, the professor next to him. It was hard to see their expressions. Jo suddenly felt very small.

'I've just had a call from the hospital,' Mr Fraser said, sounding weary. 'You'll be relieved to know Sheila will make a full recovery. That's one positive thing from today.' He turned, his eyes like flint. 'Now, maybe you'd like to explain why the five of you allowed yourselves…no, went out of your way, to put yourselves in such danger? Didn't Darren specifically tell you to get to the cottages and stay out of sight?' They nodded in silence. 'How can I possibly trust you in the future when you pull ridiculous stunts like this?'

'But it wasn't like that at all, Dad,' Dan began.

'No, we didn't have any choice.'

They talked over each other, both desperate to explain. Mr Fraser held up a hand. 'Stop! Jan, would you mind?' Jo had forgotten anyone else was there. Jan planted chairs behind them and handed Jo two ice packs.

'Sit,' Mr Fraser ordered. He looked at them and sighed. 'You, Daniel, will explain from the beginning. Joseph, stay quiet unless he gets it wrong, understood?'

For the next ten minutes Jo kept his eyes down. His head was a mess. He hardly heard what Dan was saying. Any second now it would all come out, he just knew it. They were going to be furious…and what about Zoe?

'Joseph?'

Startled, he looked up. 'Yes, Uncle Simon?'

'Maybe you should explain why you decided to do it.'

'Do it? I, um...' Panicking, he snuck a quick glance at his friend, but Dan sat rigid, eyes fixed on the floor.

Mr Fraser, his arms folded, watched him closely. 'I take it you do remember your foray into bomb disposal?'

'Oh, that. Right.' He tried not show how relieved he was.

'I'm still waiting.'

Jo's cheeks burned, he really needed to get this right. 'I, um… well,' he dithered. 'The truth is, we just sort of acted on instinct. We figured if they decided to leg it, they'd set off the bomb. We'd seen him move it, just pick it up, so we thought, why not? It wasn't until it was all over that we realised it was probably a bit stupid. Though we asked Sheila how to switch it off,' he added quickly. 'Sorry, Uncle Simon.'

Mr Fraser looked from one stricken face to the other. 'What a double-act. Looks like you and Sven will have some competition,' he said to Jan. 'Is there anything either of you have left out?'

Jo shook his head, not trusting himself to speak. At last Mr Fraser smiled. 'Debriefing is never pleasant. It is, however, best done as soon as possible.'

'So, we're not in trouble?' Dan asked, daring to glance at Jo.

'Let's say I'm holding judgement until all evidence is in.'

'What about Glasgow and Julian?' Jo said anxiously.

'They wouldn't have found him. He and his partner are long gone, I'm pleased to say. Now, scat, before I change my mind.'

Jo's knees almost buckled as the door finally closed. He couldn't quite believe he'd gotten away with the wing-flapping episode.

'That was close,' said Dan as he waited for Jo to limp down the last few stairs.

'But what about the girls? What if they say something?'

'If they do, we'll deal with it, - But they won't,' Dan added as panic spread across Jo's face. 'Come on, I'm starving. I'm going to beg some food.'

Despite the gnawing worry, Jo had to admire Dan's charm as he delivered his, poor, hungry hurt boy act to the cooks. 'I don't know how you've got the nerve. There's not a mark on you,' he said, as his friend came out of the kitchen carrying a plate piled high with rolls and cake.

'Hey, don't knock it. Remember, some of this is for you. Let's get out of here before... Too late,' groaned Dan.

'Is that for us as well?' Lucy came hurrying over. 'Just a quick bite, Zoe and I have to go talk to your dad.' She picked up a ham roll and split it between them. 'Thanks, we'll see you later.'

'Wish us luck,' Zoe murmured, her eyes fixed firmly to the floor.

'Did you see that?' said Jo. 'She couldn't even look at me.'

'Stop it, give her time,' said Dan. 'Let's go to the lounge, Paul and Ade might be in there.'

Paul's head popped up over the top of a chair as they walked in. He broke into a wide grin. 'We're safe, Ade, it's not her. We're glad to see you two are in one piece. Just shut the door tight, it'll give us a bit of warning.'

'What's up?' Jo asked, dropping onto the large sofa. 'Are you both okay?'

'Us? We're fine,' Ade assured him. 'Margaret's the one in trouble.'

'You've got to tell us more,' Dan begged, getting comfortable.

'Well,' Ade waved them closer. 'Margaret set off into Dundee, and we told her loads of times - didn't we, Paul - that someone was tailing us. Not the usual, this was a tatty green van, not one of Sven's cars. Anyway, she wouldn't listen. Man, she was like, 'you two know nothing and it's all been blown out of proportion. It's pathetic how they treat him'. Meaning you, I suppose, Jo.'

'She went on and on,' Paul continued. 'So, we get to the supermarket and she's like, 'oh, we need petrol. We'd better do it first'. She sticks the petrol in, then guess what? When she goes to pay, she only takes the keys with her and doesn't bother to lock up. We couldn't lock the stupid thing from the inside, some sort of safety system. Stupid, if you ask me.'

'She didn't even look back,' said Ade. 'Next thing, these two idiots came racing over but we were more than ready. Paul went to the front. I went to the back doors, so they'd have to split up.'

Paul took over. 'As soon as this bloke at the front pulls open the door, I kicked out. Boy, you should've heard him squeal. There was blood everywhere.'

'Me, I'm down the other end, waiting,' said Ade. 'And this guy tries to grab my legs to pull me over his shoulder. It was so cool. He leans in, I grabbed his head, sort of twisted, and 'wham', I vaulted over the top of the idiot. He turns, and before he can use this knife he's pulled out, I kneed him so hard, he just collapsed. It was brilliant. We dived under the van at each end then ran for it. There was this enormous security guard in the supermarket. he was mint. Had us upstairs in a locked room in minutes, and they got the whole thing on their cameras.'

'Wow!' said Jo. 'We heard one of the men talking about it. We didn't know you'd got away until Zoe rang.'

'You must've been so worried,' said Paul.

'And some,' admitted Jo.

'So, what happened to Margaret?' said Dan.

'She only tried to claim it was just some blokes asking directions. Can you believe it?' said Ade. 'The security guard laughed in her face. He refused to let us out of the room until Jan and Master Brampton arrived. She wanted us to carry on shopping!'

They sat in silence, digesting the news. 'What did Jan say to her when he arrived?' asked Jo.

Ade and Paul swapped grins. 'It's not what he said, more how he said it,' said Paul. 'Icebergs have nothing on him; he was cold. She started off all huffy and just deflated like a balloon.'

'Come on then, tell us your stories,' said Ade. 'Lucy gave us a very quick rundown, something about picking the lock on someone's garage, and an ice-cream van.' He leant closer. 'She wouldn't tell us why they were after you, she said you'd tell us yourself?'

'What?!' said Jo in disbelief.

'It'll keep for now, just tell us the rest,' said Paul.

Demolishing food as they talked, Paul and Ade were soon filled in. They were suitably impressed by the disarming of the bomb.

'Just don't say anything to Dad or Uncle Ian,' Dan begged. 'It's a bit of a sore point.'

'We all did alright, didn't we?' Ade said, helping himself to a roll. 'I probably won't say much to Mum and Dad though. They might think twice about letting me come on holiday again.'

'Zoe's having a rough time,' said Jo.

'Dropping a bomb probably does that to you,' said Ade. Jo shrugged and kept his mouth shut.

They all stiffened as the door opened but it was Zoe's voice that carried clearly into the room. 'And I thought being given the third degree by Dad was bad enough. At least Mr Fraser spoke to them and smoothed it over.'

As soon as she and Lucy came in, Zoe made a beeline for the chair next to Paul. Unless Jo turned right round in his seat, he couldn't see her. If that was how she wanted to play it, he thought, so be it. Trying to ignore his twisting gut, Jo kept his eyes on the carpet.

'We're in one piece, just about,' said Lucy. 'The police won't be prosecuting me for breaking into the garage and the ice-cream van. They've decided it must have been a coincidence, someone local looking for takings. Are they dense or what?'

'I was really worried Mum and Dad would want to drag me away,' said Zoe. 'Mind you, I didn't mention the 'dropped bomb' incident. Probably best to keep that bit to myself. What?' she asked, as the others began to laugh.

Jo tried to join in but his lips felt stiff. Everything felt awkward.

From the hall the chimes of the large clock could be heard.

'Five, at last,' Dan said, rising to his feet. 'Now we get to eat.'

Jo did the same, although food was the last thing on his mind. Before he could take a step, Mr Fraser called from the doorway.

'Jo, can I have a word?'

His heart sank. His uncles must have guessed the truth about the wing flapping. Dan was suddenly at his side. 'I knew it couldn't be that easy,' Dan whispered, as the others filed past them.

'Daniel, I didn't hear your name,' said his father.

'I'll wait. Promise I won't listen, Dad.'

'Let him stay,' the professor said. 'Jo's going to tell him anyway.'

'Come up to my room then, lads. This shouldn't take long.' Without any explanation he turned on his heels, the professor following.

'Great, we'll miss out on the first trays of food,' Dan grumbled.

Jo gnawed at his lip. 'Do you think they know?'

'How can they, no one said anything'

'Here, Jo.' Mr Fraser waved him over to the window. At the opposite side of the room Sven and Jan were in quiet

266

conversation. Mr Fraser smiled and gently brushed the hair from Jo's forehead. 'A haircut is due, I think, lad.'

The professor continued, 'Simon and I need to ask you about something, Jo. It's becoming obvious that these attempts to kidnap you are pretty serious.'

'I'm really sorry.' Jo tried to quell a rising sense of dread. 'I know I've put everyone in danger. If you think I should...'

Mr Fraser shook his head firmly. 'Stop; this has nothing at all to do with you putting anyone in danger, or with us wanting you to leave. Do you understand?'

'Yes, Uncle Simon,' he whispered.

'Just listen. For us to protect you properly, Sven and Jan need to know why these men are so keen to track you down. Do you understand what I'm saying?'

'You want me to show them?' Jo's tension eased a little.

'Makes sense, Jo,' the professor said. 'This Rand, when he can finally talk coherently, is likely to know more than the rest. So, it's best coming from you, we think.'

'They don't suspect anything?' Jo glanced over at the two men.

'Not a thing,' said Mr Fraser.

Jo hesitated. 'Do you trust them Uncle Simon?'

'With my life.'

'And they've saved mine on several occasions,' agreed the professor.

Jo began to unbutton his shirt whilst Mr Fraser called Sven and Jan closer. 'Jo agrees with us that you understand what's at stake. Are you ready?' Dan had to turn away to hide his sniggers.

'So, this is some sort of skin condition?' Jan asked.

'Not exactly,' said the professor. 'Stand back here by the window. You too, Dan. Simon, did you lock the door?'

'I did. When you're ready, Jo.' Mr Fraser winked and moved aside.

Though Jo badly wanted to see their faces he turned and began to roll his head. A familiar tingle ran up his spine as the two sacs opened. Pulling his shoulders forward he felt the wings spring out.

For a brief moment there was utter silence.

'My, my...' Jan babbled in Norwegian.

Sven muttered under his breath words Jo could not understand.

'This is not possible. No, it cannot be,' Jan finally declared, in English. Jo turned and laughed at their shocked expressions 'You can come closer,' he offered. 'I don't bite.'

27 An Ending

The relief Jo felt was short-lived. As he and Dan finally made it to the dining hall, it was like walking into an examination room. Everything went deathly silent. Darren and Sarah were nowhere to be seen, but the other four turned as one. Jo wanted to swivel on his heels and run.

'Everything okay?' called Lucy. To Jo's ears, her voice sounded strained.

'Suppose.' He shrugged and slipped onto a bench, grateful to have Dan beside him.

'We saved you some,' said Paul, pushing over half a tray of steak pie. 'There's extra gravy as well.'

It was an effort to swallow anything at first. Things got better when everyone started talking again, not that Jo could think of anything to say. Once they'd all finished, and the others were heading to the lounge, Jo pulled Dan to the side.

'I'm heading upstairs. I'm not feeling so good.

'Jo...' Dan began.

'Seriously. It's my side and chest.' He tried to sound convincing. He just couldn't face sitting there, pretending everything was alright. He knew Dan was watching him as he limped away, but he just wanted to be alone.

He tried concentrating on his book, but after reading the same page six times he threw it onto the bed. Turning his music up louder, he sat on the wide windowsill, staring moodily across the fields.

Nothing was ever going to be right again. For a few brief days he'd really felt part of something. Now it was back to the same old rubbish. Only everything was worse, because now they were all in danger, and it was his fault. He was so wrapped up in his miserable thoughts he didn't see or hear the door open.

'Jo?'

Startled, he slid off the sill and landed in a heap on the floor.

'Lucy! Zoe!'

'Sorry. We did knock. And text,' said Lucy, hauling him up.

Jo glanced at his mobile, still on silent. 'You're not supposed to be up here,' he said, embarrassed about falling more than anything else.

'Dan lent us this.' She showed him the wristband. 'He's keeping watch outside, just in case.'

'Why does he need to...?' Jo started.

'Because I felt bad, and we need to talk,' Zoe announced. 'I'm worried you think I don't like you because of...well, you know.' She pointed to his back.

'They're wings, Zoe,' said Lucy.

'Yeah, those.' She cleared her throat, obviously searching for the right words. 'It was a bit of shock.' Lucy gave a snort of laughter.

'You're not helping,' Zoe scolded, before trying again. 'I had to watch Paul take his foot on and off a few times before I got used to that, so you can imagine,' she paused. 'Suddenly, you had these enormous, great wings sticking out of your back. It was so weird, you know?'

The knot inside Jo's stomach loosened just a little.

'Do you want to see them again?' he asked. 'Would that help?'

'Why not?' she said, sounding as if she was preparing for a sky-dive, or something equally as dangerous.

'You'll need to move back a bit,' he cautioned. He waited until they were near the door and slipped out of his shirt. 'Ready?'

'Go for it,' said Lucy. 'Wow!' she cried, as they fluttered gently.

'They're huge!' whispered Zoe.

'Take a closer look,' Jo encouraged. He tried to fold them a bit, so they weren't as intimidating.

'How the hell do you get them inside you?' Lucy asked.

'They sort of concertina together,' he said self-consciously. 'If I'm honest, I'm not too sure. I'm just glad they do. It's why I look so big on top.'

'Can I touch them?' Zoe asked tentatively.

'Sure. It just tickles a bit.'

'They're so soft! Feel this Lucy.'

Jo had to bite his lip to stop the giggles as they rubbed their hands over the surface of the feathers.

'Can you show us how you put them away?' said Lucy.

'Sure.' He did it as slowly as he could. Again, he heard gasps as the wings disappeared inside the sacs.

'Unbelievable,' Zoe murmured. She felt for the edge of Dan's bed and sank down. 'I can't imagine how you managed to hide them when you were little.'

'They've only just developed. Believe me, they're as much a shock to me as everyone else! Here, I've got a picture somewhere.' He began rummaging through his wallet and pulled out the photograph the driver left at the campsite. 'This is how I looked when I first met Dan. It was taken at the beginning of term last year.'

'So, Dan didn't have a clue either?' said Zoe.

'No. When we first met that lump covered most of my neck and upper shoulders. I could hardly look up at him.'

Lucy ran a finger over the picture. 'Did it hurt when the lump moved down your back?'

'Oh yes,' Jo said unable to hide the shiver.

'Doesn't it make you angry?' asked Lucy, her eyes wide.

'Why would it make him angry?' said Zoe, still studying the photograph.

'I guess whoever is after Jo knows exactly what's going on. Am I right?'

'That's terrible,' said Zoe. 'You mean, a doctor let that lump grow, knowing what would happen?'

'They planted the cells in my neck when I was a baby,' Jo explained.

'No way!' Zoe stared, open-mouthed.

'Have you lot done?' Dan's head appeared round the door.

'Why, is there a problem?' said Lucy.

'Ade's just sent a text. He and Paul are on their way over.'

Zoe touched Jo's hand. 'Are we alright now? Only, you're my friend. I don't want a stupid pair of wings to get in the way.'

'Thanks.' The words caught in Jo's throat and he had to swallow before he could answer. 'Yeah, we're great.'

Ade and Paul strolled in with several bags. The room suddenly felt very crowded.

'Midnight feast,' announced Paul. 'Well, a feast at least. Your dad knows, Dan. He said as long as we're out by eleven and don't wake Sarah or Darren, we're good.'

'Where did you get the food?' asked Jo, as they began unpacking boxes of biscuits, cake, crisps and dips.

'The supermarket. Ade and I divvied up our money. We told the store staff what we wanted and they got it for us. They did us a great deal. Here you go.' Paul threw Jo a large packet of crisps. 'But payment is needed, I'm afraid,' he said. Jo reached for his wallet.

'Not money,' said Ade. 'You've got to come clean. Start dishing the dirt.'

Once again, Jo took off his shirt while everyone else stood near the door. 'It's going to be a bit of shock at first,' he warned.

'We're fine,' Paul insisted. 'How did you get those cuts down your... Mega hell on wheels!' he spluttered.

Beside him, Ade's eyes looked as if they were going to pop out of his head. 'The...they're wings,' Ade managed to splutter.

'Big wings,' Paul added. Dan laughed helplessly; Lucy and Zoe tried hard not to join in.

Jo lifted a wing, dipping his head underneath. 'Are you alright?' he asked.

Paul took a gulp of air and nodded. 'Can we have a closer look?' Jo waited patiently as they walked around him.

'This is going to be so cool,' Ade murmured, his eyes shining. 'You've got an inbuilt hang-glider. How wicked is that?!'

'And you won't need a licence, or have to pay for lessons,' Paul said, sounding equally excited. 'What's it like to fly?' he asked, as if it was the most normal thing in the world.

'I haven't been allowed to try yet,' Jo admitted. 'I've only had these about five weeks.'

'Man, I bet you can't wait,' said Ade.

'Scared, more like. I keep seeing birds doing swoops and dives. What if they suddenly stop working, or they break?'

'You'll be fine,' Lucy interrupted. 'And anyway, I don't know about anyone else but I'm going to be up there, flying with you. Darren does para-gliding. I bet he'd teach us, if we lean on him enough.'

'Great,' Dan said dryly. 'Hanging in mid-air, from the end of a piece of canvas and string is just what I want to do!'

Much later, when everyone had finally left for their own dorms, Jo lay in bed, grinning into the darkness. It had been one of the best evenings ever. Once the initial excitement over his wings was over, he'd explained about the clinic and Amy. The rest of the time, they'd stuffed their faces with food and just talked or told stupid jokes. It was all so normal.

'Are you asleep?' Dan murmured through the shadows.

'Not yet. Why, what's up?'

'What did you say to Zoe about me when they first arrived?'

The question stumped Jo for a moment. 'Why? Has she fallen out with you, or something?'

'No, she was really nice, you know?'

Jo raised an eyebrow; his friend sounded embarrassed. 'All I did was show her and Lucy that photograph of me at school. You remember, when we first met?'

'Girls are weird,' muttered Dan.

'Yeah, but a nice weird,' Jo said, thinking of Lucy.

'Suppose. See you in the morning.' The bed creaked as Dan turned over.

It was hard getting up the following day. Everyone, apart from Sarah and Darren, yawned their way through breakfast. 'Worth it, though,' said Zoe, buttering another slice of toast. 'Margaret was furious when we got back. Apparently, the professor stopped her marching us all off to bed.'

'Were Sven and Jan alright when you got back to your dorm?' Jo asked Paul.

'They weren't there,' he said, with a mouthful of cereal. 'Darren was snoring like a trooper. I heard Jan coming in later, not sure what time.'

'Now, he can snore!' Ade sniggered. 'Sounds like a train going through a tunnel.'

Normality rocked, Jo thought cheerfully. Well, as normal as things were ever likely to be around him.

When they arrived at the sports centre, it was just as crowded as the day before. Jan and Sven escorted everyone upstairs to the balcony, and again, issued warnings about staying together.

'Like we need telling after yesterday,' said Paul.

They arranged themselves along the rail, cheering and clapping the various contestants. When Sarah finally appeared for her semi-finals match Jo could hardly watch, it was so tense. Lucy's yell of excitement when she won had his ears ringing for minutes afterwards. Darren's round wasn't quite as exciting, but he still won in style.

'I can't believe they're both in the finals,' said Zoe, looking thrilled. 'This has to be the best holiday ever.'

'What, even after yesterday?' Lucy said, laughing.

'It proved we can stick together,' she said. 'And I've still got all my fingers, so that's a bonus.'

Paul and Ade came hurrying back through the doors, holding several bags of chips. 'Here you go, the professor gave us some money for these,' Ade said, as he handed them round. 'Master Brampton said that Sarah's final will be on in a few minutes, then Darren's is practically straight after.'

'So, what do you reckon her chances are?' Jo asked Dan, as they watched Sarah and her opponent warming up.

'Well, she's fighting a black belt. It's not going to be easy. She's the same height and weight though.'

'She's looking good,' Jo said, his nerves kicking in.

Jan and Sven stepped up to the balcony to watch. 'I've been looking forward to this final; they're well matched,' said Sven.

'Ya, and it's good to see so many people,' said Jan. 'It makes a huge difference to the atmosphere.'

The hall was packed. Every seat was taken. During the first round Jo closed his eyes several times, half expecting to hear the tiny bell ring out to say Sarah had lost. It literally went to the last thirty seconds. Sarah managed a brilliant throw, pinning her opponent down as the bell rang. 'I think my heart's going to stop,' Jo complained. 'Maybe you should just tell me when it's all over?'

Below, the two women straightened their jackets and waited for the signal to start again. At least he didn't need to worry about the third round; Sarah won in the second. With a massive hip throw and a clean hold, the other competitor was down and out. As soon as she finished bowing, Sarah leapt out of the arena and danced around a thrilled John Brampton.

'I won! I won!' she yelled. On the balcony, the group erupted, cheering and shouting at the tops of their voices.

'Very good. She improves every time,' Jan said, applauding loudly. 'She uses her brain, not just her weight.'

'Unlike you then, my friend,' teased Sven.

'How's Sheila?' Jo asked Jan, while they waited for the next match to start.

'Much better, she will be discharged later today. She's a good woman, I know her very well.'

'I see you've dropped the accent,' noted Dan.

'Sven threatened to disown me and tell my wife many bad things.'

He gave a rolling laugh and turned to wink at his partner. 'Anyway, I shall save it for another time. Annoying him is a favourite hobby of mine.'

At last it was Darren's turn. 'Least he's a black belt as well, so it should be a decent fight,' Jo whispered.

Jan and Sven provided a commentary as the bout got underway. 'See that move? No confidence,' explained Jan. 'He needs to believe what he's doing. Now watch Darren and see the difference, the focus.'

'His opponent needs to watch his own feet - he's going to tip himself up!' said Sven. 'Does he really expect Darren not to spot something so obvious? See how Darren's countered that attempted neck throw? He's moved his centre of balance. He's in a position to pick his opponent up…'

Once again, it was a shoulder throw that sent the opponent slamming to the floor. It was over in two rounds, seemingly without Darren even breaking a sweat. His look of pure concentration gave way to a beaming smile.

'YES!' Dan punched the air. Lucy pulled them all into an impromptu celebratory jig. Jo felt as if he was going to burst, he was so happy.

'From such a small club, it is very good,' said Jan once the noise died off a little. 'This could be you one day, Dan?'

'Now Mum's not interfering, who knows? Hey, Jo, we'll be able to practice together.'

A warm sensation started somewhere in the pit of Jo's stomach. He couldn't stop grinning. 'Yeah, I know. And go to the cinema, and meet up in cafes.'

'You don't ask for much in life, do you, Jo?' said Sven.

'It's everything I've always wanted. I suppose you're going to tell me now that's not going to happen.'

'I'll do everything in my power to give you as much normality as I can. You're right, though, the things others take for granted we need to plan carefully.'

'But at least it's still possible? Not like before, when all I had was…well, nothing but a big black hole.' Jo frowned. 'I can still live with Uncle Simon and Dan, can't I?'

'Whatever it takes, Jo,' Sven promised. 'I couldn't do that to you.'

'In that case, I can put up with pretty much anything.'

The medal ceremony began. Mr Fraser, clad in formal robes, stood with the other judges. The hall echoed with shouts and cheers, as first Sarah then Darren stepped forward to receive their gold medals.

'What a holiday,' Dan said over the noise. 'Best ever.'

'Yeah, and some,' agreed Paul.

'Even getting blown up and being attacked at the supermarket? I can think of better things to do,' Jo said with a laugh.

'I wouldn't have missed any of it,' said Paul.

'Nor me,' agreed Dan. 'Though I reckon things are going to be pretty boring after this.'

About the Author

Born in Newport, South Wales, I have lived in many different parts of the country and am currently to be found roosting near Pontefract, West Yorkshire.

For those who have read and enjoyed *A Fistful Of Feathers,* the second book in this series *Flight or Fight* will be published very shortly.

Also, a writer of children's short stories and poems, I've just finished the first book for younger readers, aged 7 years and upwards called, *Deadwood Hall.* It's a magical, fantasy adventure and it's OUT NOW! You can find out more on the next page…

With frequent stops for fruit cake, ginger biscuits, chocolate cake, and the occasional apple, the next year promises to be *very* busy.

As this book is one of millions to choose from, I'm honoured that it was the one you picked up. It's great that there is so much choice, but it also means authors rely on readers sharing their thoughts about A Fistful Of Feathers with their friends.

You can do this online, by posting a review on Amazon, or mentioning it in relevant discussions. I'd also be hugely grateful if you could share a link to it on your social media platforms, so other readers can find it and enjoy it, too.

Remember: Authors are nothing without their readers!

https://www.facebook.com/LindaJonesukAuthor/

About Deadwood Hall

An illustrated magical fantasy adventure.

It's midwinters eve and *everything* is about to change.
For Dylan and his sister Emily being shrunk down to three
inches is the *easy* part.

They end up racing through underground tunnels – riding on
the back of a Very angry centipede – and trying to outsmart a
whole army of slimy Whivicks

Deadwood Hall is about secrets, friendship, magic, weird
creatures and looking out for each other when things go *very*
wrong.
This adventure is just the beginning – that's if Dylan and
Emily can survive until Midnight!

Read it as an e-book on Kindle
Or you can buy a copy from Amazon

ISBN978-1-9993248-0-3

Printed in Great Britain
by Amazon